The Wild Flowers
Lavender

The Wild Flowers
Lavender

MELISSA JEAN

TABLE OF CONTENTS

*This book is for my babies; Leo, River and Daisy.
I love you more than all the stars, as big as the moon and as
bright as the sun xx*

Chapter 1

"Excuse me miss, I've been waiting ten minutes for my toasted sandwich and coffee," calls a stern voice to my left, shaking me from my frantic coffee making.

I glance up from the coffee machine in surprise, searching for the owner of the voice. Someone I don't recognise. She must be a tourist. Her fingers are dancing, tapping away on the bench, highlighting her impatience. I glance around at the busy coffee shop before looking back at her, a little stunned. Can't she see that I'm working alone here and have spent the better part of her waiting time, madly dashing around while juggling coffee and meal orders. My hands are literally covered in ground coffee beans.

Nonetheless, I apologise profusely and hurriedly finish making her order, pushing hers to the front of my list.

I hand over her sandwich and coffee, politely thanking her for the patience she clearly does not have. She snatches the order from my hands and rushes out without so much of a thank you. The joys of tourists. A local would never be so rude.

A sigh escapes me, louder than I expected. I glance around quickly. Thankfully, no one noticed.

Brushing a loose strand of hair behind my ear with the back of my hand, to avoid coffee grounds smearing through it, I get back to making orders. I love my little store and normally thrive on the busyness of it all, but today I am not feeling it. Today, I wish I had an employee I could hand over the reins to, so I could take a break, even for twenty minutes. I could call out to my sisters, but a quick peek at their corners of the shop, tells me they are just as busy. It seems like the people who have stopped in for a coffee, have then made their way to the bookstore or flower shop and vice versa.

I feel a tug on my jumper that is loosely tucked into my apron. Looking down, I come face to face with my sweet nine year old. My mini me, stares up at me.

"I can help, mum," says her sweet little voice.

My heart melts and I'm all gooey inside. She has a heart of pure gold. I all but forget the crowded shop for a moment. Wiping my hands clean, I run them over the length of her brown hair, the same dark shade as mine and stare into those big, green eyes that mirror my own. Azalea got her dads sense of humour, but in every other way, she is me.

"You don't have to do that darling, but I appreciate the offer all the same. You just enjoy your hot chocolate and cookie."

She shakes her head and crosses her arms. Ah, there it is. Her stubborn streak. Also, me.

"I want to help, and I've finished my milk and cookie anyway. Besides, I didn't like that lady who spoke unkindly to you."

Internally, I agree with her.

Instead of answering, I grab her hand, dropping a quick kiss to it before turning back to the coffee orders that are now piling up. I really do need to hire someone.

"Sweetheart, why don't you go and see if your aunts need any help? I think I heard Aunt Goldie say earlier that she needed help trimming the flowers for a big order."

That seems to satisfy her urge to help, and she skips off to the other side of the shop, calling out to my sister. I'm so grateful and incredibly proud of this business that my sisters and I have built together. I know if they weren't flat out themselves right now, they would be over here offering their help too. But I won't ask that of them. Being the oldest, I try my best to not burden them. Instead, I'll just manage everything myself. As much as I can, anyway.

I spend the next thirty minutes catching up on orders before the café quietens and I can finally stop for a break. It's the first time all day, I can steal a moment to catch my breath.

I make a cup of coffee, and holding the hot mug close to my chest, I let the warmth soothe my sore hands. The rich aroma of coffee beans fills the air, and I take a deep breath in, savoring the smell. I lean against the bench, resting my elbows on the cool surface, letting it support my weight. I take a huge sip, and a groan escapes me. Just the boost I needed before the afternoon rush.

I stare out across my little corner of the shop, to my youngest sister Juniper's bookstore. As always, she is caught up in a book, oblivious to what is going on around her. Laughter bursts from me as I watch some poor guy who is clearly interested in her, try and catch her attention. He wanders past her over and over again, pretending to look at the books. As he makes his fourth trip around her store, I wonder how many more laps he might do before he gets up the courage to speak to her.

Juniper is oblivious to how beautiful she is. She has the same green eyes that we share with our sister Marigold. Juni has long curly hair, a mix of blonde and brown, where mine falls in dark soft waves past my shoulders. Neither of us has ever coloured our hair. Marigold on the other hand, has had every colour of the rainbow on her unruly mix of curls and waves. Her hair was a similar colour to Juni's until a few years ago when she started switching it out with shades of the rainbow. It's currently a soft pink and my favourite of all the colours she has done. Now I can't picture her with anything else.

Where Marigold lives up to our family name, 'Wild', Juni and I do not. Juni's perfect night in, is curled up by the fireplace reading a book. She is all things good and sweet and a total romantic at heart. Juni favours sundresses, where Marigold is all things wild and loud. She wears the most glorious array of brightly coloured clothing. Her favourites being seventies style fitted overalls with cute, collared tops and sneakers. She truly brings the colour to our lives.

I glance down at my own outfit. I'm more of a fitted jeans with a t-shirt gal with my hair thrown up in a barrette or pony. I would call my taste, comfortable yet stylish. But really, it just screams mum. And seeing as that is my most favourite thing in the world, I'm okay with it.

My mystery friend in the bookstore finally musters up the courage to approach, and I hear him ask her a question. She smiles but glances up only for a moment when she answers, before turning back to her book. Looking dejected, he puts the book back on the shelf but surprisingly doesn't leave. He randomly picks up another book and makes his way over, trying again, but gets the same response. Poor guy. He clearly likes her and is trying to flirt but she will have no part in it.

I watch this interaction go on for another five more minutes, before he finally gives up and leaves. Another laugh bursts from me, and this time Juni looks up from her book in my direction. I give her a wave and a wink before my afternoon's entertainment is interrupted by someone clearing their throat. A manly, husky, clearing of the throat. I turn my attention to the customer waiting at the counter and I'm nearly floored. Wow.

I'm greeted by the most gorgeous man I have ever seen in my thirty-five years of life.

And he looks annoyed. Glaring even. How can someone who looks like that, be so grouchy? I'm at the tail end of my day and my patience is wearing thin for rude customers. I mentally cross my fingers that he is going to be kind, but from the look on his face, I might be out of luck.

Attempting to ignore the tall, strong, muscular looking body with the black, run your fingers through, messy on top hair, and deep blue eyes that almost look grey. I grab my pad and pen to take his order.

"Umm, hi. What can I get for you?"

He stares back at me in silence for a moment before answering. And when he does, he continues his glare, speaking slowly to me like I might have trouble understanding his order.

"I would like a double shot black coffee. If you have the time to tear yourself away from checking out your pal over there in the bookstore."

Umm, what? I glance over at the bookstore and realise he is talking about the guy I was watching trying to flirt with my sister. The one who I was definitely not, checking out.

Anger bubbles up in my chest and I know it's mostly because I'm exhausted and hungry.

But also, who does he think he is?

I open my mouth to tell him so before I quickly clamp it shut, reminding myself he is a customer. 'The customer is always right' is so far from the truth, but I still have to abide by it.

"I'm sorry sir," I grit out between clenched teeth, "I was just looking over to see if my sister needed any help. I'll grab you that coffee now. Is that to go?"

My smile is forced and my words come from between clenched teeth.

I pray he wants the coffee to go. But also weirdly, part of me wants him to stay so I can look at him a little more. What can I say, I'm a glutton for punishment. I can't remember the last time I felt butterflies just from looking at someone.

"Yes thanks."

I got a thanks. I'll take that as a win. I make his coffee, sneaking a few glances at him from the corner of my eye. He still looks pissed. Tourists. Hopefully he is only passing through. I can enjoy checking him out for a moment, but I certainly don't want his grumpy attitude gracing my shop's presence again.

Just when I think I'm on the home stretch, and almost finished with his coffee, he pipes up again.

"Also, it didn't look like you were trying to help anyone. Least of all me. It looked like you were winking at your friend over there and ignoring me standing here."

I'm gobsmacked.

'Remember he is a customer' runs through my head again but I'm struggling. Today was not the day for this man to come into my store. Those little butterflies I felt only a moment ago, have all but disappeared now. I don't care how good looking he is. He's a jerk.

Screw him being a customer.

"Well, you're wrong. I'm thinking maybe that's hard for you to grasp. Being wrong," I say sharply, raising an eyebrow, giving him a pointed stare.

He squints his eyes, glaring back at me.

Okay, I have no idea what just came over me. That was so out of character for me. But really, he deserved it. He doesn't say anything else, so I continue making his coffee.

Once it's ready, I quickly hand it over. It sloshes over the side a little and I pray he doesn't ask me to make another cup. I get a grunted "Thanks" and a raised eyebrow before he turns away.

I watch him walk out and as there are no other customers in the coffee shop, I poke my tongue out at his back as he leaves. He must somehow sense it though, because he turns around, catching me. Mortified, I quickly smile and wave, doing my best to cover it up. He raises an eyebrow and shakes his head as he pushes the door open. He definitely saw me.

I groan and cover my eyes with my hands. What the hell just happened right now? That is totally not me to act that way.

Laughter rings out across the room. Goldie, my younger sister, holds up a peace sign at me, having busted me too.

She makes her way over and takes a seat at a table closest to my coffee counter.

"Your daughter is in her element pruning some of my flowers for tomorrow's arrangements."

She points at her tall desk, in her little section of the shop and I smile, watching Azalea focusing intently on the task at hand. She will happily continue until it's time to head home. I have a strong feeling she might follow in Goldie's footsteps one day and become a florist.

Goldie calls out, "Juni, the shop is empty. Pop your book down and come and join us before the next rush."

Juni looks up distractedly from her book, confusion furrowing her brow. "What did you say Goldie?"

Rolling her eyes, Goldie jumps back up and walks to the door, locking it and turning the 'Back in fifteen minutes' sign over. On her way back to the table, she gently takes the book from Juni's hand and places it on the desk. She grabs her hand and walks her over and it would be almost comical if it wasn't so Goldie and Juni.

Goldie points at the chair.

"Sit Juni. I'll make you a snack."

Our youngest sister is twenty-five and not in any way incapable, but we treat her like she is at times. Everyone in our family babies Juni. Juni's head is usually found in a book, oblivious to our babying of her.

Juni places her hands under her chin, framing her face, and stares dreamily at her bookstore. "I've been thinking I could maybe hire Fox to make me some new bookshelves.

Now that the store is doing so well. I can just picture the beautiful intricate wood panels. What do you both think?"

I'm nodding before she has even finished. I had been thinking of doing a few upgrades myself. A new coffee machine and some new wingback chairs for the corner by the fireplace. Maybe some new plates too. My own eyes mist over, imagining it all.

Goldie sits up straighter and fist pumps the air.

"Oh, me too! I would love some new flowerpots and maybe a new hanging floral display behind my desk. Maybe Fox could build me some new planter boxes too. Is he coming to family dinner next week? We can ask him then Juni."

Goldie continues to talk about the shop and her ideas for upgrades, but I tune their conversation out.

I scan our store, built from the ground up, by the three of us. The three Wild sisters. For as long as I can remember, we had dreams of opening a store together. One big store catering to each of our special interests.

At the front of our shop is one big window that lets all the natural light in. To the right of the window is a big, beautiful door in sunny yellow. Fairy lights, loop like ribbons across the front of the building and above our sign, '*The Wild Flowers*'.

We spent close to a year preparing to open, each of us working on the finer details from the cups and saucers, the floral ribbons and the bookmarks we would sell in the shop. What we didn't focus on was the name. For months, we went back and forth on possible names without ever settling on one. One month before we opened, the signwriter told us if we didn't give him a name, our sign wouldn't be ready for our grand opening.

So, we piled over as a group to our parents' house to chat names one evening.

After we each embraced mum at the front door, she sung out her usual call to let our dad know we were there. But today it hit differently.

"Tom, the Wild flowers are here!"

We each turned to the other as if in slow motion. Goldie cheered, Juni had a soft knowing smile cross her face and I verbalised what we were all thinking.

"The Wild Flowers?" I whispered, hopeful.

And that was that. Our store name was decided. And I have loved it every day since.

You can't miss our shop on the main street of our small town. It's a gorgeous lavender purple, with more twinkling fairy lights strewn across the hanging flowers above the windows. It's magical. Walking into the shop, customers are first greeted by Goldie's flower shop to the left. Big, beautiful blooms adorn her store, and smaller bouquets are placed in buckets outside, just below the front window, and to the right of the main entrance against the wall in the shop. Walking in the door, you are greeted with the scent of all kinds of flowers and greenery. It's our own room diffuser, as the scent of fresh flowers, carries through the whole store. Moving past the florist counter, sits Juni's bookstore, in the left nook of the store. It's the heart of our store, just like Juni. Juni has spent the better part of the last six years, carefully curating the book selection and it's the most popular bookstore in our town. In the far-right corner, opposite Juni's shop, is my little section of the store. The coffee shop. I love my little corner space that has enough room for a cash register on the counter, a coffee machine and food prep space, as well as a few tables and chairs and what I call the cosy corner. Most people gravitate to the wingback chairs there to enjoy the warmth of the fireplace, a coffee and cake, and one of Juni's books. Goldie's floral arrangements adorn the tables and always draw customers to her shop on their way out, looking for a little bouquet of their own, to take home.

My love for coffee has only grown over the years, as has my love for our little business. What started out as a dream, became a reality for us when I was 'let go' from my barista job when Azalea was two. The owner wanted someone younger she could pay a lot less, and I needed flexibility as a newly single mum.

My sisters banded together, and we opened up our store, where I could work as much as I liked, and my daughter could be a regular feature here in a space where she was welcome and safe. Win win.

"Earth to Lala." Goldie starts waving to me and I'm snap out of my thoughts.

"I was asking if you wanted to come over for pizza tonight, Lala?"

Goldie's pizza is infamous in our family but after the day I've had, I'm ready to just head home and go to bed when it's closing time.

"I'll pass tonight love but thank you."

"What about Zaylee? She can come for pizza and a sleep over. I'll drop her at school tomorrow."

My mini me pipes up from the flower desk before I even get a chance to answer.

"Yes, please Aunty Goldie! Can we watch a movie too? Pleeeease."

I laugh, nodding in agreement, while Goldie shouts "Yes!" My sisters and I all live on the same street, which is convenient seeing as we spend all our spare time at each other's houses, or at our parents' house. When we aren't here of course.

Azalea runs over and fist bumps Goldie, before sitting on Juni's lap for cuddles.

I know how lucky I am to have such a wonderful, supportive family. Between her dad, my sisters, my parents and I, Azalea is surrounded by so much love.

"Make sure you call your dad before bed okay Zaylee."

She nods eagerly. She adores her dad, and he adores her, but his work keeps him away for long stretches of time, so it can be weeks, sometimes a month, before she sees him again.

Josh was my high school sweetheart, and we worked hard to make our marriage work, but we drifted apart more and more over the years, until we just became passing ships in the night. Eventually we reluctantly conceded that it felt more like we were friends, than lovers, around the time Azalea was two. So, we decided to separate, and later divorce.

Since then, it has just been Azalea and I in the house. Just the way I like it. I have zero time for relationships between the coffee shop and Azalea, and that won't be changing any time soon.

Chapter 2

THE NEXT DAY, I'M YAWNING at the counter, when one of my favourite customers walk in.

Ebony is one of my dearest friends and lives down the road from me. In our small coastal town, almost everyone lives down the road from one another.

Ebony, her husband Ryder and their two children Molly and Asher moved to our small town three years ago and we became fast friends over our love of coffee and running. Molly is four and just adorable and Asher is two and toddles behind his mum and sister everywhere they go. Today she is child-free, and I just know she deserves an extra-large coffee. I get started on making her one without asking. She loves coffee just as much as me.

"Hi, love how are you?" She asks, leaning over the counter and kissing my cheek.

"I'm tired. So tired. Counting down the minutes till closing time if I'm honest."

Eb laughs and flicks her hair over her shoulder. Her name suits her to a tee, with her long black hair always up in a ponytail. She picks up a cookie packet from the display tray, cracking it open and offering me a piece. I take it and savor the soft, chocolate gooey centre. I haven't had lunch today and its already afternoon. This week in the store has been killing me and I can't wait till the end of the week when I can take a day off.

Her expression turns sympathetic. She pats my hand, rubbing the back of it soothingly.

"Can I help in any way? I can do dishes or clean tables if that would lighten your load, Lala?"

I give her the first real genuine smile I have had today. She's an absolute angel. Warmth spreads through me. I'm so lucky to have such wonderfully supportive friends.

"I love you, Eb. You're too good to me. I'll keep your beautiful offer in mind."

I won't take her up on it unless I'm desperate, but it's so nice knowing the offer is there.

My thoughts wander back to yesterday and I shake my head thinking about it, dying to tell her what happened.

"You wouldn't believe the guy I had in here yesterday, Eb. He was so rude. I mean incredibly good looking, but a total jerk. I think he was just a tourist passing through thankfully, because I've never seen him before. He had the nerve to tell me to basically do my job and serve him coffee. Can you believe that?"

Eb shakes her head, again in sympathy. "Sounds like a real jerk love. Argh, tourists. Hopefully he has moved on already." Her tone is a little absentminded, but I don't think much of it.

I nod in response, taking another bite of the cookie she offers me again. She will insist I charge her for it, and I will insist that I won't. Only a small handful of people get freebies in my shop. Ebony, my sisters, my parents and our family friends Wolf, Bear and Fox.

Ebony starts tracing circles on the bench, and I know now, something is definitely up. I stop chewing and place the cookie down on the bench, brushing crumbs off my fingers and then wiping the counter down with a cloth.

"Out with it, Eb."

She looks up at me with innocent eyes as if to ask what I am talking about. I give her a pointed stare and she shrugs, a laugh bursting from her.

"Okay, okay, you've got me. Lala, before you say no, I need you to just agree and say yes."

I laugh in response. Eb has the most wonderful way with words. And she can get me to agree to pretty much anything.

"Okay… yes. I think. So, what am I agreeing to?"

She smiles and flutters her lashes dramatically, laughter exploding from her.

"You just agreed to a date with my brother."

Okay, she can get me to agree to almost anything. Except for that. I'm already shaking my head.

"Uh uh. Nope, not happening Eb. You know how I feel about being set up. Besides, I love you too much to date your brother. What if it was disastrous? And not to mention, I've never even met him."

She's nodding, ready to answer, already prepared for my response.

"I know Lala, I know. But remember I told you he was moving here to be close to us, for his daughter? Well, he did it. He finally moved here. After talking about it for the past six months, he just up and moved. His daughter is eight, just a year younger than Azalea. Besides all that, you guys would be so perfect for each other I just know it. He's thirty-eight, very good looking so I'm told and he's really kind. A perfect gentleman. And honestly you two have so much in common. Please, please, please?"

She throws puppy dog eyes, and I groan. I know she is going to keep asking until I agree. She is tenacious. She has some good points though. She has mentioned her brother to me a lot since we met, and he actually does sound pretty wonderful from her description of him.

I sigh, resigned to it. She grins. She knows she has me cornered.

"Do you at least have a picture of him? He's never in your family pictures on social media. I have no idea what he looks like."

She quickly scrambles for her phone, her eyes lighting up. She spends a few minutes flicking through photos on her phone.

"Argh, I can't find any. I haven't seen him in a year until yesterday and he isn't on social media because of his job. He's a police officer. Very reliable by the way."

She winks at me. She has me and she knows it.

"Okay fine. Just one date though okay. And just as friends. A very friendish friend date."

She laughs and claps her hands, jumping up and down with excitement.

"Yay! This will be wonderful. I just know it! Okay, I'm going now. I need to convince him of the same. I'll call you later!"

She jogs out, throwing a wave over her shoulder at me. I shake my head, laughing. I can't help but smile at her enthusiasm for this. Who knows, maybe her brother and I will become friends. I don't dare to dream it could be anything more than that. And I'm really not looking for more anyway.

I throw myself back into the rush of the day and forget all about the date until two days later when Ebony texts me. She has a day and time for the date. Crap.

'Hey gorg, Brax has agreed to meet up! Yay! If I'm honest though, and you know I always am, he was also reluctant. But I think this is going to be fun. Can you meet on Thursday night around 6pm at Armaretto's?'

My favorite Italian restaurant. Yes please. Even if this goes nowhere, I'll at least enjoy the food and it's been too long since I've been there. Actually, too long since I've relaxed and let loose a little. Maybe I'll even have a few wines. I smile at the thought. This could even be fun.

I flick her back a quick text agreeing to the location and time.

It clicks then that it's Wednesday, which means dinner is tomorrow night.

Nervous butterflies swarm my stomach. Suddenly I'm worrying about something I wasn't even fazed about before. I haven't been on a date in years. What do people even talk about on dates? What do I wear?

I shake it off. Ebony is one of my closest friends so any brother of hers will be just as great. I don't need to impress him. This is going to be easy.

That afternoon after closing the shop, I make my way across the road to the grocer just down the street. I wave at friends and locals that I pass on my way there. I love this little town. Aside from the tourists who seem to be growing in numbers every year, it has a peaceful vibe, and I like that I recognise most faces I pass on the street. More than half of the people in my small town have known me since I was a baby. I love that I get to raise my girl here, where she gets to have the same experience.

I glance at my watch and quicken my pace. I need to get to the grocer before they close. I push through the door and the bell chimes, a cold blast of air from the cooling hits my face. The cashier is busy serving someone, so I know I have a few minutes before they turn the sign at the door to closed. I rush through the aisles before heading back to the first one, closest to the door. The little bell rings again, signalling someone else has come in and a sigh of relief escapes me. I won't be the person holding up the shops closing time after all. I look up to see who it is, fully expecting to recognise the face. I do recognise them. Except it's not a friendly local.

It's the guy from the coffee shop yesterday. Argh.

I had hoped he might have left town already. Not my luck. Here's hoping he leaves tonight.

He's on the phone, so hopefully he is distracted enough that I can sneak to the register without him seeing me. I'm really not in the mood to talk to anyone, let alone him. It's been a long day, and I just want to get home and eat dinner. He makes his way into my aisle, and I scurry to the next one over. A little further away from the register and my chance of escape. Damn.

I overhear something that catches my attention, and I stop, grabbing the shelf before I stumble into the condiments. I pick up a random sauce bottle and pretend to read the ingredient list. It's tomato sauce. Yuck.

He is speaking loudly on the phone, and my blood starts to boil at what I hear next.

"Yeah, I'm just grabbing a jar of coffee." A bitter sounding chuckle escapes him and my eyes narrow.

"Yeah, they do have cafes. Apparently, the best coffee in town is where I went yesterday, and I refuse to go back there." He pauses, before responding to whatever question is thrown his way.

"Oh yeah, the coffee was really good. No issues with the coffee. Probably the best I've had honestly. But the service was terrible. The worker was rude."

He laughs again at something the other person says, and I practically snarl. Who does he think he is?

But damn right I make good coffee.

He isn't finished. I grit my teeth and place the sauce back on the shelf before shuffling down to grab a jar of pickles. I don't even know if I need pickles, but I need to keep my hands busy. I toss them in the basket not even bothering to check what type they are. Azalea loves pickles so I know they will get eaten.

I tune back in to his conversation. If steam could pour out of my ears, it would.

Travis, the young cashier, wanders down my aisle and starts to open his mouth, likely to offer me some help or have a chat. Normally we would talk for a good ten minutes, catching up on his schooling. Travis is about to graduate and head off to university. I babysat him when he was a toddler, and I have a soft spot for him. I try to explain to him with hand gestures and silent mouthing that I can't talk right now. His expression becomes puzzled, and I know he is on the verge on unintentionally outing me. I pull my phone out of my back pocket and quickly type a message, flashing the screen to him when I'm done.

'I'm listening to this phone call. Can't explain now, will explain later.'

I point towards the next aisle over and he raises his eyebrows and nods. He thankfully keeps walking.

I'm acting crazy and I know it, but I'll explain later. Right now, I need to hear the rest of this conversation.

"Callan, I would rather drink instant coffee than go back to that shop."

Oh, I can make that happen. I'm mentally preparing a sign that has his gorgeous face all over it, banning him from ever entering again.

Besides, he's not really that gorgeous anyway.

Okay, who am I kidding. He really is, but he's a jerk. His next comment solidifies that thought.

He laughs again. "She was incredibly beautiful that's for sure, but her attitude was something else."

Oh. He thinks I'm beautiful. A blush warms my cheeks, before I quickly shake it off. That part doesn't matter. He called me rude and said I had an 'attitude'.

He was the one who had the 'attitude'.

I'll show him 'attitude'.

I storm out of the aisle I'm in and past the one he is occupying, slowing to give him my best scowl. I hope it screams that I heard his conversation. I no longer care if he sees me.

He glances up, my stomping doing the trick, and does a double take when he spots me. The hand not holding his phone, reaches up to cover his face and he groans. Busted.

"Hey Cal, I'm going to have to call you back. Yeah, I screwed up."

Yep. You sure did buddy.

Deciding I'll just order takeout, I ditch my half full basket by the counter and march over to the door, pushing through the exit. I take a deep breath of the fresh night air and let out a frustrated grunt. I turn left towards home, still fuming. How dare he say I was rude. And why the hell is he still here?

I hear footsteps pound the pavement behind me but don't bother to turn around. I'm guessing it's him and I refuse to give him the satisfaction of looking behind me.

A deep, husky voice calls out behind me.

"Hey, wait up. That was rude of me to be talking about you like that. Please let me apologize. I am sorry."

I spin around, almost bumping into him he is so close. "Damn right it was. Except the part about my coffee. It really is the best. But other than that, you were rude. So rude."

He crosses his arms, frustration now crossing his face.

"Yep, I just admitted that didn't I? But in my defence… I didn't know you were there."

"Oh, so that makes it better? You didn't realise I was there, so that excuses your behaviour?"

Shaking his head, his hands go to his waist. "Hang on a second. I apologised. Sincerely. It was a mistake. That's it. Don't make this bigger than it needs to be."

My blood starts boiling once again. What is the go with this guy getting under my skin? No one has ever made my blood boil like this. No one.

"Oh, that's it? I have a reputation here pal, and you going around bad mouthing me is going to ruin it." My chest heaves from the energy this conversation is exerting from me.

Throwing my hands in the air, I laugh dryly. "You're so frustrating! I'm never this angry. I'm level-headed. I'm calm."

I point at him. "You. You're frustrating and rude."

His laugh sounds more like a bark, it's so loud and assuming.

"So other than pointing the finger at me, is there anything you might want to own up to?" he asks slowly, aggravation written all over his face.

I think about it for all but a second.

"Nope."

I spin around and continue my walk home, not looking back once. I hear a laugh burst from him behind me. Jerk.

Chapter 3

I SPEND THE NEXT DAY and a half focusing on work and not on my date. And also stewing on the grocery store incident. Most tourists only stay for a few days, so I imagine he has left by now.

It's 5:00pm Thursday and I'm rushing out of the store at closing time to head home and get ready. I give Azalea a quick kiss on the cheek and wave goodbye to Juni and Goldie. Juni agreed to mind Azalea at my house tonight till I get home from the date, and they have settled on a reading marathon with burgers and fries. Right up both of my girl's alley.

Once home, I head to my wardrobe, pulling out the dress I borrowed earlier from Juni. Thankfully we are the same size. Just another perk of having sisters.

It's a colour I gravitate to, and as soon as I spotted it in Juni's wardrobe, I knew it was the one I wanted to wear. Although initially I had planned on just wearing jeans and a nice top, my go to for dinners out. But Goldie convinced me I needed to make more of an effort than that, and looking at the beautiful, soft fabric, I'm glad she did.

It's a forest green floaty summer dress with a tied waist, that falls just below my knee. The spaghetti straps are delicate, and I pop on a silver chain to finish off the look. Juni tried to get me to wear her strappy heels, but I'll always be a sandals girl. I pop on my favourite brown pair and do a little turn in front of the mirror. I keep my hair loose in waves and my makeup light, with just a little mascara and a rose-colored lipstick.

Thankfully I live only one minute's walk from the restaurant, and I'm on main street in no time. I wander at a leisurely pace, in no rush to get there. As usual, I'm going to be early. I pass locals who all stop to say hi or wave as they pass. The air is slightly cool with a crisp breeze that rustles the leaves on the trees and lifts my skirt slightly. I watch as the ends lift and twirl in a dance of sorts, and I feel content. Happy.

I can see clear across the harbour, where the ocean meets our little inlet and as always, I'm mesmerized by the slow waves trickling in. My favourite thing to do every night, once Azalea is tucked in, is to sit with a cup of coffee in my cosy reading chair by my big wraparound window and look out at the ocean.

The breeze picks up again, shaking me from my thoughts, and I think to myself that I should have bought my cardigan for later when the sun is completely gone.

For now, I enjoy the cool breeze of the early evening night. I much prefer that to the heady, hot, salt in the air kind of days, like earlier today.

Pushing open the door of the restaurant I step inside, and the smell of fresh pizza dough mixed with tomatoes, garlic and cheese hits me. My mouth waters. It's a busy night and the restaurant is filled mostly with locals and peppered with tourists. Thankfully I can't see my friend from the other day.

As I look around, I realize I didn't even think to ask Eb what her brother looks like. I do another quick scan of the restaurant looking for a guy who looks like her. I crane my neck trying to see the other half of the restaurant that's hidden behind some large pillars. No luck.

"Lavender, my dear. Are you eating in tonight? We are full, but I can wrangle you a table if you give me five minutes."

I turn in the direction of the voice and give him a smile. Tony has owned Amaretto's for what feels like my whole life and is like the towns grandfather. He is adored by everyone.

I blush a little at my next words.

"Thank you, Tony, but I'm actually meeting someone here tonight. It's kind of a... date."

I shrug my shoulders at him, and he grins back at me, wide and joyful.

"Oh, Lavender, I'm so happy to hear that. You do so much for your store and your sweet Azalea. You deserve a little fun too, no? Who's the lucky guy - who are you meeting?"

I grin sheepishly. "All I know is that it's Ebony's brother. And his name is Brax."

I shrug again, trying to look nonchalant, but nerves have set in. He turns his head to the side thoughtfully and glances over at the tables.

"Yes, I think I know who you are meeting. I'll walk you over."

He abandons the front desk and ringing phone to escort me over to my date. He takes my hand in his and pats the back of it, before leading me through the restaurant. He confidently weaves in and out of tables, and I try to keep up. I can't see in front of him. He leads me to the back corner of the restaurant and stops suddenly. He pats my hand again, before stepping aside, gesturing at the table.

"Here you are my dear. I'll send Marie over soon to take your order."

He gives me a quick wink, before rushing back to the front desk. I tentatively step forward towards the empty seat, when the person sitting at the table with his back to me turns, mid hello.

His words trail off and I stop short of pulling out the chair and sitting. My mouth drops open at the same time, as his eyes squint in my direction.

It's the guy from the coffee shop and the grocer.

"It's you," he says accusingly, crossing his arms and leaning back in his chair.

To avoid a scene in front of people I have known my whole life, I roughly pull out my chair and take a seat, tossing my purse onto the table.

"I could say the same to you. What are you doing here?"

He smirks, raising an eyebrow.

"What am I doing here? What are you doing here? I thought I was meeting up with my sister's friend. The one she raves about. Yet here you are, and I just know you can't be the wonderful Lavender she talks about all the time."

Oh, the gall of him. If I could shoot daggers out of my eyes right now, I would.

He sits back, appraising me. Something akin to desire flashes across his face and I'm momentarily thrown. It passes quickly.

I squint back at him and mimic his stance in my chair. If he thinks he hasn't met his match, he is sorely mistaken.

"And here I thought I was meeting up with my friends amazing brother. Yet here you are. Seems like you have poor Ebony fooled about your character."

I send another glare his way. This time it's delight that flashes on his features and he laughs. Momentarily I get a glimpse of a charming smile under there. Momentarily, being the key word.

"I'm curious. Are you always so rude to your sister's friends?"

He leans forward in his chair and places his elbow on the table, his cheek resting on his hand. It kills me to admit it, but he looks good. I'll never admit that to him though. Why does he have to be so good looking but also an absolute jerk?

"Ebony only told me your name. She never mentioned where you work. Whenever you came up in conversation before I moved here, it was just Lavender this, Lavender that. Never anything about your job. So no, I'm never rude to my sister's friends."

I grunt in response "Doubtful."

"Are you this rude to your friends' brothers?"

I ignore his question, instead asking one of my own.

"So, you are our new police officer. I thought police officers had to be charming. And helpful. And kind." I raise an eyebrow at him and wait for his response.

Okay, I don't know where this side of me has come from, snarky and argumentative, but he has unleashed a monster.

He scowls, before leaning back and crossing his arms again.

"And I thought café owners needed to be hospitable to their patrons. Or did I incorrectly see you poking your tongue out at me the other day? Maybe I just imagined that?"

Oops, he did see. Okay, he's not wrong there. A snort bursts from me, and I quickly cup a hand over my mouth. It was petty of me to do, but I have zero regrets about it.

This date is sinking like a ship and sinking fast. I'm not getting caught in it, when it capsizes.

I push my chair back and stand, grabbing my purse off the table.

"I should have known it was you. You and Ebony have the exact same eyes," I tell him, pointing and waving my finger in his general direction.

He narrows his gaze, and a smirk lifts the corner of his full bottom lip. Argh. Why am I even noticing his lips?

I draw my shoulders back and stand taller. I'm not done yet.

"And you're right. I should be hospitable. So, this is me being that. Getting out before I say something I really regret. You have reminded me tonight why I never say yes to blind dates. So, thank you for restoring my faith in them. Not."

A brief look of remorse crosses his face before it closes off again.

I push my chair in, because even angry, I'm still a good customer.

"Also, I recommend the margarita and olive pizza. And the bruschetta. Grab a chocolate mousse too. It's to die for. And FYI. I am only recommending it because I love Tony, and he deserves a big sale out of you."

I waggle my fingers at him, before stomping off. I hear his laughter echoing behind me long after I reach the front door of the restaurant.

Chapter 4

School drop off - done. Coffee shop orders for the week - done. Bills paid. Food shopping - done. Check, check, check and check.

Monday is going well so far and its only eleven in the morning. The shop is closed Monday's and it's my day to relax, but I usually spend it doing odd jobs. Not today. Today I worked through my list as quickly as I could, to try and get some down time in before I pick Azalea up from school.

I stroll down the boardwalk with one destination in mind. Leo's bakery. My mouth waters at the thought of his cinnamon scrolls. It's been weeks since I've been able to get here and I'm ridiculously excited for that cinnamon pastry goodness.

I run up the few small steps and push open the door. I'm giddy. Euphoric almost. I've missed these scrolls, and it has been that kind of a week. I still haven't spoken to Eb about the date. She text me last night to ask how it went, so I am guessing her brother hasn't told her yet either.

Making my way to the glass cabinet, I spot the cinnamon scroll shelf. It's empty. I glance around, hoping they have moved its shelf. They haven't.

"Oh, hey Lavender, are you here for a scroll? Um, I just sold the last one…" Leo has the good graces to look upset on my part, even though he doesn't need to. He has done nothing wrong. But Leo knows just how much I love those scrolls.

I smile reassuringly at him.

"It's okay Leo. I'll try and get in earlier next week."

He double taps the counter. "I'll put one aside for you next week Lavender. I'm sorry. If I had known you were coming in…"

I'm distracted momentarily from the conversation. Out the corner of my eye, I spot a familiar looking shape. He turns and as he does, I see him take a big bite out of the cinnamon scroll that he is holding.

"You have got to be kidding me" my words trail off. I feel the anger slowly bubbling up inside.

I throw my hands in the air. "My god! You're everywhere."

Brax simply stares at me and takes another bite. Slowly. He is mocking me.

I point my finger at the scroll. I know I'm being childish, but I can't seem to help myself. I regress to a teenager in his company, and it is irritating.

"You…. You took the last scroll."

He nods and continues to take bites. God that scroll looks so good. Maybe even the best one that I've seen Leo make. My mouth waters.

I vaguely hear Leo offer me something else, but I'm too focused on the scroll thief in front of me.

"First you come into my shop and act like a jerk, then you tell me I have no customer service on the worst blind date I've ever been on - and trust me I've been on a few crappy ones."

"Yeah, I've got no doubt about that," he mutters under his breath, cutting me off. Oh no he didn't just say that.

"Damn." I hear Leo say. I'm with you on that one.

"Argh!" I stamp my foot. Acting like said teenager again. "You stole my scroll!"

I'm being irrational of course, but at this point, I just don't care.

He scoffs and gestures to the cabinet where said scroll lived only moments ago.

"I can't see your name on anything in this shop Lavender. So, it looks like you're out of luck."

He flicks a wave to Leo, "Thanks for the scroll, it's the best I've ever had." He turns to me, taking a huge bite out of it again, before he storms out of the bakery.

He is so frustrating. Leo clears his throat.

"Lavender… I can drop one over to you at the shop tomorrow?"

I smile at him sheepishly. "I'm sorry Leo, that was so out of character for me. He just makes me so mad! Long story there, I won't bore you. It's fine, I'll pop in next week and pick one up."

He chuckles at my response. "I could tell Lavender. I've never seen anyone make you so mad and I've known you since the day you were born. It might be worth thinking about why it is that he evokes such a response in you."

He gives me a friendly wink before walking off to restock the bread rolls.

What is he talking about? I shake my head and head back out the door, forlorn and a little defeated. I'm cinnamon scroll-less and a lot sadder for it.

Once home, I stubbornly try my hand at making my own cinnamon scrolls. I make most of the pastries and cakes in my own coffee shop, but I've never even attempted a cinnamon scroll. Leo's are absolute perfection, and I've always known I couldn't do it justice. And I wasn't wrong. I'm on my third failed batch. I toss them all into the bin.

I turn to a task that always soothes my soul, and one that I am good at. I plug in the coffee machine and scoop the beans out, tamping them down. I listen to the bubbling, the calming scent of coffee wafting through the kitchen. I pour a small pitcher of milk and begin the frothing process, my hands warming as the liquid heats and expands.

I wipe the machine over and holding the mug in my hand, I take a seat at the breakfast nook. My mind wanders over the events of earlier today. Shame fills me. I can't believe I reacted that way in Leo's shop. Something about Brax drives me to insanity.

I should definitely apologise to Leo, and I probably should apologise to Brax too.

Maybe. I'll think on that one a bit more. But I was, out of line.

I unlock my phone and send Ebony a quick text, finally filling her in on our date and then the events of earlier today. She doesn't disappoint in her response and a laugh bursts out of me.

'Whaaaaaat?! He hasn't told me anything and when I asked him how the date went, he told me he would tell me in person at our family dinner. Sounds like he deserved the blow-up after the way he acted in your store and on the date. No apology necessary honey.'

Another text quickly follows before I can reply.

'Did I ever tell you he pushed me into a puddle when I was five and he was seven? He does not deserve that last scroll. Thanks for avenging us both!'

I smile widely at that. More text bubbles appear, and I patiently wait for her next message.

'But in all seriousness Lala, he really is the best guy (other than my wonderful husband). I have no idea what's taken over him when it comes to you. This is so out of character for him.'

I frown at that and turn my phone over, taking a sip of my coffee. I have no idea either.

Chapter 5

A FEW DAYS AFTER MY bad date and bakery run in, I'm serving at the counter when I spot a sheepish Ebony walking towards me. She is with her daughter Molly, and a young girl I've never seen before. She has long black hair like Ebony and Molly. I wave to Molly and her friend. Ebony seats them at a table near the counter, before walking over to me, holding up a small bag of candy in front of her.

"Peace offering," she says, before gently placing it on the counter and stepping back to wait for me to finish the coffee order I'm making.

I hand over the to-go cup to my customer, giving them a smile, before turning to Ebony.

I reach for the candy. She knows the way to my heart is always sweets. Sweets and coffee of course.

"You don't need to give me any peace offerings. You did nothing wrong Eb. It's not your fault your brother lost his manners the other day. And the day after. Or the few days after that too."

I laugh to lighten the mood, but I'm still frustrated with him and our abysmal date.

"Ouch, but absolutely fair call. No, you're right. I don't know what got into him. It is very unlike him." Eb replied.

I find that hard to believe, but I don't challenge her on it. I have to remember this is her very much-loved brother.

"It's ok Eb, never mind… So, who do you have here with you today?" I gesture at the young girl close in age to my own daughter, sitting at the table with four-year-old Molly.

"Well… this is Beth. Beth is actually Brax's daughter."

Beth looks up at the mention of her name and gives me a sunny smile and a wave. She's a real cutie. I give her a beaming smile and wave back.

"She is actually starting at Azalea's school tomorrow. I was hoping Zaylee might be here today to meet her. Just to help Beth feel comfortable about starting at a new school."

I'm nodding before she can finish. Her dad might leave something to be desired, but that's not Beth's fault. The brief interaction I had with her is enough to tell me that she is a little ray of sunshine.

"Yeah, Zaylee is here. She is out the back helping Goldie plant flowers."

I turn to face Beth. "Would you like to join my daughter and my sister in the back garden, Beth? They are planting some flowers."

Beth nods quickly and Ebony reaches over, taking her hand and giving her a small affectionate smile. Molly hops up from the table too, and races over, giving me a big hug before grabbing her mum's hand.

"I'll head out there with her Lala. Can we grab dinner this week?"

I smile wide and it's a genuine one for my sweet friend.

"Of course, I would love that, Eb. Juni and Goldie have planned a Mexican fiesta night Sunday - if you wanted to join?"

She blows me a kiss as she walks through the back door. "Sounds fab, I would love to! I'll message you later gorg. Sorry again about my bonehead brother."

She mouths the last part above her niece's head, so she doesn't hear. I give her another smile, reassuring her it's okay.

It's not her fault that her brother misplaced his manners in the move to our small town.

A week passes by, and the name Beth has become a household regular. Azalea has found her new bestie and it's freaking adorable.

We are sitting down to breakfast at the nook one morning when the inevitable happens.

"Mum, can Beth come over for a play date?"

Ah there it is. The question I was waiting for. I can't check with Ebony about this one. This is a parent-to-parent question. Beth is an absolute sweetheart, and I love Azalea's newfound friendship with her. So, it looks like I'm going to have to speak to Brax again after all. The last time we spoke was at the bakery, and I wouldn't exactly call that speaking. If I'm honest, I was maybe a little, or a lot, to blame for that scene. Hindsight is a wonderful thing.

"Yes, sure honey. I'll speak with her dad, and we can organise something soon."

I'm deliberately vague about when that will be.

My answer is not good enough for my girl and I knew it wouldn't be. She needs to lock it down.

"Thanks mum. How about this weekend?"

"Umm… I'll check Zaylee. Leave it with me. So, ah, what are you taking in for news today?"

Steering the conversation down a different path works, and my mini runs a mile a minute talking about her news article for class.

I keep thinking about the conversation I will need to have with Brax and butterflies fill my stomach.

I usher her off to get ready. Picking up my half full mug, I make my way around the house, picking up jumpers, bags, shoes and schoolwork, while sipping my coffee. The delicious aroma drifts through the house as I walk, leaving a warm trail in its wake.

I love my cosy little home. It's the perfect size for Zaylee and I. We have worked hard over the years to make it our own. After Josh moved out all those years ago, I felt this urge to reinvent the space, to replace and remodel everything I could, for my fresh start. In time, Zaylee has added splashes of her personality here too. Our back porch overlooks the ocean in the distance and at night, we can hear the waves crashing. It's pure magic.

Lamps adorn every side table in each room, and cushions pile onto every space of our wrap around couch. I went with a neutral coastal vibe, and I still love the peaceful feel my home has. The only real mix of colour here, are Azalea's artworks on the fridge, the art we have framed on the walls in our hallway, and the fun coffee coasters that Goldie has painted for me over the years. Being a coffee connoisseur, coasters as well as beautiful mugs, are my quirk.

I rush through getting ready, throwing on my 'unofficial' work outfit. Jeans or leggings are my go-to, but today it's leggings and a black oversized tee. I pop on my scrunchy socks and sneakers. I like to think of my look as casual, stylish mum. Azalea would tell me to add some colour if she was helping me get ready, but thankfully she isn't. Colour is Goldie's domain. Juni's is more moody hues.

"Mum, I'm ready, let's go!"

I head to the kitchen and pour the rest of my coffee in a to-go cup. Now I'm ready.

After dropping Azalea to school, I make my way over to the shop, flipping the sign to 'open' as I breeze through the door. Thankfully the school is only a two-minute walk from the shop. I can do drop-off and then get to the shop fifteen minutes before we open. If I'm running late, Juni steps in and sets up the coffee shop for me. Gosh I love her.

Juni glances up from the tables where she is restocking napkins, and I blow her a kiss in thanks. As I pass Goldie in the florist, I give her a quick squeeze.

"Morning sister," Goldie says, squeezing me back.

The day moves along surprisingly fast, with a steady stream of customers trailing through our doors. We take turns minding each other's shop section while the other goes on a break. I love getting to sell books and make floral arrangements each day. Before I know it, it's almost closing time. I breathe a sigh of sweet relief.

Lately I've been feeling a little run down with how busy the store has been. I haven't had a solid few days off in a row, for a while. Maybe a little vacation with Azalea is in order.

I'm busy daydreaming at the counter, thinking about possible holiday destinations, when the bell over the door tinkles.

I glance up shaken from my daydream, and turn to refill the machine with coffee, almost spilling it in the process. It's Brax. In his uniform. Oh, my lord.

I may not be a fan of his attitude, but I am certainly a fan of him in this uniform.

His eyes find mine and a look I can't quite place, passes over his face. Dread maybe?

Whatever he is here for, he isn't looking forward to it. Nerves bubble up in my stomach, wondering what it might be about.

He saunters over and I brace myself for whatever he has to say. Hopefully I'm just reading into it too much, and he's only in need of a coffee. I step out from behind the counter and wring my hands behind my back.

"Lavender." Okay, I do not like him, but I do like his voice. Especially when he says my name.

He continues. "I think it's pretty obvious that we don't get along."

I stop myself from rolling my eyes at that one. Yes, captain obvious. I stay silent still, waiting to hear the rest. I don't know where this sarcastic side of me has come from, but Goldie would be proud.

"But it seems my daughter Beth, is a little infatuated with your daughter. A lot actually. I've heard about her all week, and now she has moved into playdate territory."

Ah, he has been grilled for a playdate too. He clears his throat.

"It means a lot to me that Beth has found a friend. I was worried about moving her away from everything she knew, and all her friends back home. But this week she has been excited to go to school and has been happy. The happiest I have seen her in a while. Your Azalea has had a lot to do with that."

Oh. I didn't expect that at all. I still don't like him, but I can empathise with wanting the best for your child and for them to be happy. I thaw slightly. Only slightly though.

My tone is a little friendlier than it was before. "You're here to call a truce?"

He grimaces but nods. This is killing him. Oddly, I feel comforted by that.

"Yeah, I am. Just in front of the kids. If we can be civil and not shoot each other down, metaphorically speaking, I think we should try. It's very clear we don't get along, so I'm not asking to be friends. Just cordial to each other."

I know it took guts to come here and do this. If he can do this for Beth, then I can do this for Azalea.

I put my hand out in front of me, and he glances down at it, like it's repulsive to him. What a way to make a girl feel good about herself. I almost withdraw my hand before he hesitantly reaches out, his clasping mine. A sharp tingle shoots up my arm, and he pulls his hand away so suddenly, that I know he felt it too. I take a step back, nodding at him.

"Yeah, sure Brax, I can do that... ah, I need to get back to work. Would you like a coffee to go?"

He rubs the back of his head with his hand, looking unsure about how to answer before placing his hand on his hip and nodding.

"Yeah sure, a black coffee would be great. Thanks."

I turn and make my way back to the counter, making sure not to look over at him until I'm finished. I make his coffee as quickly as I can and hand it over, making sure to not touch any part of his hand in the exchange. He looks to do the same, and snatches the cup away, almost spilling it in the process. I quickly ring up his order and he taps his card, almost as fast.

"Okay, thanks Lavender… I'll speak to you soon about the girls having a playdate."

Then he is gone. And I'm left standing at the counter wondering what the hell just happened.

Chapter 6

Brax

I HATE THAT THIS IS the best damn coffee I've had in years. Maybe ever if I'm honest with myself.

I take another sip, and I already feel calmer. That went better than I expected. I hop back in the squad car and head home. I've finished my coffee by the time I pull into the garage, but I haven't finished thinking about Lavender.

Lavender Wild. Wild is accurate. In that she drives me wild. I've never met someone so infuriating in my life, and that says a lot with the job I do. I usually let things slide and not affect me, but she certainly has. The other cops I work with tell me I have the patience of a saint, and I really do. So, what the hell is going on?

I change out of my uniform and throwing on a t-shirt and sweats, I grab my keys and slip my feet into my runners by the door.

The cool night air gives me a minute's reprieve from thinking about her, as I make my way down the street to my sister Ebony's. I don't bother knocking, I never have at Eb's house.

As I open the front door, the smell of a roast dinner hits me, and my mouth waters. I kick off my shoes as my girl comes racing into the room, diving into my arms.

"Daddy! I missed you."

I hug her tight and kiss her on the top of her head. "I missed you too Bethy Bug. Loads. Have you done your homework? After dinner at Aunt Eb's, it's straight home to bed okay."

She nods up at me grinning. I'll never get sick of her enthusiastic and loving hellos. She's the best.

Beth takes off to join her Uncle Ryder in the lounge room, where they were watching a TV show. Ryder is one of my oldest friends. He and Ebony started dating when Beth was three and married when she was four. But he was always Beth's uncle, long before he officially was. I call out a "Hi" to Ryder. I'll catch up with him over dinner.

Right now, I need to vent to my sister.

Walking into the kitchen, I throw my arm over Eb's shoulders and kiss her lightly on the head.

I lucked out with siblings. Ebony is the greatest. It's always been just us two for the majority of our adult life. Our parents are travelling sports team doctors and have been since before we were born. It's meant that for most of our life, they have travelled with their football team, often leaving us at home with family, friends, or nannies. My parents are great, but they never had that parenting instinct and so it's always been Eb and I, supporting each other. We speak to our parents on the phone once every few weeks and we see them once a year and that suits us all just fine.

In the three years that Eb has lived here, she always came to us in the city. Beth and I have only visited her once and it was for two days and so quick that we didn't even leave the house except for a trip to the beach. But that was enough of a taste of this town, to know it was the best place for Beth to grow up.

I walk around the bench and pull out a stool, taking a seat and bracing against the kitchen bench. I clear my throat, and Eb looks at me suspiciously.

I point at the bread rolls she is buttering, and she nods, handing me a knife. I take over her job, while she plates the hot food.

I try to be casual, knowing full well I need to tread lightly here. Instead, I blurt out my question, frustration bubbling to the surface.

"What is the go with Lavender. Why is she so frustrating?"

Ebony's head rears back in surprise. Then a laugh bursts from her.

"Oh brother, you are speaking in tongues. You must be the only person on this planet, and very definitely in this town, that would ever use those words to describe Lavender Wild."

She laughs again, finding this hilarious. It's not. I frown, glaring at her, which only makes her laugh louder.

"Seriously Eb. She's infuriating! The first day I met her she was too busy checking out some guy in her store, to serve her own customers, and then she had the nerve to act like I was in the wrong."

I lean back on the stool, crossing my arms and scoffing at the memory.

She sends me a pointed look before going back to buttering.

I know a lecture is coming and I feel like we are kids all over again. I might be three years older than Eb, but she's always acted like it's the other way around.

"Brax Chance Madox. She was not checking out a customer. I spoke to her about it, and she told me she was watching some poor guy trying to get her sisters attention. Lala didn't know she had a customer waiting. I know you had just moved that day, and you were tired, but you've got her all wrong. She's wonderful. She took me under her wing when I moved here. She unconditionally loves, and mothers everyone. She is adored in this town. Rightfully so."

Interesting. Lavender supported Eb when she knew no one here. Now Azalea is doing the same for Beth. I'm starting to think maybe I should be a little more grateful and a little less of a jerk about all of this.

I was a little harsh with her that day. I was tired. Overall, it was a shit day. Beth was upset about moving and cried the whole drive talking about the friends she would be leaving behind, and I got a flat halfway here. Maybe I did overreact.

"Okay, if what you're saying is true, then fair call. Maybe. And I admit, I was pretty rude that day. I was also out of line in the supermarket. I shouldn't have spoken about her to Callan like that. Bethy was still upset about moving and I took out my frustration on her. But what about the cinnamon scroll? You have to admit, that was ridiculous."

Ebony puts the knife down on the bench and braces her hands on the edge of the countertop. Looking frustrated at me.

"Brax. From Leo's account, you might have encouraged her meltdown a little bit. You're not innocent here big bro. Don't even start on that bad date either. Of course she was offside. You picked her up and put her there."

Eb stares at me daring to argue with her. I open my mouth ready to argue but let out a sigh instead. I won't win this argument. Ebony has already made it clear she thinks the sun originated from Lavender, and now she is using football references which for her, is bringing out the big guns.

I hold up my hands, chuckling. "Okay, okay. I come in peace. You're team Lavender. I get it."

She shakes her head. "Uh uh, I'm team both of you. Have you wondered at all why I even set you up in the first place?"

"Actually yeah, I have. The thought has crossed my mind. A lot." My sister's judgment is generally good, but I'm questioning it in this scenario.

"So, why did you set us up?"

"Aside from wanting my best friend to become my sister-in-law and wanting my big brother to find a wonderful love like I have, you're both similar. Really similar."

I'm already shaking my head at that. Not possible.

"You are! You're both kind and thoughtful. Brax, you give to the people you love and care about. Lavender does too. She mothers everyone. You're both really funny and sometimes when she makes a joke, I can't help but think how you would have said the exact same thing. You are both amazing parents. You have two daughters, almost the same age. It's a perfect pairing if you ask me."

I'm stunned into silence. When she puts it like that, I can see what she means. But there's no way it would work. Sure, she is hot as hell. Maybe the most beautiful woman I've ever seen. If I put my shit aside and was honest with myself, that first day I met her in the coffee shop… I was the one checking her out. But then I thought she was looking at some other guy and it irked me. More than I care to admit. Every time I have seen her since, I've noticed something else about her. The unique green of her eyes that sparkle like emeralds. Or the way she looks when she laughs at something and doesn't realise anyone is watching. Carefree. Her whole face lights up. Like that day in the coffee shop, or when she was talking to Leo in the bakery.

But the catch is - I can't be in her space for longer than five minutes before I get annoyed and want to argue with her.

Why is that? And why the hell can't I stop thinking about her?

Chapter 7

I FLICK THE SIGN ON the door to open and take a seat behind Marigold's counter. She is running late this morning, so Juni and I are manning the entire shop. It's one of our slowest days of the week, so I don't expect the morning rush to kick off until ten.

I glance around Goldie's space. Her shop is the most wonderful burst of colour. Every possible flower you can think of adorns walls, baskets, tubs and hanging spaces around the shop. Soft, floaty, velvet ribbons in every colour imaginable, trickle down the wall behind her shop desk.

It's the most warm and welcome space for customers who come into our store, and I'm so proud of what Goldie has created here. The scent of flowers envelopes you as you walk through the door. Particularly the Peonies, Lavender and Magnolia's, mixed with the earthy scent of greenery and foliage. It's heavenly.

I get started on putting together an arrangement that is looking rather sad in my less than capable hands, when the bell tingles over the door.

I look up and surprised by who it is, my finger slips on the thorn of a rose.

"Ouch." I shake my finger, blood pooling on the end. I pop it in my mouth, to stop the bleeding.

Brax watches, concern etching his face as well as another emotion I can't pick, that quickly disappears when he notices that I'm watching him.

"Are you okay?" He asks me tentatively.

I nod, popping my finger out of my mouth.

"I'm fine."

"Thank you," I add, as if it's an afterthought.

I run my hands down the front of my shirt, brushing off flower scraps, suddenly nervous. Why am I nervous?

"So, uh, what can I help you with Brax?"

He rubs at the back of his neck, turning his head to the side.

"Is Goldie here? I'm just after some flowers."

He glances around, looking for her, coming up short.

I shake my head, "No she's running late. But I can help you… sort of." I laugh, a genuine smile spreading across my face.

Brax cracks a small smile. A smile. No matter how small, it's still one.

I'm a little stunned.

"Well, uh, I can try and make you a bouquet and if I screw it up, I can get Goldie to redo it. Is that okay?"

He nods. "Yeah sure, let's do it."

"So… who are you buying flowers for?"

It's none of my business, but I've heard Goldie ask customers that question and then explain that it helps her to hone in on the vibe of the arrangement.

What I don't say, is that I'm also just really keen to know who he wants to buy flowers for. Is it a date?

He doesn't seem phased by my question or show it if he thinks it's an odd one.

"It's for Beth. I wanted to surprise her when I pick her up from school."

Oh. He is buying flowers for his daughter. That's the sweetest.

"That is so nice Brax. I bet she will love that. Does she have a favourite colour?"

He runs me through her favourite colours, and I get to work, doing my best to make an arrangement with flowers that I think she will like.

I work in silence, aware that he is watching me the entire time. I pick an assortment of colours and flowers. They look okay to me. There's a mix of pink roses, sprigs of lavender, a few sprays of babies breath, a few yellow daffodils and red dahlias. I have no idea if this works, but I think it's pretty.

I finish it off with a hot pink ribbon. I twirl it in my hands, studying it from all angles. It's not bad at all. But it's certainly not up to Goldie's level. The more I look at it, the more I feel deflated.

I place it on the bench. "I'm sorry Brax, its nowhere near as good as Goldie can do. She should be here soon. If you don't mind coming back, I can get her to redo it."

He looks at the bouquet and looks at me, confusion clouding his features.

"Lavender, it's great. Beth is going to love it. I don't want it redone; I'll take this one. How much do I owe you?"

Oh, he likes it. A blush fills my cheeks and spreads down my neck and across my chest.

I fumble around for her price list and work out a price, giving him a small discount. He pays me, grabbing the bouquet off the bench.

"Thank you for this," and he holds the flowers up, pushing the front door open.

I really wish Brax would go back to being a jerk so I could go back to hating him. Instead, each interaction with him has me thawing, just a tiny bit more.

Goldie walks in, wild and wonderful, hair half up, contained in a bow atop her head, the rest flowing in a glorious mess of pink curls and waves behind her. Today's overalls are hot pink, and her tee is a pastel blue. Her canvas shoes are decidedly tame today. Just a plain white shoe she has painted some flowers on the side of. Usually, her shoes are as bright as her clothes.

She is as cute as a button.

"I'm sorry Lala. I had to go to the hardware store to grab some more wire. My supplier hasn't had mine in stock for a while, so this will have to do." She waves the bag in front of me.

"All good Goldie, I didn't mind. You know I love your shop and It's fun to play with flowers for a change."

She winks at me. "You know you can work in the shop whenever you like sweetheart."

A warm smile spreads across my face. "You're a ray of sunshine Goldie girl. Thank you."

She reaches under the bench and brings scissors, spools of ribbon and foam pieces to the surface.

"So, did anyone come in for flowers while I was gone?"

I pull out the order book, turning today's order page to face her.

"Yep. So, a few orders and purchases of your premade bouquets. Two birthdays, one anniversary and one thinking of you, bouquet. When Steph was in ordering for a birthday, I overheard her say to someone on the phone that she was off to order her wedding flowers… I'm sorry Goldie."

She screws her face up and groans. "When will I crack this damn wedding market. It's so frustrating!"

I nod, understanding her disappointment. She has worked so hard to try and get into the wedding market, but for now, everyone orders from another local florist. In my opinion, Goldie's flower arrangements are unmatched, but people are concerned that maybe she can't do wedding flowers since she hasn't had her own. It's antiquated and ridiculous.

"It is frustrating," I agree. "I know you will one day though, for sure. Maybe once you have your own wedding." I give her a wink and blow her a kiss.

She laughs, pulling out tubs ready for bouquets.

"Me, get married? In your wildest dreams Lavender."

"Who's getting married?" Juni pipes up from her corner of the bookstore.

"No one," Goldie and I say in unison.

"But maybe Goldie, one day," I add.

Goldie shakes her head again and Juni looks thoughtful, considering my words. She nods adamantly, in absolute agreeance with me.

"Oh Goldie, you're a closet romantic at heart. You'll get married one day," she says.

Goldie throws up her hands, exasperated with us both. "I am not a closet romantic Juni. I am free spirited and live my life exactly how I want to. I can promise you I am not secretly pining for a man or a woman over here. I don't need someone telling me what my house should look like or that there's too much colour everywhere. No thank you."

Juni, the real romantic, shakes her head. "The right guy won't try and change you, Goldie. He will love you and all your colour, just as you are."

Goldie shakes her head, quickly changing the subject.

"Anyway, I saw Fox in the hardware store today… I asked him why he hasn't been coming to our family get togethers recently. He mentioned he has been really busy… and work is going well. Did you happen to need any work done in the bookstore Juni…?"

Goldie shoots me a quick glance and I try to hide my smile. I know exactly what she is doing. Sneaky.

Juni innocently looks around the bookstore, completely oblivious to the implied meaning behind Goldie's words. She never makes the connection when it comes to Fox. Now if he was written as a main male character into one of her stories, that would be a whole different ball game.

"I have been thinking of getting new shelving, now that the store is doing so well."

She looks off into the distance, very serious and contemplative.

"But actually, I might hold off till just before Christmas."

Goldie looks over at me, sighing and shaking her head. She will try, till the end of time, to get those two together. Everyone in our two families, knows that Fox is majorly in love with our Juni. But Juni is too oblivious to catch on, and there's no point in telling her. She would feel awkward around him after that. We all decided years ago that she needs to come to the realisation on her own. But it's painful to watch them together. Juni floats around in his presence and she doesn't even realise it. She glows around him. And Fox absolutely swoons over her.

Maybe one day they will get it together.

"Stop meddling," I mouth to Goldie.

She rolls her eyes, leaning close and whispering, "You know she likes him, she just doesn't realise she does, because she's too caught up in those books. Her real-life prince charming is right in front of her. He's the only guy she likes spending time with. And the only one she actually wants to talk to!"

I swat her away when Juni looks over at us, her eyes narrowing. "What are you two whispering about?"

"Nothing," we say in unison.

I turn to Goldie, quickly changing the subject and hoping Juni doesn't push for more information.

"So, ah, other customer you had pop in this morning was Brax… He came in to get a bouquet for his daughter Beth."

"Awww" they both chime in response.

Goldie gives me a huge grin, her eyebrows raising up and down.

"I know we are supposed to hate him, but he really does seem sweet. And oh, my goodness, is he sexy. I think we should forgive some of his past transgressions so you can test out the goods," Goldie says laughingly.

A groan escapes me, and my hands fly to my face, covering my eyes.

"Argh, no thank you. I will admit however that getting his daughter flowers was very sweet. He also liked the bouquet I made."

I scramble through my bag, searching for my phone. "Here, I took a picture of it to show you."

I scroll across to the photo, shoving it in her direction.

Goldie squints her eyes looking at it and uses her fingers to zoom in. She glances at me and then looks at the bouquet again.

"It's… lovely Lala. Really nice. He um, loved it did you say?"

I give her shoulder a light push. "Yes, I know. It's not professional looking at all. But I think it's kind of cute."

I turn my head, studying the picture a little more. It is a little lopsided and I maybe didn't pick the best flower combo. Okay, I need to stop looking at it, or I'm going to pick it apart even more.

She nods, a little too eagerly. "Oh yeah, it's really cute. You did a great job."

She slides off the stool adding, "And I take it back. We are not supposed to hate that man. He is a saint for loving your bouquet Lavender," and she laughs, ducking out of the way of the flower stem I throw at her.

Chapter 8

A WEEK GOES BY, AND I can't avoid it any longer. I brace myself for what I'm about to do. I hit send and close my eyes. Although I've thawed a little towards Brax, I still don't want to hang out with him for a whole morning. But I'll do it for my girl. Just like I know he is going to do it for Beth.

We have that in common at least.

I squint at the screen, rereading my message. I probably do need glasses. I'll add it to my never-ending list of things to get done as a single parent who owns their own business too.

'Hey Brax, it's Lavender Wild. I've done my best to hold off for as long as I could on this, and I know you aren't looking forward to it either, but Azalea has not stopped

asking to see Beth. Do you think we could just meet up at the walking track, so the kids can ride their bikes? Let me know what you think. I really did try my best to drag this out. Promise.'

The little sent icon finally pops up. It's done. Now to wait for a reply. Part of me is hoping he says no, and I can at least say I tried. But I really don't want to let my baby girl down either.

I sit, nervously fidgeting on the couch before I turn on the TV and absently flick through channels. Ten minutes go by, and a text alert screeches from my phone.

I peer over the arm of the couch at the lamp table, not daring to touch my phone.

It's Brax. Of course it is.

Reluctantly I pick it up and open the text.

'Hey, Lavender Wild. It's okay, I'm in the same boat. Although I am glad it's not just me getting asked every second of every day to organise this. Let's do the walking track and hopefully that will keep the girls happy for a while longer. Saturday 10am work for you? I've been running the track every morning since I moved here, so I know where it is.'

Oh, he is a runner too. I mentally file that in the back of my mind as another thing we seem to have in common.

I flick a quick text back, agreeing to meet at that time and date. Unsurprisingly, I get no reply back. Although his text back was perfectly nice, we both seem keen to keep our interactions at a minimum where possible. I think back over how sweet he was for getting Beth flowers the other week. It's really what helped me feel comfortable to message him to catch up.

Taking in a deep breath, I cement in this catch up. No going back after this.

"Hey Zaylee," I call out. "Beth's dad agreed to a catch up. We are meeting them on the walking track Saturday. You can take your bike."

Before I even finish, I hear excited squeals from her bedroom. Azalea comes racing out and dives into my arms on the couch. Laughter bursts out of me and I pepper kisses on top of her head.

"Thank you, Mum! You're the best! The best ever."

She jumps up and does a happy dance before racing back into her room. I can hear her cheering.

The awkward catch up I'm going to have with Brax, is by far worth the excitement she just had.

A smile spreads across my face, and I settle back into the couch. Excited for my mini to spend time with her friend. But not so excited to spend my morning with Brax.

Saturday rolls around far too quickly for my liking. As this isn't a date, and never will be, I make zero effort with my appearance, in comparison to my last catch up with Brax.

The dreaded 'date' that we won't speak of again. I hope.

I throw on some leggings, my baby blue runners and my favourite lemon coloured, long sports crop. My hair is up in the messiest of buns, and I pop on my sunglasses for good measure. Azalea on the other hand, dresses up as if she is going to a concert. She meticulously chooses a glitter top, sparkly silver leggings and her hot pink runners. She looks fabulous.

I give her a big squeeze on the way out, and we leisurely stroll to the walking track, Azalea pushing her bike along as we chat.

As we round the corner, I spot Brax, leaning against the streetlight, a huge smile on his face. I'm thrown momentarily. I've never seen him look so happy.

He is watching Beth rollerblade up and down the path. He cheers her on, every time she picks up speed.

Against my better judgement, I recognise he is exuding good dad vibes, and I'm honestly here for it. In a platonic, not interested, but still going to check him out way.

As we get closer, he looks up in our direction, his face closing off. The easy way in which he smiled at his daughter and laughed along with her, is now gone and replaced by a more cautious one. But not entirely unfriendly. I think our florist experience, thawed the ice a little for the both of us.

He pushes off from the light post and gives me that same cautious smile, before turning to Azalea and giving her a wave.

"Hi Lavender. Hi Azalea. It's so nice to meet you. I have heard so many wonderful things about you from your mum and from Ebony and Beth."

Okay, well that was nice of him. Not only was he kind, but he also aimed that charming smile at my daughter. The easy, natural one.

There goes that ice thawing a teeny tiny bit more.

He glances up at me and the easy smile stays there, albeit a little more dimmed. I decide after that interaction just now, that I am more than okay with that. More than okay with someone who is kind to my daughter and helps her to feel at ease.

I smile back, my own a lot less hesitant now.

He gestures to the path and the girls rush ahead, giggling and talking loudly.

Their joy is infectious, and a real smile bursts from me. Brax looks over at that exact moment, and from the corner of my eye, I spy him do a double take, before turning back to look out at the water.

We are both silent for a few minutes, walking side by side, when he clears his throat.

"It's a beautiful place Lavender." He gestures out to the ocean and the path in front of us. "My sister has been at me for years to come here to raise Bethy. Since she moved here really. I wasn't ready till now."

Surprised by his candidness, I don't respond immediately. He doesn't volunteer any more information than that or about why Beth's mother isn't on the scene, and I don't ask.

I nod, acknowledging his first comment.

"I've lived here basically my whole life, and I can't picture being anywhere else. It's heaven on earth. Well, that's how my sisters and I feel anyway. Which is lucky, because we are together almost all the time."

He looks up at me with a quizzical expression.

"I know you own the store together, but do you all live together too?"

I laugh at his question and his puzzled expression. It's not the first time I've been asked that, and it won't be the last, I'm sure.

"No, we don't live together, we all have our own homes. Mum and dad made sure we all bought houses in our early twenties to be financially 'sensible'. God, I hate that word. But they were right. We do all live on the same street though and it's the absolute best. Our neighbours often see us running up and down the street at all hours, for a quick catch up, some milk, to borrow something or for a sleep over. I really couldn't have asked for better siblings."

He nods at my words and a small smile lifts the corner of his mouth. I watch his mouth a little longer than is comfortably appropriate. He starts talking and breaks me out of my stare.

"Yeah, I see that. It's pretty obvious how close you all are, from the glares they shoot in my direction whenever I go into the store."

Laughter bursts from me again. I love them. I can picture them doing exactly that.

He smirks, but this time in an amused way.

"But really, it's very cool. Eb and I get along really well, but we aren't as close as you and your sisters. I'm hoping being here will change that. She's a fantastic aunt to Beth and she really needs more female figures in her life. There are things I can't quite understand, no matter how hard I try. Eb just gets it."

He glances at me from the corner of his eye, as if weighing up what he says next, deciding whether to confess it.

"Beth's mother and I were never together. As in, never in a relationship together. We went on a few dates together, and that was it. We went our separate ways. The chemistry just wasn't there. She called me nine months later, to tell me that she had just given birth to a baby and asked if I wanted her before she gave her up for adoption. I got on a plane hours after that call, raced to the hospital and within twenty-four hours, I was a father. Without a doubt, the best decision I've ever made. Beth is the best thing in my life."

Surprise floors me and I'm lost for words. I scramble my thoughts together, wanting to say the right thing. I mean Brax confiding in me? What on earth is happening right now?

I think back to Ebony telling me how her brother is one of the most amazing men. I'm starting to see why she praises him so much. I'm also wondering why she never told me about this. But then, come to think about it… I don't tell anyone half of the things my sisters tell me.

Before I can think about it too much, I reach out and gently squeeze his forearm. He looks down where his arm and my hand meet, before looking up at me, that quizzical look crossing his face again. My hand retracts back to my side quickly. I take a deep breath before responding.

"Not a lot of guys would do that Brax. That must have been really hard and such a surprise. Not having time to prepare for a baby or even knowing about her till she was born. If you don't mind me asking, has she ever tried to see Beth?"

I couldn't imagine giving up Azalea, but I know life happens and for some people, it's their only option. I wonder if she herself had much support in her life, and my heart crushes at the thought. I won't pass judgement on someone I don't know.

He shakes his head, turning to look out at the ocean again. I take the opportunity to check on the girls, asking them to stay close.

Brax continues staring out at the ocean and worry fills me. Was my question too personal? Before I can apologise, he turns back to face me, giving me a wistful smile.

"No, she hasn't asked to see Beth. I honestly wish she would, but I also think Beth is better off not having contact, if her mum can't make a genuine effort with her, you know? I'm just so grateful to Ebony. In those early days, she really stepped up to help me work it all out. She lived near us for years until she moved here. We missed her a lot after she moved, and I know her absence really hit Beth hard. I was stubborn to hold out on moving here for so long. I can see, Beth is already flourishing here."

I'm nodding in response to his words, that ice continuing to thaw in me even more. How can I hate, or even dislike someone who did all of that. Who not only took on sole care of a baby he didn't know he was having, but also just adores her. Although I'm still confused about how we are even opening up to each other, I decide to be honest in return.

Even then, I'm still surprised by what I say next.

"I understand that, Brax. You don't want her to come back if she isn't going to stick around and hurt Beth in the process. Azalea's dad is wonderful, a really great guy, but we just couldn't make it work. We have known each other, most of our lives. We got married just out of high school, and we were just too young. Over time, we ended up moving like ships in the night, never quite meeting in the middle."

He looks over at me, watching me carefully but not saying anything. I decide to continue anyway.

"Eventually, we just decided together that things weren't working anymore. That we both deserved more from a relationship. More than we could give each other. It was all very amicable, and we are great friends now. He is away a lot with work. He's a travelling engineer for big projects across the country and sometimes overseas too. But he calls Zaylee every night and they write to each other all the time. He travels back once every month or so and lives a few streets down from ours."

I don't know why I add the next sentence, but it slips out before I can stop it.

"But he wasn't my great love."

Brax's head whips around at that and he smiles. It's big and genuine and it floors me.

"So, you're a romantic at heart Lavender? I didn't expect that from you at all. You believe in great loves?"

Shoot. Why did I say that? I'm kicking myself internally.

I shrug my shoulders. I'm not embarrassed about it; I'm just annoyed at myself for confessing too much to Brax of all people.

"Yeah, I believe in great loves. I mean, you do realise I part own a store that has a coffee shop, a florist and a bookstore in it. That is the ultimate romance lover's dream, and I get to live it every day. Is it so surprising that I'm a romantic at heart?"

A laugh bursts from him at the same time as a giggle escapes me, and surprise flashes across his face.

I've thrown him. Good. It seems like maybe we both had the wrong idea about each other.

He shakes his head, a smile still gracing his lips.

"Actually, the more I think about it, it's not that surprising to me. Ebony told me you're a champion for your friends, and the first person to put their hand up to help someone you care about. It's not a stretch at all, to think someone like that would love love, too."

I blush at his words.

He peers over at me from the corner of his eye, before looking ahead again. He clears his throat before speaking again.

"You weren't discouraged by what happened with your ex though? I tried not to be after Beth's mum, but I lost a lot of trust after that."

Of course he would lose trust after that. But our situations are different, and Josh has been nothing but good to me since our separation.

"That makes sense. But no, I wasn't discouraged. A little hesitant to just dive into anything until I was sure, because of Azalea. I've not met anyone I was sure about though. I'm hopeful one day I will."

I quickly realise how that sounds. I don't want him to think I've been a nun or anything. Although thinking back, I probably have lived closer to a celibate lifestyle than not. I am not telling him that though.

"I mean, I've dated over the years, but it never goes beyond a few dates. I suppose the romantic in me lives on another day. Or so my sisters would say anyway."

He smiles at that. This is nice and surprisingly easy, this back and forth. I check on the girls again. They are having a blast, happily playing together.

"Are you and your sisters very similar?"

I scoff at that, giving him a quick smile.

"Definitely not. I mean, I guess we are similar in some ways, but mostly not. I think I'm somewhere in the middle of the two of them. Goldie is very pragmatic, loud, fun, logical, the life and colour of a party. Juni is quieter, more reserved, an idealist, who loves to get lost in a story and romanticises life. I think sometimes I'm a little mix of them both, though they would probably describe me as too mature, too level-headed and much too sensible."

I chuckle, thinking about how they would describe me.

He looks serious before he speaks again.

"I can't help but think you might be wrong there. It seems to me like they would say only the loveliest of things about you Lavender. I can't imagine them knowing you and thinking anything other than you're wonderful."

I'm taken aback by his words. I also know they are true. Yes, my sisters would jokingly say I'm sensible and level-headed. But they would also say I'm kind, smart, funny and caring. We have each other's backs, and nothing could change that. Although I was joking with him about their description of me, I'm surprised by his take on it. And I'm touched.

"You're right, they would say lovely things about me. They aren't just my sisters; they are my best friends."

We share a quick smile. I change the subject, still reeling a little from his observation.

"Anyway, thank you for meeting up with me. I know you didn't want to, but the girls are having so much fun."

To punctuate my point, I gesture towards them on the path ahead of us.

We walk in silence for a little longer, watching them laugh and ride alongside each other.

As if in slow motion, I see Azalea hit a large rock and fall from her bike. Even from here, I can see she has landed awkwardly on the ground, her bike landing at her feet.

My heart speeds up and I gasp.

"Shit." He mutters beside me.

We take off, running towards her, her wails getting louder as we get closer.

"Mum! My ankle. Ow!" She howls in pain.

I skid to a stop, just shy of cutting my own knees, knowing that will hurt later but not caring.

Brax lifts the bike from her, and I scoop her into my arms, frantically checking her over.

"Where does it hurt Zaylee?"

She cuddles into me, pointing at her foot.

"My ankle."

Brax crouches down and gently lifts her foot, carefully inspecting her ankle from a few angles.

"Can I take your shoe off Azalea? I just want to take a look at your foot."

She gives him a teary nod and my heart breaks. My brave girl. I cuddle her in closer and kiss her head.

Carefully removing her shoe and sock, he takes a proper look at her foot and ankle.

He looks up at me, giving a reassuring smile.

"It's okay Lavender. I think it's just a sprain."

Oh, thank goodness. I let out the breath I didn't realise I was holding.

"Thank you," I mouth, and he nods back.

He turns to Azalea and pats the back of her hand.

"Your ankle is going to be fine Azalea. But to be safe, I'm thinking maybe you might need to get it checked out. Do you think you can walk on it?"

Brax is so kind to her and without intending to, he makes me feel instantly calmer too.

She tearily shakes her head, but thankfully the sobs have subsided.

"If it's okay with your mum, I can carry you back. Would that be okay with you Azalea?"

She nods and her little arms reach out to him. Surprise flashes through me. Azalea is a super friendly kid, but I didn't expect her to be comfortable with someone else carrying her.

He gently picks her up and stands. He reaches his hand out for me to help me up. I try to stand on my own, only to realise my legs are shaky and unsteady. Instead, I take his hand, letting him help me up. I slide my hand slowly out of his, giving him a weak smile when his eyes find mine.

I quickly turn my attention to Azalea, and he does the same, turning to Beth and checking in with her too. Who is this soft, gentle man?

"Bethy Bear, how are you? Azalea is going to be just fine okay. Let's get her to the doctors and then back home, okay pumpkin?"

I grab Azalea's bike, pushing it along behind them, lost in my thoughts.

I was prepared to hate Brax. I was prepared to put up with him today, to find him annoying and be counting down the minutes till I could get out of here. What I didn't prepare for, was to like him.

Brax walks slightly ahead of me, one strong arm holding up Azalea, the other holding Beth's hand. He glances back at me briefly, a concerned look on his face.

"Are you okay?" He mouths.

I nod a little too eagerly. I'm not okay, but I don't want him to worry about me. I keep replaying Azalea coming off her bike and twisting her ankle. I feel sick just thinking about it.

Brax doesn't buy my response but he is juggling holding one child and the hand of another so he can't be worrying about me. Even still, he comes to a stop and turns to face me. The girls chat away, not noticing he has stopped.

"Lavender, talk to me. I can tell you aren't okay. Do you need us to stop for a minute?" He asks me softly.

My face flushes but not from embarrassment. I'm uncomfortable. Because I haven't had anyone show me this kind of concern in years. Other than family and friends of course.

A shy smile crosses my face. I might be strong, independent and not easily impressed, but I am a sucker for a thoughtful gesture or a kind word.

"I'm okay Brax, just a little shaken. It's hard seeing her in pain, but she seems to be feeling a lot better." I nod my head in her direction, soaking in the loud giggles coming from her as she talks to Beth.

He studies me for a moment, likely assessing whether I'm telling the truth. I had forgotten he is a cop. I stare back, unflinching and he nods, seemingly convinced.

We continue our walk in silence, with Brax making the occasional joke that has my girl and Beth giggling over and over.

At the end of the walking track, Brax turns to me.

"Which way Lavender?"

"Um, sorry?"

He points towards the town.

"Which way are we going?"

I stare at him puzzled. Which way are *we* going?

He lets out a sigh, like he might be a little exasperated with me.

"Where are you headed? Back home or to the doctor?"

"Oh, the doctor. He's just down the road."

I reach out to take Azalea from him, when he frowns.

"I'm not going to leave and make you carry her all the way there, Lavender. I'm coming with you."

I'm speechless. He isn't asking me; he's telling me. And it's hot. Really hot. I wordlessly point in the direction of the doctors, and we continue on the path.

As supportive as Azaleas dad is, he is always off on his work travels, and I'm left to do the day-to-day life stuff. It's rare that he has been here when she has been sick or needed something like this. I'm used to handling things on my own. But I feel myself overflowing with gratitude at Brax's stepping up to help, when he really didn't have to.

We reach the doctor's office, and instead of leaving us at the door, he walks us through the entrance and sets Azalea down on the chair. I start to say thank you before

I quickly close my mouth. Brax has already taken a seat next to her with Beth. Okay then. He is staying.

I'm flustered as I make my way to the desk to sign in. I steal a few glances their way, as I wait for the receptionist to enter in our details. Azalea is laughing at something Brax said, and they all have smiles from ear to ear.

I rejoin them, sitting on the other side of Azalea, gathering my thoughts while they talk and joke. I fire off a quick text to Josh, letting him know what's happened. I know he won't see this till he finishes work and by then I hope to have more answers about her ankle to update him with.

The doctor's surgery is quiet, and we are called in almost as quickly as we sit. I stand, taking Azalea's hand and leading her in. She can walk the short distance to the door with my help and I thank Brax, giving him and Beth a quick wave as the door closes.

The doctor examines her ankle and reports that it is a sprain and should heal in no time. He wraps it with a bandage, and we are done.

As I pull the door open, Dr Thompson says loudly for everyone in the waiting room to hear, "Lavender Wild, don't forget my offer a few months ago to set you up with my son Liam. He is a nice boy and is studying medicine too. A real catch. You two would be perfect together. Let me know next time you're in."

I internally groan. This is the third time he has offered to set me up with his son and each time I politely decline but he still asks.

He doesn't wait for my answer, ushering me through the opening. I pull out my phone, ready to ask one of my sisters to come and pick us up when I realise Brax is still here, waiting for us.

"Oh," the shock clear in my voice.

I shake it off, "You're still here."

He nods, surprise crossing his features.

"Of course. We wanted to make sure Azalea is okay. Can we help you get home?"

I can't hide my grin at his words. Brax continues to prove me wrong. He isn't as bad as I originally thought. Nowhere near it at all.

Chapter 9

CRAP, IS THAT THE TIME? I'm running late and it's sports carnival day at school. I volunteered to help weeks ago, and now present-day Lavender is regretting it big time.

I usher Azalea out the door and down the front steps. She grabs her bicycle and helmet from the front yard, her ankle having almost healed, but feeling good enough to ride again. Another great thing about living in a close-knit small town, is that people leave doors and cars unlocked, bicycles in yards and side gates open. I don't bother locking my front door when I leave this morning.

Azalea rides her bicycle to school while I get a quick run in. It's been two days since my last run, and I'm itching to move my body. Being late is the perfect excuse to make that happen.

I keep pace with her, and we talk about school and her friends. It's an easy, comfortable chat until it's not.

"Mum, will you ever marry anyone again?"

I stumble, quickly righting myself before picking the pace back up, doing my best not to show her how frazzled her question has made me.

She's never asked me that before.

Thankfully she mustn't have noticed me almost face-plant to the ground, because she keeps going.

"Zeke's mum and dad split up a few years ago and they are both married to new people now. Don't you want to marry anyone else?"

As we round the corner, with the school now in sight, I start to slow to a jog, and she slows down too.

"Umm I'm not sure. Would you be okay with that baby doll? I mean, I have no plans to marry anyone else. I don't know if I will. Would that be okay if I did?"

I'm cautious with my words, not wanting to commit to anything in this conversation. Do I want to get remarried one day? Yes. I do. Because like I told Brax on our walk, I am a romantic at heart. But that doesn't mean I will meet the right person, and I won't remarry otherwise.

I'm on the edge of my seat waiting to hear her answer.

She seems to think about it for a moment and I don't rush her.

Then she says confidently, "Yes that would be okay. I used to be sad and want you to be with daddy. But not anymore. I like that you and daddy are friends, and I get two houses and two rooms. And that we are still one big family. Maybe you might have another baby, and I'll get a brother or sister!"

That one almost definitely knocks me over, but I right myself quickly, muttering out loud, blaming a loose piece of gravel. We slow even more as we reach the school driveway and make our way to the bike rack.

I ruffle her hair lightly when she takes her helmet off.

"I don't know about that sweetheart but thank you for the thought. I'll keep you updated if that changes, okay?"

She seems satisfied with my answer and giving one of her big, beautiful smiles, reaches up and kisses my cheek, before rushing into school calling out behind her "See you in there, Mum!"

I watch her, a tender feeling melting into my heart. My sweet baby girl.

A voice from behind, interrupts me from my thoughts.

"You got sucked into this today too?"

Without turning, recognising the voice, I answer Brax. "Yup. But these days are usually pretty fun, so I don't mind."

He comes to a stop next to me, putting his hands in his pockets and angling his upper body towards me.

"Are you a runner Lavender?"

Surprise flickers through me at his words. He must notice, because he smiles briefly.

"I wasn't far behind you guys on the turn into school, and I saw you running. It looked effortless, like you run often. Not just the run of a parent who is late." His words end on a teasing tone, and I raise my eyebrows.

"Yeah, I'm a runner. Most days anyway, but as Azalea gets older and the shop gets busier, I struggle to fit it in. But when I can, I do. It's important to me. I'm currently training for a small ten kilometre run we do here around the town in a few months. I do it every year and try and better my time."

A series of emotions cross his face, from surprise to landing on being impressed.

"I'm blown away by that Lavender. Is there anything you can't do?"

I laugh at that, shaking my head. "Lots Brax, lots. Make good cinnamon rolls for one. But thank you."

He laughs and shakes his head at that.

We stand there for a few moments, and I feel more awkward by the minute. Or nervous. I can't quite tell. I never feel awkward or nervous around anyone and yet here I am in a seemingly constant state of either or both, when I am around him.

"Okay, well I'm heading in. Bye Brax!"

I hurry in after Azalea, listening to Brax's laugh follow me all the way in through the gates.

I spend the rest of the day trying to avoid him but as the day progresses, that gets harder and harder. Particularly when we are placed into a group together.

When the sports coordinator calls my name, Brax's and another mum Adina's name out, I cringe. Great. Not only am I paired with Brax, who I have been trying to avoid, wanting to escape looking like a bumbling teenager in front of, but I've also been paired with Adina.

The second being the high school bully that made my life tough back then and does her best to still do it now.

And the first, being the man that I am finding confusing the more I see of him. One minute he is frustrating me endlessly, and the next, I'm checking him out and thinking how lovely he is.

Despite trying to avoid him, I'm not blind to his good looks. I've seen the other mums taking notice of him all day and I've heard the chatter. And who could blame them. He has spent the better part of the day running up and down the oval, refereeing teams and setting up sports. There was one spectacular moment where he reached up to secure the top net on the goal posts and we all caught a glimpse of a very toned and very muscular abdomen. I started sweating in places I never knew could sweat when I saw that.

And not only that, I've caught him staring my way a few times.

His smile right now, is genuine and warm and I like it too much. I give him one in return. It doesn't last when I spot Adina making her way over too.

We are tasked with preparing the fruit platters for the kid's afternoon tea. Right up my alley.

To my surprise, Brax picks up a knife and starts chopping up oranges. I stare at him a few moments longer and he glances up, catching me.

"What? I have an eight-year-old Lavender, I do know how to chop up fruit."

Of course he does. I'm reminded of Azalea's dad Josh. He would never touch the kitchen and when he has Azalea, they live on frozen meals and takeaway. I usually prep some food to send over for them to eat while she is there.

"Oh, yeah of course. I'm sorry, I didn't mean to offend you."

He sends me a puzzled look and almost like he can read my mind, he says, "I'm guessing Azalea's dad doesn't do any cooking?"

I let out a snort and my hands shoot up to cover my mouth. He chuckles at my embarrassment.

"Definitely not. Josh is fantastic, but cooking is not his strong suit. Actually, he doesn't do it at all. He makes up for it in other ways for Azalea, and that's all that matters."

He glances up at me quickly, and an expression crosses his face that I can't quite place.

He turns back to chopping and says quietly, "That's nice Lavender. Really nice. How kind and respectfully you speak about your ex. I don't know a lot of people that have so many nice words to say about their ex-partner."

My cheeks flush and suddenly I feel warm. Other than my sisters and close friends, I don't get a lot of compliments.

I shrug. "I'm not anything special. He just doesn't deserve for me to be unkind. He does his best and he adores my girl. That's enough."

Adina finally appears at our table. Great. It couldn't be worse timing for her to hear this conversation. She had the biggest crush on Josh for the longest time and has never let me forget I wasn't 'worthy' of him. She doesn't disappoint today.

"Oh Lavender, you really were so lucky to have Josh weren't you. To be honest, we were all so surprised when he married you. Most of us thought the football player would choose the popular girl… but anyway, that was his mistake, wasn't it?"

Although I'm used to her little digs, it still hurts. I roll my eyes at the popular girl comment though. She was the so called 'popular girl'.

I'm interrupted from my thoughts by Brax's voice. And it has a harsh ring to it.

"Actually Adina, it sounds to me like it was the other way around. I don't know Josh, but everything I'm hearing, tells me he was the lucky one. Sounds like he would also agree with that too."

Oh damn. I did not expect that.

Adina's mouth gapes open. She looks like a fish, gasping for air and it really brings me so much joy. I usually shuffle away when she makes her comments and do my best to try and ignore them. But not today. Today, I'm staying right where I am. She can be the one to shuffle away this time.

I sit up a little straighter in my chair and watch as she awkwardly does just that.

My hands fly to my cheeks, and I turn to Brax, still stunned.

"That was… amazing Brax. I don't think that has ever happened. I've never seen Adina lost for words either. Thank you, thank you!"

He simply nods and gives me that look I can't quite place again.

It's quiet between us for a few minutes except for the sound of our knives on the chopping boards. I'm lost in the pure joy I just experienced at seeing Adina finally put in her place.

Brax clears his throat loudly.

"So, no one has ever stuck up for you with her Lavender? I'm guessing this isn't the first time she has done this. You didn't seem surprised."

He says it so casually, but an undercurrent runs beneath the surface of his words, and it doesn't sound casual at all. It sounds anything but calm and casual.

I shrug my shoulders, trying to make it seem like it's not a big deal, when it really is. Adina has been a bully to me before I even knew what the word bully meant. Brax standing up for me means a heck of a lot.

"I guess no one ever really hears her say it. She's usually forthcoming with her feelings towards me when she catches me alone. Or if she says it in someone's company, they usually just tell me not to worry about it. What she said then was pretty tame in comparison to what she says alone."

He doesn't say anything, but I see the cords in his neck strain at my words. Feeling like I need to explain more, I continue on.

"Adina has loved Josh since we were teenagers. But he never gave her the time of day. She hated that. Although I did nothing wrong, she still acts like somehow, I stole him from her. It probably doesn't help that he just brushed her off rather than tell her outright he wasn't interested. So, she blames me for them never getting together. Would you believe she is married? But she hasn't moved on."

I shrug again, realising how ridiculous that sounds. He seems to think so too.

"That's crazy. I'm sorry you've had to put up with that. And that no one has ever said anything to her in your defence before. It makes me kind of mad if I'm honest."

Brax turns away, focusing back on the fruit he was chopping a few minutes ago. Except this time, the chopping is much more aggressive. Poor fruit.

"Oh, my sisters would if I let them. I've begged them not to over the years. I don't want Adina to target them. The most I've let them get away with is giving her solid glares when we are in her vicinity."

Brax and I both laugh at the image I paint of my sisters.

He nods, "I can see them doing that for sure."

I nod too. They would defend me to the end if I let them.

"But Josh has never said anything to her? Never pulled her up on speaking to you like that?"

I shake my head. "No. He would if I asked him to, I'm sure. But I never did. And he never offered. He would just tell me to ignore her and reassure me he was never interested in her. He always said she wasn't worth our time. I guess he wasn't wrong about that."

Brax puts the knife and fruit on the bench, bracing his hands on the edge. Anger rolls off him in waves.

I jump in, needing him to know I'm not a damsel in distress here.

"I've asked her to leave me alone over the years. There have been a few times where she has backed off and kept away the next time I had seen her. But she always comes back eventually. I don't see her that often thankfully."

Brax shakes his head and turns to look at me, crossing his arms and leaning back against the table.

"So, you said something, and she didn't stop. And then he didn't say anything after that?"

I slowly shake my head. Yeah, it doesn't sound good when he says it like that.

"Look, I know you won't say anything bad about your ex and I think that's great, but he should have fucking defended you, Lavender. Every single time she said something. Not just once, or if you asked. It should have been each and every single time. I would never have let that slide if you were mine. Not for a second."

His words flow over me, like a rich balm, soothing me. It feels like a tiny piece of my heart heals a small open wound. If I'm honest, it always did bug me Josh never said anything to defend me. I remember coming home from baby playgroup, crying at how awful she was to me. Josh would just comfort me and tell me to ignore it. I don't offer up that information to Brax. For some reason I want him to get along with Josh. I want them to be friends too.

But now I see, Brax is right. Josh should have said something.

I shrug it off. I can't change it now and thinking back over it won't make me feel any better.

"Thanks Brax. That means a lot to me."

We stare at each other over our places at the work bench. I break eye contact first.

We continue chopping, this time in a comfortable silence. For the first time since he has arrived, I feel completely at ease in Brax's company, and I don't know what to do with that.

Chapter 10

Sisters beach day. Well, sisters and Ebony beach day. And her husband Ryder is coming along too. So more like group beach day really.

I love our beach days during the summer months, and I can't wait to see Ebony and Ryder today. The kids are with the babysitter, so they're coming along for a child free date. They have both been so busy with work and family life that I haven't seen them as much as I like, and I miss them. If anyone gives me hope that a true love story might be out there for me, its Ebony and Ryder. He idolises her beyond anything I could put into words, and she really deserves nothing less.

It's early when I get to the beach and as usual, I'm first to arrive. Everyone else will trickle in shortly, and thankfully the tourist crowds haven't swarmed yet. Most of the town complains when it hits tourist season, but we are pretty lucky that we don't get anywhere near close to the number of visitors, the larger towns around us get.

Whenever I first touch the sand, I always take a moment to ground. It's my calm, soothing, happy place. I watch the waves trickle in, and I scrunch my toes in the dry sand, watching as it slips between them. I feel the sun beaming down on my bare arms, warming me, ready for a swim.

I beeline to the shady corner of the beach, grateful no one has taken it and lay claim to it, placing my beach towel down and my picnic basket off to the side of it. I peel off my mini sundress. The only time I wear a dress is to the beach or on a date, and this one is a favourite. It dips low in the back with a cute little bow at the base, and sits high at the front, in a soft yellow polka dot pattern. It's so far from what I usually wear, and I think that's why I love it so much. I pop my sunglasses on and lay down, smoothing out my swimmers. My red one-piece dips low in the back too and has a sweetheart neckline with thick straps. I've had it since Azalea was a baby, but I can't part ways with it. It's the only time I wear red, and I love it. There's something about the beach that makes me feel more confident in brighter colours.

I close my eyes, blocking out the sun and without meaning to, I fall asleep. It's been a busy week at the café, and I haven't had a lot of sleep. I'm startled awake by the sound of a bag landing next to me and when I open my eyes, a shadow looms over me.

I sit up fast, accidentally knocking the sunglasses off my face and on the brink of what feels like a heart attack, before I realise who the shadow belongs to. Brax.

"Oh my god, Brax you scared the crap out of me!"

I groan and fall back on the towel covering my eyes with my hand. I hear his low chuckle before I feel him kneel next to me.

I peek out from between my fingers, spying on him. He is laying out a towel next to me. And not just next to me, but right next to me. If I move my shoulder six inches to the right, I would be touching his towel. I slam my fingers shut before I start to hyperventilate.

"I'm sorry, I really didn't mean to startle you. I know I shouldn't laugh, but I've never seen someone move that fast. I think you scared me, more than I scared you," and he chuckles again. In that sexy, low voice of his.

I burst out laughing too.

"I'm sure it was a sight you won't forget," I tease, thinking about how funny I must have looked sitting up so fast, sunglasses flying off my head.

He clears his throat. This time, his voice is all husky, the stuff of dreams.

"No, I certainly won't be forgetting that sight."

I drop my hands from my eyes, resting them by my side on the towel. I stare over at him, searching his face. My face flushes with heat, not from the sun. I don't think he was talking about the same comical sight I was, somehow.

He stands up and I realise he is in swim shorts and no t-shirt. No freakin' t-shirt. And what I am staring at is all kinds of amazing.

Toned and tanned skin as far as the eye can see. Brax doesn't have an inch of anything spare on him. He is all strong, muscular and solid, his height even more pronounced when he is standing and I'm laying at his feet.

I don't know how long I stare for, but I realise it's been longer than is socially acceptable, and I turn my head to the side, cheek resting on the towel.

"Lavender," is all he says in that husky low tone. I turn my head to look up at him again, biting my lower lip, nervous he has caught me out.

He lets out a ragged sigh.

"Don't do that."

"Don't do what Brax?"

His hand rubs his chin, and I can't quite make out why he does it. Only that I've seen him do it a few times before.

"Bite your lip."

Understanding dawns on me and without meaning to, I do it again. I do it when I'm nervous and I am all kinds of feelings when I'm around this man. Anger, frustration, nerves, pent up sexual tension.

He shakes his head and looks up at the sky, his hands resting on his hips.

Deciding I need to break up this tension between us, I tentatively ask, "Uh Brax, can you help me up?"

He doesn't reply immediately, still staring up at the sky, focusing all of his attention on it.

"Brax?"

He looks down at me, and for a moment we are caught in a heady stand-off, neither of us saying anything. Goosebumps consume my body despite the heat of the day.

Finally, he says hoarsely in that sexy voice, "Sure, honey."

Honey? If I thought I was hot before, I am now steaming. Sweat beads pop up, dancing across and down my chest. My immediate thought is that I need to get into the water.

Not letting me think about it for much longer, he reaches down and takes my hand, gently pulling me up to standing. Right into his chest.

It's not till I'm up, that I realise how close we are. With only a few inches between us, I can smell his minty toothpaste, and the aftershave he must have sprayed on his neck.

I breathe in the intoxicating aroma of citrus, pine and wood and I'm instantly transported to a forest and that feeling of breathing fresh air for the first time. It kinda feels like I'm having a moment like that right now. Breathing in fresh air for the first time in a long time.

I'm brought back to reality, when a familiar voice calls out, "Lala! Get your cute butt over here and help me carry this ice chest!" Goldie's here.

I take a quick step back and gesture over at my sister, "I better go, uh, help with… that. Be right back!" My voice is a little off and very high pitched. I hurry over to her but can't help a quick glance back. Brax is still standing in the same spot and hasn't taken his eyes off me.

Well then.

It clicks as I'm running away, that I am wearing only a bathing suit. A quick peak back tells me that Brax has noticed that too, and I watch as he scans me from my feet up. When his eyes reach mine, I can feel them smouldering from here. When did we move from utter disdain for each other, to checking the other out?

I give Goldie a hug and grab the ice chest from her, while she unloads her car with her beach bag and towel.

"So, Brax is here? This is a development indeed, Lala!"

I roll my eyes at her. "There is no development here Goldie. I actually don't know what he is doing here. I'm guessing maybe Eb invited him?"

I shrug nonchalantly. Or try to anyway. Before she catches on that I am totally lying, I gesture towards him, "Should we go?"

She smiles at me knowingly but doesn't say anything more thankfully.

We make our way back to Brax and are joined on the way by Ebony, Ryder and Juni.

We greet each other with hugs and a lot of laughter. I love this group so much.

Eb grabs my hand lightly, swinging it between us as we walk.

"Lala, I hope it's okay that I invited Brax. I should have checked with you first. I thought it would be okay – I know you guys have made amends and I really want him to get out and see what the town has to offer."

Her voice becomes a little wobbly and I glance at her in alarm. "I'm worried if he doesn't like it here, he might move back to where he was living before."

The worry in her voice and on her face is evident and worry fires through me. Brax could leave? Why does that worry me so much. I tell myself it's because I don't want Azalea to lose her new friend, but I know it's more than that.

That thought bugs me more than it should.

I think back over our conversation from the other day and what he said about wanting to be here, near Ebony, and liking the slow-paced life for Beth.

I squeeze her hand. "Of course, it's okay that he came today. We won't let that happen okay. We will make sure he falls in love with this town. But honestly Eb, the way he spoke the other day, he is happy to be here and doesn't want to go back. I doubt he will, okay?"

She nods, looking more reassured. I put my arm around her, giving her a quick squeeze. I hope for her sake that he stays.

"I thought maybe he was just saying that to me. It's reassuring to know he told you that too. Oh, I feel better now, thanks Lala."

She throws her arm over my shoulder too, squeezing me tight, and we walk towards the group like that, chatting and laughing.

My eyes meet Brax's, and he is watching us, smiling. I give him a quick smile in return.

Everyone sets about organising our picnic spot. As I make my way back to my towel, I realise Brax's towel is still situated right next to mine. I like that a lot.

I sit back down and pull out my book, eager to get in some reading time before our next book club meeting.

I don't look up, but I feel Brax take a seat beside me on his towel. I try to focus on my book, but I read the same line over and over. I'm about to toss it down, when I hear a deep chuckle from him.

"No way." I peak over the top of my book. He gives me one of those genuine, sultry smiles, reaching down into his backpack.

"So, Eb told me you guys eat, play some games and mostly relax and read, so I brought a book with me…"

He pulls his book out and an involuntary laugh bursts from me. We hold our books out together. It's the exact same murder mystery.

"Is this a set up?" I laugh, staring pointedly over at Eb and my sisters. I have a hard time believing it isn't. Brax is reading our book club selection.

He shakes his head. "Nope, I had no idea you were reading this. I just really like this genre, and I saw it in your sisters shop last week. I don't get a lot of time to read. But when I can, I like to."

Ebony chimes in from her towel, obviously listening in on our conversation. I'm not surprised in the slightest. "Uh guys, definitely not a set up. We are all reading this book remember," and she pulls her own copy out. Goldie and Juni join her in pulling theirs out too.

We all start laughing.

"Ah okay, so it's not so special to us then," Brax pipes up, giving me a wink. We are winking now?

I keep it cool on the outside, but internally I am one big melting pot. I'm so wishing that we were special right now and I could explain a little more about the book club selection, but I don't.

Juni decides for me, and speaks up, "Actually it is Brax. Because while I do run the book club, Lala helps me choose the books every so often. And she chose that one. Because she loves murder mystery's too."

Thanks for outing me, Juni. Brax looks back at me again with a wry smile on his face.

"Ah, weren't going to tell me we had that in common then? Or are you trying your best to disprove we do have things in common."

It's not exactly a question but at the same time it, kind of is. And he's not wrong.

I'm enjoying this newfound flirting, or whatever it is we are doing. But I'm cautious not to get too invested in this. We didn't have the greatest of starts to this friendship and I'm still not entirely convinced he isn't a possible jerk under all that kindness.

Although I keep getting proven wrong in that category.

I shake my head. "Nope. I wouldn't want you to think we might actually have some shared interests and could potentially get along," I joke, hoping he won't see through me.

"Guys! You both have a lot in common!" I whip my head in Ebony's direction, both wanting her to stop talking and dragging this out, but also waiting for her to continue, curious to hear more.

"Well, you both love mystery and thriller books, you both love coffee beyond what a normal person should, you are single parents to girls almost the same age, Italian is your favourite food, you guys love old movies and you both secretly love country music."

We are both quick to jump in and deny that last one, proving her point. Everyone starts laughing and chiming in about how much we both do love country music.

While they all chatter amongst themselves about those little facts Ebony shared, I take a peek at Brax shyly from the corner of my eye and mutter, "Well it really is the most heartfelt of all music types if I'm honest."

His hand reaches out for a high five and he nods enthusiastically, "Right! I'm with you on that one Wild."

Warmth flows through me at his words. When Ebony lays out our similar interests like that, I can see why she set us up to begin with.

I clear my throat, "It's also nice to have another country music lover in my corner. I don't know anyone else who likes that style of music."

He nods, rubbing his chin. "My best friend Callan is a rancher. A few hours inland from here. We met at a summer camp when we were ten. His parents thought it would be good for him to get away for the summer, give him a break from the farm, but he hated it the whole time. All he talked about was his cattle," he laughs.

"He never went to another camp after that. But on the last day, we hit it off over a game of poker after lights out. We stayed in touch, and the next summer he invited me to visit his family on the ranch. From then on, I spent every summer with his family till I went to college. Every summer we would go to a barn dance, and they always played country music at his house, from morning till night. That's where my love of country music began."

I rest my head on my arms, where they are laying on my tucked-up knees, face to him.

"I love that story. He sounds like a wonderful friend to have Brax," I tell him softly.

He nudges my leg with his. The conversation from the others becomes background noise.

"I stayed that night after you left the restaurant. I stubbornly refused to go without eating, so I stayed. I ordered the pizza you recommended too. I think initially I ordered it hoping I would hate it so I could add it to the list of things I didn't like about you. But it was so good.

I didn't want to tell you this, but I've had it a few more times since."

He gives me a sheepish smile and I return it.

"It's so good. I order it once a week, I can't live without it. I'm glad you like it… but I should confess that I almost suggested another option that is the worst thing on their menu. Just to punish you."

His laugh is infectious, and I join him, grateful he didn't take offence to that.

He nudges me again with his leg.

"On three, tell me your favourite country music singer. One, two, three."

We both call out the same singer, at the same time. After our laughter subsides, Brax turns to me.

"You're not so bad, Lavender Wild."

The sentence alone doesn't say much, but the loaded meaning hanging behind it, does.

My voice comes out almost as a whisper. "You're not so bad yourself Brax Madox."

Chapter 11

I'VE BARELY KNOCKED ON THE door, before it swings open. Ebony pulls me in for a hug before turning to Azalea to do the same. She ushers us in, before closing the front door.

"So, I hope it's okay… but Brax is here for dinner too. He's out the back with Bethy, Ryder and the kids."

Azalea fist pumps the air, and without even bothering to ask, takes off through the house to the backyard.

I sigh, "I guess Zaylee approves."

Eb's laughter rings out from behind her, as she leads me down their hallway, into the kitchen. Eb and Ryder's house is open, light and airy. Although you can't see the beach from their home, you can hear the waves tumbling onto the sand from their backyard. I love their home. It's a lot bigger than my own, and the kitchen opens onto a large, covered veranda, where I spy Brax standing.

Eb waves me over to the kitchen bench, "I'm just prepping the salad."

I take a seat at the bench, where Ebony wordlessly hands me a knife and the cucumber, and I start chopping.

Do I go out and say hi? Is it rude if I stay in here? Every possible thought about how to tackle this, soars through my mind. I settle on staying in for now, and heading out to greet him after food prep is done. Ebony needs me after all. Who's going to chop these cucumbers if I don't?

A snort escapes me at that thought, and Ebony glances up curiously.

I give her what likely looks like a deranged smile, before distracting her and asking about her day.

We chat about work, life and kids. Molly and Asher come tearing in, giving me a hug as they run past. They race back outside, and as I glance over at the back door, I spot a picture on the shelf I've never noticed before. I slide off the stool and walk over, picking it up.

"Umm, how long has this been here Eb?"

She looks up and squints her eyes to see the picture clearer from where she stands behind the bench.

"Oh that one? Years love. Have I never shown you?"

Years? How is it possible that I have never spotted this?

"No, you haven't! If you had, I would have known it was Brax I met in the coffee shop that first day."

Eb covers her eyes and groans.

"I honestly don't know why I've never shown you that picture. Especially with all the times I've talked about him. We could have avoided all that drama when you first met."

I'm nodding in agreement, but I'm not angry at her. It's not her fault. Brax and I were just wrong place, wrong time. Is the time right now? I push that thought away as quickly as it pops into my head.

"Lavender. Hey." Brax's voice rings out from behind me, almost as if he knew I was talking about him.

I swing around, putting the picture behind my back.

Argh, why does he get more and more good looking, every time I see him?

"Hey Brax, how are you?"

Before he can answer, Ebony pipes up.

"Look at you two being all nice and stuff. I'm so proud of you both."

I roll my eyes at the same time that Brax groans.

"We have been 'nice' for a little while now Eb. And besides, I'm always nice."

Ebony laughs, and I chime in "You are not. You were decidedly very 'un-nice' when I first met you."

I'm smiling as I say it though, and he smiles back too.

"I could say the same for you too, Ms Wild," he jokes back.

Ebony watches on with an amused expression.

"What?" I ask her pointedly.

Hands in the air as if to defend herself, Ebony backs up from the bench. "I'm just enjoying the show. That's all. It's a show I tried to buy tickets for before that were returned. But looks like the show is back on."

She giggles to herself. I feel my face flush at the inuendo and while Brax is shaking his head at her, I discreetly pop the picture back up on the shelf, walking back over to the bench seat.

She taps the table, suddenly remembering something. "Although… rumour is going around my dear girl, that Dr Thompson is trying to set you up with Liam again."

Nothing gets past anyone in this town.

The laughter dies off my lips when I turn to Brax. He looks annoyed. His hand rubs across his chin and the other, is resting on his waist. Tension rolls off him, and he doesn't look like he finds this funny at all.

I abruptly stop laughing, feeling uncomfortable now. Did I say something wrong? What just happened?

Understanding dawns on me. Is Brax jealous? He can't be. I shake the thought off.

Eb looks between us both, before continuing. Knowing her, she is rubbing salt into this wound.

"I heard he asked you about Liam, when you were at the doctors for Azalea… I think you mentioned it after, Brax? About how inappropriate it was…"

I sharply inhale. So, Brax heard and didn't like it? Butterflies dance in my stomach at that and suddenly I'm nervous.

I tune her out, sparing another quick glance at Brax. But he isn't paying his sister any attention. He is focused on me.

"I just came in to let you both know that the barbeque is almost ready."

I smile sheepishly at him, and we stay locked, staring at each other for a few moments. Ryder calls out to him, breaking the spell. Brax gives me a coy smile and winks at me before backing away, making his way back to the barbeque.

I watch him through the door a little longer than I should, before turning back to find Ebony smirking at me.

I hold up my hand at her. "It's nothing Eb, don't jump the gun. We are just getting along, okay? It's nice. Our girls are friends. And maybe we do have a few things in common, I'll give you that. But that's it."

"Oh honey, I know that's not it, but I won't push I promise. I'll just stay in my own, very excited little lane. For now."

Giving me another wink, she goes back to cutting up salad.

I stand, "I'm going to head outside and check on my girl. You need a moment to rid yourself of those delusional thought's Eb."

She cackles loudly, as I make my way out to the back yard. The conversation is all but forgotten when I walk onto the deck. Brax and all the kids are playing a game of football, on the large space of grass, just below the deck. The older girls are helping the younger kids, and Brax is trying abysmally to tag them all. They are all laughing and having the best time. They dodge around the large jacaranda tree in the back corner of the garden, and I spot Ebony's vegetable patch, growing beautifully, thick and luscious. When Eb has an abundance of vegetables and fruits, she will drop a wicker basket of fresh delights at my front door. It's always a welcome surprise. I lean against the railing, staying a little out of sight, and I'm transported momentarily to a daydream. Where this place and moment, is my everyday life.

I daydream that Brax and I have come here to Ebony's house with our girls for a family dinner night. We all have a beautiful night, and at the end of it, Brax and I go home. Together. The girls fall asleep in the car, and we tuck them into bed when we get home. Our home. Then we curl up on the couch and watch a movie together. This little daydream that has popped up so unexpectantly, surprisingly fills me with so much joy. I didn't realise how much I had wanted that. How much I had missed out on, all these years, by not having that. Going to events solo or going home solo when Azalea is with her dad. Spending nights on the couch by myself, after she goes to bed.

I touch the corner of my eye and it's wet. I'm tearing up at this thought. A sharp pang hits my chest and suddenly I feel so alone.

A warm arm wraps around my shoulder, interrupting my thoughts. I quickly dab at the corner of my eyes and clear my throat, leaning into Ryder's side hug for a moment, before resting against the railing again.

"How's it going at the shop Lala? Eb said you had some trouble with your coffee machine last week. You know you can call me if you ever need help. You know that right?"

I smile, watching the game play out in front of me.

"Do you mean like last time you tried to fix it?" And a laugh bursts from me. Ryder laughs, looking a little sheepish.

"Ouch! That hurts... but fair point. Maybe don't call me. Might be safer," he chuckles.

We stand in silence, both watching the kids play.

"It's nice isn't it," Ryder says, pointing at the game.

"It really is. He's so good with them."

"He's the best Lala. There's not a lot of people I trust, but Brax is at the top. Did you know he introduced me to his sister?"

I shake my head at that, surprised. "No, I didn't know that. Did you know Brax before you knew Eb?"

In the three years Ebony and I have known each other, I've never asked them how they met. Thinking back, I haven't asked her a lot about her life before here and suddenly I'm feeling like a crummy friend. I make a silent vow to myself to squeeze every last drop of information about her life before she came here, when I see her next.

"Brax and I have been friends since we were young. But because Ebony is a few years younger than us, she didn't come along to anything. So, I never met her. I heard about her often and I would also overhear their conversations on the phone sometimes and think she had the most beautiful laugh. I didn't meet her until Beth came along, and even then, not until she was two. We had almost met at her first birthday party, but Ebony had to leave early, and I got there late. What are the chances? But she was dating someone at the time, so it wasn't meant to be. Anyway, since Beth was born, Ebony had been helping him out occasionally when he was at work, and one day I had gotten to his house early and he wasn't home yet. But Eb was."

He looks wistful as he reminisces on their story. I feel so much affection for him. Ryder treats Ebony like a queen. It's Ebony and Ryder's love that inspires me and gives me hope. They adore each other.

"Would you believe that first day we met, we didn't hit it off," he shakes his head chuckling. "I can't recall what it was, but I did something to annoy her that first day and I was not a fan of hers either if I'm honest. Despite that, I thought she was the most beautiful woman I had ever seen. It didn't take long before I wanted to be around her all the time. She had me hooked not long after. I had to convince Brax to let me tag along to their catch ups and I did everything I could to be around when she was looking after Beth, till she finally noticed and gave me a shot. Best decision I ever made was to not give up on her when she kept rejecting me. I think she thought all guys were jerks after her last boyfriend. Now that guy was an absolute jerk."

He pats me on the shoulder, before heading back to the barbeque, calling over his shoulder.

"It's not how you start Lavender. It's how you finish. Anything is possible."

I let his words settle in my chest, while I continue to watch the game playing out in the backyard.

Maybe how things start isn't the most important. Maybe it's where they finish.

Chapter 12

"Where the hell are my keys?" I mutter scrambling through my bag. I'm perched on my front step and have been for the past ten minutes. I've also looked through my bag at least five times already, hoping each time will be the one when I find my keys.

I resort to emptying it on the step. Nope, not in there. I check my jeans pockets one last time and my jacket a final time too. Also, not there.

I let out a frustrated groan. Today is not the day for this to be happening. I'm tired and just want to get inside. The air is warm and sticky, and I need a shower.

I usually don't even lock my front door if I'm out, but for some reason today, I did. And it has to be the weekend that Juni and Goldie have gone away with my parents, to visit our aunt up the coast.

And because they are all away, they have locked their homes too. I hit the call button, hoping Josh might have left his spare key under the garden rock, so I can then get my own spare key from in his house. No answer. He's away overseas right now, and checking the time, he is probably already asleep. Great.

Thankfully Azalea is staying at a friend's house tonight, so I don't have to worry about her being locked out with me.

I sit on my front step, staring blankly at the stars that usually bring me so much comfort, except for tonight, contemplating my next move. Maybe I could jimmy the window open or break one and get it repaired tomorrow. Or I could just go back to the shop and sleep there for the night. I could also stay with any of my friends in town, but I just can't be bothered to message anyone or turn up unannounced at dinnertime. My fault for thinking I would stay back at the shop tonight to do inventory and deep clean the store.

Just when I resign myself to sleeping at the store, a patrol car pulls up, the window going down. It's Brax.

I haven't seen him since the barbeque and a thrill races through me at the sight of him.

"Hey Lavender, are you okay?" he calls out.

I nod, "Yeah I'm fine, I've just locked myself out of the house!" I call back.

The ignition turns off and he hops out of the car.

As he gets closer, I get a better look at him in his uniform. Why does he look better in it each time I see him? It should be illegal for him to be wearing it really; it looks so unbelievably good.

"Does anyone have a spare key?" He asks, his deep husky tone sending a chill down my spine.

"Yep, but they are all out of town," I mutter, a frustrated laugh escaping me at the irony of it.

He nods and looks like he is contemplating something, before he nods again.

"Right. That is shitty luck. I have a tool at home that will get me into your lock. But I'm starving. I haven't had a chance to eat all day. I was heading home from my shift to have dinner when I passed your house. Wanna come over and have some dinner with me and I'll drive you back after and get you in?"

I pretend to weigh up his offer, knowing full well I want to, but I also don't want to look too eager. But I am. I really am. I want to spend more time with him, get to know him better.

"That would be great Brax, thank you."

I scoop the contents of my bag back into it and hop up, dusting off my jeans. We walk alongside each other in a comfortable silence, and I as I walk around to the passenger side of the door, he meets me on the other side.

Opening the car door for me.

I can't remember the last time anyone opened my car door.

He must sense my hesitation and mistake it for unease. But it's not. I'm just surprised.

"Ah, the door handle jams a bit sometimes. I just wanted to help you with it in case it was stuck," he says quickly. I slide in, smiling at his excuse and he hurriedly shuts the door.

On the short drive over to his house, I glance around at the controls on the dash and the radio and ask a bunch of questions that he patiently answers, the awkwardness from before all but forgotten.

"Ebony is going to drop Beth to my house after dinner, so she will be here soon too."

Warmth flows through me at the thought of seeing her. Beth is a little ray of sunshine.

"Oh, I'm glad, it will be nice to see her. Azalea will be jealous she missed out on catching up with her."

He glances over at me quickly, "You're both welcome to come over any time you like."

Oh. I didn't expect that. I smile to myself and glance out the window before replying.

"Thank you, Brax," I reply quietly, touched by his offer, and surprised again, by how much I love the thought of seeing him more.

We pull into his garage, and the door handle easily opens. No jarring in sight. I chuckle softly at that, and he gives me a coy smile.

We make our way into his house through the internal garage entrance, and it is not at all what I expected.

It's warm and inviting. A mix of rich warm browns and dark woods, complimented by soft furnishings in varying shades of blue and cream. It's lovely. Really lovely. I instantly feel at ease.

He gestures to the couch, and I take a seat. Its open plan, so I can see him in the kitchen from where I sit and I get comfortable, grabbing a cushion to hold while I watch him move around, pulling things out of the fridge. I hear the faint sounds of music playing from his speakers and it's a band I like. A country music band.

"Nice music choice," I say coyly, singing along softly with the chorus.

Brax joins me for the last few bars. "It's my favourite song from them. It's on repeat a lot here."

"It's on repeat a lot at my house too," I reply softly, giving him a quick smile.

He flashes me a smile of his own, before clearing his throat, breaking the moment, and grabbing some plates from the cupboard.

"I was just planning on making an easy dinner, if that's okay. I was going to make toasted sandwiches with cold meat and salad. Does that work for you?"

My stomach grumbles, reminding me I didn't have time for lunch today. It sounds amazing - and even better that I don't have to make it myself.

"Sounds great Brax, thank you. You really don't have to make me anything though."

He stops what he is doing and stares at me, his gaze suddenly intense. "I want to," he says before going back to fixing the sandwich.

He brings over two plates and hands me one, taking a seat beside me.

We settle into an easy conversation, and I spend the majority of the time laughing at his jokes, and he laughs at mine. It's comfortable. It's nice.

Ebony arrives with Beth and after a quick hello, rushes off, but not before she gives me a raised eyebrow and a wink. I roll my eyes at her, but she just laughs in response.

Just as I'm about to suggest that I head off too, Beth sits next to me on the couch, curling up into my side. "Can we watch a movie together Lavender?"

Her sweet little face looks up at me, eager for me to say yes. There's no way I can say no. Besides, I really do love spending time with her.

I squish her back and smile down at her. I glance up at Brax and see he is watching our exchange with a soft smile on his face.

"It's up to your dad Beth. I don't want to impose."

Brax is quick to reply. "Not at all. Please stay Lavender."

He quickly adds, "If you want to, of course. I can take you home if you need to get back."

With Azalea at a friend's house for a sleepover, I have nowhere else to be. And if I'm honest, I really don't want to be anywhere else either.

"I would love to stay and watch a movie then. What are the options Beth?"

Beth runs me through all her favourite movies, and I nod along, most of them being Azalea's favourite movies too. We decide on an animated movie about a princess and a mermaid who swap roles for a day. I take note of the name, knowing Azalea will want to watch it too when she gets home.

I settle in with the popcorn Brax makes for us. While chatting to Beth about the movie, a cup of coffee is placed into my hands. I glance up in surprise as Brax hands Azalea a mug of warm milk, before laying blankets over both of our legs.

I'm touched. It seems to come so naturally to him to do things for others, and I think back to when I first met him and my impression of him then. It was so far from the truth of who he really is.

Brax settles in on the other side of Beth. Part way through the movie, I feel his hand rest against the back of the couch. For the rest of the movie, I can't focus on anything else. Every time he moves slightly, his hand grazes my shoulder. I sneak a quick look over at him and our eyes meet.

Beth suddenly starts talking about the movie and we quickly jump apart.

I turn back to face the screen, keeping my eyes on the TV till the movie finishes.

As it's ending, I can feel myself starting to drift off to sleep. I yawn, exhaustion hitting me. It's been a huge day. I glance up at the clock on the wall. It's nine o'clock. I stretch, trying to wake myself up a little, before turning to Brax and Beth.

"I loved that movie Beth, thank you for letting me stay and watch it with you. Azalea will love it too. I'll have to show her when she gets home."

Folding my blanket and placing it on the lounge beside me, I slowly stand, not wanting Brax to take Beth out so late.

"Thank you for a wonderful evening, Brax. I really needed this. I always miss Azalea when she is away for the night."

He gives me a quick smile and nods.

"I'm glad you came over. Beth loved having you here. I did too…"

I fire off a quick text to Ebony and she responds almost immediately. I take my mug and the popcorn bowl to the kitchen counter, Brax following behind me.

I turn, resting my back against the kitchen counter.

We stare at each other for a little longer than is polite. Warmth spreads from my chest, up my neck and I break eye contact.

"It's late. I better be going."

Brax crosses his arms over his chest, cocking his head to the side. He is silent for a moment, and I wonder if he is going to say something. He shakes his head slightly and smiles.

"I'll just get Beth's jacket, and we will drive you, home."

He walks past me, and I reach out, grabbing his arm to stop him. He glances down at my hand on his arm. My eyes flash up to his and when he looks at me, his gaze increases in intensity. That warmth from before floods through me again and my hand lingers a little longer, before I slowly let it drop.

When I speak, my voice is husky. "Stay here. It's too late for Beth to be heading out to take me home. I'm just going to stay at Eb's tonight. My parents are back tomorrow and they can get me the spare key then."

"Are you sure? I don't mind Lavender, and I know Beth won't mind either."

I'm already nodding, wanting to quickly reassure him, "Its fine. I've already messaged your sister, and she is expecting me."

He must realise arguing with me is futile because he concedes, "Okay sure. Can we at least walk you over to Ebony's?"

I laugh at that, and he rewards me with a coy smile. Ebony's house is at the end of his street. He could see me walk to her house from his front door if he wanted but I appreciate the sentiment. I don't think I've ever had anyone offer to walk me home.

"Sure. I would really like that."

"Beth, grab your jacket, we are walking Lavender down to Aunty Eb's."

The evening air is balmy and warm. We take the short walk to Ebony's, Beth running ahead of us. Eb and Beth embrace as if they haven't seen each other in so long, not just hours before. It warms my heart, and I just love it. Brax and his family are close, and being from such a tight knit family myself, I appreciate it.

Beth runs back to Brax's side, and he gives Eb a wave. I wave at her too.

Crouching down, I give Beth a hug, feeling her squeeze me back. I wait till she lets go first and then I stand, turning to Brax.

"Thank you for a really fun evening. I had such a lovely time, you two."

Beth waves, "Bye Lala!" and starts skipping back up the street.

Brax chuckles at her use of my nickname. I love that she feels so comfortable with me already.

He takes a few steps backwards, and his voice deepens when he responds.

"Me too Lavender. I'll see you tomorrow at the coffee shop?"

The words are simple, but the undertone speaks volumes.

"I would like that... I'll see you tomorrow."

I stand there for who knows how long, watching him walk away. When he reaches his front door, he stops and turns back towards Eb's house. We stand there like that for a moment, before I quickly wave and hurry in, a little embarrassed that I was caught, but a lot giddy about that whole exchange. And the whole evening really.

Chapter 13

"Mum, I have a party invitation."

Uh oh. The words most parents don't want to hear.

"Okay sweetie… when is it for?"

Please be in two weeks when Josh is back. Please be in two weeks.

"This weekend."

Great. I am definitely not getting out of this. Could I bribe Goldie to take her? My mind starts ticking over with the possible options. My parents?

"This weekend? That's late notice for a party Zaylee."

She looks sheepish before adding, "Well… I was given it two weeks ago and I forgot to give it to you. It's been in my desk at school."

Her eyes widen at my expression, taking on a pleading expression. "Can I please still go mum?"

I take a quick look at the invitation. Its Brianna's party. Her mum Andrea won't mind a late rsvp. I send off a quick apology text, letting her know we will be there.

I sigh, "Yes Zaylee you can go. But remember to bring invites home straight away next time kiddo. I need notice to close the shop, okay?"

She looks guilty and I feel bad instantly. "It's okay kiddo, I know you didn't mean to. Just try and remember for next time."

I fire off a text to the group chat that includes my parents, sisters, Wolf, Bear, Fox and their parents. They don't disappoint. Within five minutes we have a plan worked out. Juni is going to run the coffee shop that day and my parents will cover the bookstore in the morning, followed by Wolf at lunchtime and then ending the day with his parents Patricia and Jeff finishing the cover.

It's times like this, that I know how lucky I am to have such supportive family and friends.

Saturday rolls around much too quickly. It's been a few days since I've seen Brax and I'm missing him. It's crazy how far we've come. From not being able to stand him at all, to now missing him.

I brush that thought aside. Zaylee and I grab our bicycles and I'm thankful I chose to wear denim shorts and a t-shirt for this party.

We chat as we slowly ride over, but then race the last leg, pulling up to the party laughing. I park my bike on the front lawn. Things hardly ever get stolen around here, so it doesn't even cross my mind to lock it up or put it anywhere else. As I drop the bike, I glance over to see Brax standing by the side gate entrance to the party. I walk over as Zaylee races past, barely stopping to say hi to Brax as she heads into the backyard.

"Hey you," he says.

"Hey yourself."

He points over his shoulder grinning, "You got sucked in too?"

I groan, covering my eyes, and then laughing.

"It's the worst way to spend a Saturday, right? I have to now cover Juni next week on my day off to make it up to her. But the smile on Azalea's face this morning was worth it."

He nods, "Yep, I hear you. Beth has been singing and dancing around the house all morning and just now before you got here, she told me this was the best day ever. Which is pretty much what she says every time she goes to a party." He chuckles at that, and I do too. I really like that we both have girls around the same age and understand this stage of life.

We make our way into the party together, side by side and it's nice. Really nice. It almost feels like we are here together, and I daydream momentarily that we are.

I walk around greeting the other parents and saying hi to the kids. I love that everyone here and all their kids, have grown up together and I'm reminded that kids parties are a good opportunity to catch up with the other parents.

Brax gets along with everyone like he has known them all his life too.

We mingle separately at the party but I can feel an invisible force connecting us. As the party goes on, when I look around for him, he's already staring at me. I lose track of the conversations I'm having, but I don't care.

Somewhere along the way, we slowly meet in the middle of the party.

Brax walks away from one of the single dads at the party looking frustrated and I'm surprised. Nick is really nice and gets along with everyone. We have occasionally caught up for coffee when his son and Azalea have had a play date.

"Not a fan of Nick's I'm guessing?"

He tips his head to the side. "What makes you say that?"

I point at his face. "The look on your face," I say as I laugh.

He shakes his head and glances back at Nick who is now talking to another parent.

"No, he's okay… did you know he likes you?"

I screw my face up in surprise. "He does? I don't think so… I mean we have hung out when the kids have played together. And he has suggested we do a movie or something but never implied or outright told me that he likes me. Are you sure?"

I glance over at Nick again, and this time it's Brax who screws his face up.

"Yeah, I'm sure. Are you interested in him Lavender? He seems to think he might have a shot with you."

He looks increasingly annoyed. And jealous.

I don't make him wait for my answer, not wanting to give him the wrong idea about Nick. Although the jealousy thing looks good on him, and I wouldn't mind seeing it just a tiny bit more.

"No, I'm not interested Brax, and he doesn't have a shot with me. We are just friends. Well, that's all I want anyway. He's never hinted at anything else, but if he did, it would be a no."

Relief washes over his face.

"Dad! Come and check out my painting!" Beth calls out to Brax, interrupting the moment.

He stares at me, a questioning look in his eyes, studying me like he isn't sure whether to believe me or not. Beth calls out to him again and he turns, walking away, before glancing back at me once more as he walks away.

Like clockwork, Nick wanders over and doubt floods me. If he does like me, how did I never spot it?

I'm sure Brax just has it wrong. At least I really hope so anyway.

"Hey Lavender I've been meaning to ask you… would you like to go to dinner sometime? Just you and I… like a date."

Oh. Brax wasn't wrong then. I look over in his direction, surprise clear as day on my face, to find he is already watching us. Arms crossed. And this time it's most definitely jealously I can see across his face.

"Lavender?"

I break my staring contest with Brax and turn back to Nick.

"Oh… Umm, thank you so much for the lovely offer Nick. But… I'm sort of interested in someone else. I'm really sorry. You're a great guy, one of the best truly, and I love our friendship. I'm hoping that won't change?"

I take his hand in mine and squeeze it gently before dropping it. I really don't want to offend him. He is so lovely, and his son Smith and Azalea are great friends. I'm praying he takes the rejection okay.

He nods and what looks like is a forced smile, crosses his face. "Oh yeah, that's fine Lavender, I understand. It was worth a shot hey." He laughs, but that also sounds forced.

We stand there awkwardly for a moment before he excuses himself and makes his way over to another group.

A sense of dejection floods me. I suspect we won't be doing any more playdates, and I hate that. I let out a groan, covering my eyes before turning away.

"Everything okay?" Brax asks in a low voice behind me. It startles me and I jump before quickly turning around. His hand reaches out to steady me, softly grabbing my arm.

"Geez Brax! Don't creep up on me like that, you scared me."

His thumb rubs at my arm quickly before dropping it back to his side.

He nods towards Nick.

"Was I right?"

He looks a little smug, but that jealousy I spied before is still very much there.

"Maybe…"

His arms cross his chest, and he suddenly looks annoyed. Very annoyed.

"Did he ask you out?"

I laugh. "What is this – a game of twenty questions?"

He raises an eyebrow but doesn't say anything else. I quickly put him out of his misery.

"Yeah, he did. I politely told him no and asked if we can still be friends. I'm not holding out hope though which is a shame."

Relief briefly crosses his face, and he nods.

"I can't help but feel a little relieved… but I am sorry that you think your friendship might be over. Do you want me to speak to him?"

I appreciate his honesty about feeling relieved and his offer to speak to Nick on my behalf, but I realise then that the friendship isn't that important if it's over in a flash.

I shake my head, "Thank you, but no need to. I think maybe it has run its course."

Brax looks relieved again and I can see why. I already know that half of the mums at school have a crush on Brax. He's a hot topic at school drop off and it drives me wild every time I get dragged into it. So, I know exactly how he feels.

"Ah, sorry to interrupt. I just need to grab a drink from the ice chest…" Sounding uncomfortable, Nick looks between the two of us. I realise then that we are blocking the drinks and take a step back, so he can walk through.

Before I can say anything, Brax steps closer to me and puts his arm around my shoulders.

"Sorry Nick, we'll get out of your way," he says as he steers me in the opposite direction. Okay, if Nick didn't realise before who I'm interested in, he certainly knows now. I glance back in his direction, hoping he is okay. He watches us for a moment before shrugging and reaching into the ice chest. Looks like he recovered pretty quickly.

I realise then that Brax's arm is around my shoulders. For the whole party to see. Taking a quick peek around, I notice half the mums staring in our direction. But I really don't care.

Brax looks at his watch.

"It's been two hours. Is that long enough? Our kids are just playing together anyway. Wanna get out of here and grab some ice-cream with the kids?"

I nod eagerly, "That sounds like heaven. Let's go."

Chapter 14

AFTER A LOVELY, RELAXED AFTERNOON with Brax and the girls at the ice creamery earlier, Azalea and I are now sitting on the couch watching a movie when I get a text from Juni.

'Does my niece want to come over to have a girl's night? I've just hired some movies, and I have popcorn and her favourite chocolate milk. You're welcome too of course but only if she comes haha.'

I smile at that one. Both of my sisters have a beautiful bond with my daughter.

I've barely uttered the words when Azalea yells "Yes!" Jumping up and running to her room to pack a bag.

'Azalea and her plus one will be there soon haha x.'

Just as we are ready to head out, my phone rings.

Brax's name flashes across the screen.

"Hey Brax," I answer too quickly, cringing at myself. I should have let it ring at least a few times.

"Hey Lavender. I was hoping to get some medical advice if you have time?"

He sounds a little rushed and concern floods me.

"Yeah of course, is everything okay?"

"Nothing bad, but Beth is sick. She wasn't feeling well when we got home and had a lie down. She just woke up with a fever and I'm out of medicine. I called the local pharmacy, but they are closed for the day. Is there anywhere else around here I can get some?"

One of the downsides of living in a small town is that things close early. One of the perks though, is that most people are happy to help in a pinch.

I walk back into my kitchen and open the cupboard above the refrigerator. I grab the kids fever medicine and pop it on the bench.

"The pharmacy is the only place. But I have some. I was heading out to my sisters anyway, so I'll drop Zaylee there and then bring it around. I'll be there in ten minutes."

He's already refusing. "No, I don't want you to change your plans for me. I can try the next town over."

"Nope. I'm bringing it over Brax. I see my sister every day and Zaylee will love a night away from her mum to eat as much junk as she can without me there to tell her no. I'll be there soon."

He sighs but I can hear the relief in his voice.

"You're amazing Lavender. Thank you."

Almost ten minutes later, I'm knocking on Brax's front door.

It swings open immediately after my knock, and Brax ushers me in.

I know it's not the right time to be checking him out, but I do anyway. He is wearing sweats and a loose tee that's seen better days. But it looks amazing on him. He pads barefoot into the kitchen, and I follow behind. I think 'home Brax' might be even better than 'uniform Brax' and that is saying a lot.

"Beth is asleep in her room. But I'll wake her up for some medicine. Thank you for bringing this over honey." Brax reaches out and squeezes my upper arm. He runs his hand down my arm to my hand, before letting go.

A blush fills my cheeks, and warmth lingers where his hand trailed a path down my arm. I'm also really loving that 'honey'.

I hand over the medicine and he makes his way into Beths room with it.

He comes out a minute later, with a puzzled expression.

"Beth is asking for you. Is that okay?"

I jump up from the bench stool I had just sat on when he left the room.

"Of course."

Brax leads the way with that slightly puzzled expression still.

As I walk in her room, I'm blown away by the décor. Rainbows are painted on one wall and pale pink, colours the other three walls. A plush peach coloured trundle bed sits in the corner of the room, with a gorgeous white desk and fluffy chair. It's beautiful.

I glance over at Brax, and I just know without asking, he did this for her, no one else. I've come to realise he is just that kind of a man.

I take a seat on the edge of her bed and feel her forehead.

"You're very warm sweetheart. Can I get you anything?"

She shakes her head and rolls over to face me.

"Daddy gave me some medicine. Could you read me a story Lavender?"

I look over at Brax and his mouth widens in surprise. He looks at me and nods. I glance around the room and spot her bookshelf. I walk over and pick out a fairytale book.

"Is this one, okay?"

She nods and I walk back over to her bed. She scoots over so I can hop up on the bed and I pop my feet up on her comforter.

"Can you sit at the end of the bed daddy."

He pushes off from the door frame and walks over, "Sure bug."

He positions himself so his back is against the wall and his legs are across the bed. Landing on the floor. My feet touch his leg, and I start to pull them towards me before he reaches out and grabs them, laying them in his lap.

To my surprise, he starts to massage my feet. I want to tell him he doesn't have to, but my feet are always so sore from standing all day and this feels like heaven.

It takes everything in me to not fall asleep while he does it.

I open the book and start reading to Beth and shortly after she falls asleep. I feel her face again and look over at Brax.

"She feels a lot cooler," I whisper.

He nods and letting go of my feet, he leans over and kisses her forehead.

He points at the door, and I stand, pulling the covers up higher and tucking her in. We quietly make our way out to the living room and Brax stops, turning to me suddenly.

"Beth loves her aunt and gets along with most people but when she is sick, she only ever wants me. I've never had her ask for anyone except for me Lavender. I'm still in shock a little. But the good kind."

His words are heavy with meaning, and I'm touched. I reach out and lightly touch his shoulder, giving it a gentle squeeze.

"I'm glad I could be here to help Brax. She's a very special little girl."

He nods, a smile lifting the corner of his mouth.

"Would you like a coffee? I wouldn't normally offer someone coffee this late, but I know you drink it around the clock."

A laugh bursts from me. "Yeah, I would love that."

While he makes me a coffee we chat easily. With Brax, conversation just flows effortlessly. I've never had that experience with anyone outside of my family or close friends. I feel like I could talk to him about almost anything and it seems, Brax may feel the same. We move from topic to topic, talking about family, work, favourite movies, ex-partners, our kids, foods we love and foods we hate. We barely take a breath.

Eventually, we make our way to the couch, and he grabs my coffee for me before I can, carrying it to the coffee table.

"Can I ask about your life before you moved here? What was that like?" I say as I sip my warm coffee.

Brax settles back into the couch a little more before turning his body, angling it towards me.

"Busy, rushed, chaotic. The crime rate was high in the city, and I was slammed at work every day. I started to hate the job. We didn't get to see family often because I was always working or taking Beth to extracurricular activities. It also didn't help that no one lived close by, and I had to have a babysitter on call. Beth and I made it work, and we created a good life around that. But it was time to slow down and prioritise time, and family."

"And do you now? Hate the job?"

He shakes his head. "No, not at all. Coming here and slowing down, has helped me love it again. I enjoy the community spirit and the work here. I feel like I'm actually helping people and because of that, they are happy to have me here. In the city, cops aren't exactly welcomed with open arms. It also helps that the crime rate here is almost non-existent. There are so many perks to living here. For both of us."

I nod. I know exactly what he means.

"Did I ever tell you we moved away from here briefly? I think it was the beginning of the downfall of Josh and I, but it took us a few years to acknowledge and accept it. I don't really talk about it and as crazy as it sounds, I often even forget I left here. It's such a small blip on the radar of my life really."

He looks surprised by my admission. I'm a little surprised by it too.

"What happened?"

"Josh was promoted. More money, a bigger house, a great job. Too many incentives to pass up. So, we didn't. This was before Zaylee was born. We said our goodbyes, moved five hours away and hated it the minute we got there. Well, I hated it. Josh didn't like it, but he didn't hate it. I tried to like it more and make it work but the busyness of everything was making me miserable. We stayed for two months before moving back. I didn't have the store then."

"So, what happened when you got back?"

"Josh took another job, the one he has now, and he started travelling for work. The funny thing is, he loved the job he had before he took the city one. Things might have worked out differently, but I think it would have just delayed the inevitable. He was away all the time. We had Azalea not long after and then things just crumbled. We were too young, and we didn't prioritise each other."

He nods in understanding. "I've dated a few people in the past, nothing serious. I never met anyone I had wanted to prioritise if I'm honest, and I didn't want to waste my time or theirs."

"Did you want more kids?" I blurt and he smiles.

"I always wanted more. A brother or sister for Beth would have been nice. What about you?"

"Me too... Zaylee has been asking me for a sister for years," I tell him.

He nods, chuckling. It's funny how similar we are and how parallel our lives are in this season of life.

We sit in a comfortable silence for a little longer both of us seemingly lost in thought, before I pick up my coffee mug from the table.

"It's getting late, I should go. Azalea will be asleep, but Juni will wait up for me and will probably want to watch another movie." I wave the mug at him, "Thank you for this."

I take the cup to the sink, and he follows me out to the door.

I turn to say goodbye and he is right there, so close I can feel the light tickle of his breath. I look up into his eyes and he takes a deep, shuddering breath in.

Without thinking twice about it, I lean in for a hug. His arms curl around me instantly, squeezing me tight, and his chin rests on the top of my head.

I squeeze him in return, before taking a step back. I instantly regret ending the hug so quickly.

"Bye Brax."

"Bye honey."

There he goes again, making me all warm and tingly inside.

I can't contain the smile that spreads across my face, and biting my lip, I start walking backwards to my car. I give him a small wave before turning, reaching my car. It's unlocked like always. I only drove it tonight because I wasn't sure how long I would be here and even though I feel safe here, I'm not a fan of walking super late at night.

Just as I pull the door open, I hear him calling out.

"Lavender."

I look over my shoulder, waiting.

"I'm glad you came back here all those years ago."

I'm speechless. I stare at him for a moment watching a slow smile cross his face. What he leave's unsaid, speaks volumes.

I nod shyly.

"Me too Brax. It was one of the best things I ever did."

I don't look back when I get in the car and drive off. If I did, I would have seen Brax leaning against the doorframe, rubbing the back of his neck up into his hair and shaking his head with a huge smile on his face.

Chapter 15

"Clemmy! Can you help me move this shelf," Juni sings out from her bookstore.

"Sure, just give me one minute!" I call back.

I finish wiping the table and throw the rag at the bench. Well, that's where I aimed anyway. It's intercepted by a hand.

Mortified, I start to apologise, thinking I've almost hit a customer, before realising the hand is attached to Brax.

I start laughing when I see his grin. Thank goodness it's just him. Warmth spreads through me seeing him here. It's been a few days since I saw him last.

"Clemmy hey? Wanna tell me what that's about?"

I grin at him. We didn't get around to nicknames the other day when we shared bits and pieces of our life story with each other.

"You heard that?" He nods, smiling big. That smile gets me every time and I blush. It's intoxicating when it's aimed directly at me.

"It's my middle name. Clementine."

He looks surprised. "As in Clementine, the fruit? Like the way your names are all flowers?"

I nod, laughing. It's a long-standing joke in the town and I forget that he hasn't been here that long at all.

"Yeah, except technically the Juniper is a shrub or a tree. But yep, we are all named after flowers, or a plant and our middle names are fruits. Mum started off easy with me but went a little wild with my sisters."

He chuckles, turning his head to the side, a coy smile spreading on his face.

"There's a story there. I like it. Lavender Clementine. It's unique. Can I ask - what are your sisters middle names? Or is that a Wild family secret?"

When he winks at me, I think to myself that he can know whatever he likes with that charm. Especially when he says my name like that.

"Well Goldie is Marigold Peach and Juni is Juniper Apple. I sort of kept the tradition going with Zaylee. Her name is Azalea Lemon. When I was pregnant with Zaylee, all I wanted was lemon flavoured everything. I would call her my baby lemon. So, Lemon suited her perfectly."

"I love that, Lavender. I think it suits you all perfectly. Will you tell me the story about how you got your names?"

I used to be embarrassed telling this story and would shy away from it when people would ask. But surprisingly not with Brax. I find myself wanting to share these parts of myself with him, which is odd seeing as I hardly know him really.

"Most people think it's weird and I get it. Mum and dad have always been hippies and so no one in our town was surprised when they named us what they did. They both grew up here too, and their parents before them. But tourists always comment or new people to town when they find out our names. Mums' best friend Sophia is a 'hippy' too and she named her children after animals."

We both laugh at that.

"It's adorable really. We banded together in school, so no one teased us. In time it just became a non-thing. She has three sons, Fox, Wolf and Bear. We all grew up super close and still see each other all the time and every few weeks for a combined family dinner."

"That would have been fun growing up together. I love the community feel here. But I'm sensing that a big part of that, is your family." Brax replies.

"I know how lucky I am Brax. It's pretty rare what we have, and I wouldn't trade it for anything."

He braces his hands against the back of a chair, leaning forward slightly.

"So, Fox, Wolf and Bear hey? Also, really great names. There's three of them and three of you…"

I laugh loudly, holding my chest at the implication.

"Yep. If you want to know whether our parents hoped we would all pair off, you're correct. We are all close in age. I'm thirty-five and Wolfie is thirty-six. Goldie and Bear are both twenty-nine and Juni is twenty-five and Fox is twenty-six. They planned it that way."

He looks a little more serious this time when he asks, "So did you and Wolf ever date then?"

I shake my head quickly. I want to make it very clear how platonic we are. "Wolf is like my brother… we are really close, but we have never dated. We hang out all the time though. It took Josh a few years to get comfortable with that, even though Josh grew up with us and knew we were always just friends."

He pushes back off the chair, moving to lean against the wall. He studies me for a moment. To work out if I'm telling the truth. I want to reassure him.

"He is due in about now actually, so you might get to meet him. He always pops in for a coffee in the afternoon when he finishes work. Wolf is a…" And I'm interrupted by Wolf's voice calling out from behind me.

"Champion. Stud. Amazing person. The coolest person you know. Any other adjectives I might be missing Clemmy?"

"Ah there he is." I turn to him with a big smile, and he pulls me in for a big hug, kissing the top of my head. He throws his arm around my shoulders, towering over me.

He turns to Brax who narrows his eyes, glancing between the two of us a little suspiciously.

Goldie passes us by and her and Wolf bump fists. She must notice Brax's expression because she sings out, "Don't worry Braxy boy. Wolfie is harmless. He's not after your girl." She sends him a wink and to Brax's credit, he chuckles and shakes his head.

Meanwhile, I'm over here dying from embarrassment.

"Goldie! Brax and I are just friends…" I steal a quick glance at him and see his grin disappear, replaced by a frown.

I mean, I would like to be more than friends… but does he? I can't be sure.

As she walks away, she yells over her shoulder. "Sure you are, Lavender!"

Wolf laughs again and extends a hand to Brax.

"Looks like Lala has a bit to fill me in on. Keeping secrets are we Clemmy?"

Please make them all stop. I groan and cover my eyes and this time both Wolf and Brax laugh. Great, already in sync with each other.

"Let's grab a beer sometime. I can tell you a story or a thousand about our girl here, Brax."

Brax nods, "I would like that." He would?

Wolf turns back to me, "I'm just going to grab a coffee, but I'll make it."

He pats me on the shoulder before walking behind the counter. Wolf has helped me so many times over the years in the coffee shop and makes even better coffee than I do. I've been trying to recruit him to work with me for years.

And the customers just love him. But he loves his job in construction and home building with his brothers, I could never tempt him away.

I tell Brax that, in case he wants a coffee before he heads off. He really does make amazing coffee.

"Nah, I like your coffee the best honey. I'll pass on anyone else making my coffee from now on."

A blush colours my cheeks again. I really like the sound of that.

Wolf very obviously listening, chuckles at that and I turn to give him a glare. He holds his hands up defensively but smiles.

As he walks out with his takeaway cup, Wolf slaps my hand in a low five. He shakes Brax's hand again and says, "I like you," before singing out a goodbye to Juni and Goldie on his way to the door.

Brax watches me from his post against the wall. I watch him back, feeling like we have stepped into new territory.

"I like him too. You actually do seem like brother and sister."

I nod slowly. "Everyone likes Wolfie. He's a great guy."

We stand there in silence for a little while, the tension thick between us. The bell at the door jingles and a regular walks in for their coffee. I give her a quick wave as she heads to the counter. Checking my watch, I realise the afternoon rush is about to start.

Brax moves from his spot against the wall. "I better let you get back to work Lavender. Beth has been at me to organise another play date if you are both free on Saturday?"

I barely let him finish his sentence before I jump in, "Yes we are free."

He steps closer to me, reaching out to brush a loose strand behind my ear. His hand lingers by my ear and his fingers trail along my jaw before dropping to his side.

His eyes are smouldering, and he shakes his head, giving me a smile. "I'll call you… bye honey."

I'm all breathy when I respond, caught off guard by that intimate moment.

"Bye Brax."

He heads out before suddenly turning, walking back towards me a few steps.

He sings out, "Hey, what are your parents' names?"

I smile big at that.

"Margaret and Tom!" I yell back.

He cracks out a laugh at that and takes the last few steps to the door, giving me another quick wave before leaving.

I glance over at Juni, waiting expectantly by the shelf, a huge smile on her face. "In your own time…"

Chapter 16

WITH MY LITTLE MINI IN tow, I head down the street in my slippers. Both of us decked out in our pyjamas. It's a usual occurrence in our street to see a Wild sister walking to each other's house in pyjamas.

I don't bother knocking, letting myself in.

"Goldie! We're here."

Azalea kicks off her shoes and wanders into the backyard to play with Picasso, Goldie's foster dog. Goldie fosters dogs when she has the time, before they find their forever home. It was almost like he was meant to find her. He is the namesake of her favourite artist and has become her little shadow. I'm hoping she can keep this one.

I pop the coffee cake I made on the kitchen counter. Goldie's house is as eclectic as she is. A myriad of bright colours, florals and a bouquet of flowers adorn each room. Today, the smell of roses fills the air. Every time I'm here, a different floral scent fills her home. Other than my own home which I would describe as cosy, Goldie's is my favourite place to be. It's like a warm hug from a rainbow in here.

I wander into the backyard to find Juni laying in a hammock, book on her lap with her eyes closed, Azalea playing fetch with Picasso and Goldie weeding her garden beds. It sums us all up so perfectly, with my coffee cake inside.

Goldie's garden is a feast for the eyes and a dream for any florist. Both here and at the back of our store, she has curated the most delightful array of flowers in all colours. I could get lost in this garden and be happy for it.

I lean down and kiss Juni's forehead and she opens her eyes smiling up at me. I make my way over to Goldie and kiss her cheek. She reaches back and squeezes my hand, transferring the dirt from her own, to mine. Goldie refuses to wear gloves when she gardens, believing that her connection to the earth is impaired by the fabric. It makes for a lot of mess, but a lot of love in her garden.

I take a seat, admiring the view out here. Over the back fence, I can see the same view of the ocean that I can see from my house except here, I can also see the lighthouse. From Juni's house we see a similar view but also get the added bonus of the cliffs. I love that each of our homes offers us a slightly different view of the ocean.

"So, Clemmy. Tell me more about Brax. I've noticed he has become a regular coffee drinking fixture in our establishment," Juni says sweetly.

I knew this was coming. It's actually overdue. They usually don't last this long before they ask me questions. About anything really. Goldie has interacted the most with Brax out of my two sisters but even that has been limited. Whenever Brax pops in, Juni is usually sat behind the desk with her face in a book, lost in a story.

I toy with the tablecloth, unsure how to answer. I don't even know what this is. All I know is that there is some serious tension of the good kind between us, and we have been spending more time together. Mostly with the kids.

"Mum! I'm going inside to watch TV." Azalea tears into the house, Picasso chasing after her.

I breathe a sigh of relief now that Azalea is out of earshot.

"I honestly have no idea what it is. Or if he even wants it to be more. I mean I think he does, but he hasn't made a move in any way exactly... argh I do know for sure that he is gorgeous, and kind and he makes me laugh. Is that good enough?"

Resting my chin on my palm I fill them in on our last few catch ups.

"Also, we went to the park the other day and he sent me a text when I left and since then we have been texting every day. So, progress I guess?"

"That is definitely progress! There is some serious electricity flying between you two. I know that much for sure!" Goldie chimes in. She has abandoned her garden of flowers in favour of the conversation, having turned to face me from her cushion perched on the grass. Goldie's pink hair is in a messy knot atop her head and her outfit for today is emerald green overalls and a pink fitted tee. She is adorable and wild, our Marigold.

Juni flips off the hammock in one graceful swoop. She is dressed in her pyjamas too. Her long, light brown curls fall down her back effortlessly and I know she barely spends any time on her hair, it just looks that good naturally. Unlike mine which takes way too long to do. Thankfully, I was blessed with thick dark waves that generally look nice without a ton of effort, but it's definitely not effortless. The only thing we share, are our same green eyes. The locals in town sometimes refer to us lovingly as the green-eyed Wilds. It's what we based our store name on; 'The Wild Flowers'.

"Well, I like him. He bought a book the other day from the shop and asked for my advice about it. He was genuinely interested in my opinion on it and took my advice seriously. He told me he reads every night. Every night! How wonderful. He also told me that Lavender makes the best coffee he has ever had and was very complimentary of her."

She gives me a wide smile and winks before floating into the house after Azalea.

My mouth agape, I don't even get the chance to ask when this was. I had thought they had barely met. She doesn't come back out. I'll have to corner her later for more information.

"Wolfie and Bear are coming over soon. You know they are going to grill you about Brax."

I groan. Yes, they will. But I really don't mind.

I join Goldie by the garden bed, and we work side by side till we hear laughter from in the house. The guys are here. We wash off in the garden sink before making our way inside.

Wolf waves a hello, caught up in a video game with Azalea, and Bear walks over arms outstretched, enveloping me in a big hug. All three brothers are tall with dark brown hair, each with varying shades of brown eyes and builds. They absolutely suit their names. Wild and so far, untameable, although most of the women in town have tried. They are also kind, strong and generous and give the best hugs. We grew up together from babies and love spending time together. Our pizza and movie nights are like going back to our childhood when we would have sleepovers, watch scary movies and eat too much. The best.

"Where's Foxy tonight? Goldie said he isn't coming."

Bear leaves his arm hanging over my shoulder loosely and glances over at Juni who is curled up on the lounge in the corner, reading a book.

"Well… lately it has gotten a little harder for him to come to these catch ups. He hasn't said it outright, but Wolf and I agree on the why."

He raises his eyebrows at me and nods towards our sweet, oblivious Juni.

I frown, lowering my voice, even though I know she won't hear anyway.

"I knew he still had a crush, but I'm honestly surprised every time by it. I really thought he would have gotten over it years ago."

He shakes his head, "Nope. Still pining away. Juni still doesn't know?"

I shake my head this time, shrugging. "No, she doesn't. I've mentioned it to her so many times over the years and she would just shake it off and tell me she would know if he did. But clearly that isn't true. I stopped telling her a few years ago because I didn't want her to then get self-conscious around him. You know our Juni girl. Maybe it's time I tell her again? I don't want to push her into anything, but Goldie and I really do think she likes him, she just hasn't realises because she's so caught up in the store and her books."

His laugh is booming and fills the air.

"It's funny how two people, who would be so perfect together, can't find their way to each other."

I gasp dramatically. "Bear. Are you an undercover romantic and I never knew all these years?"

He grins widely. "You didn't know Clemmy? Shucks, I cover it well then don't I."

I grin back at him. It's impossible to not love Bear.

He pats my shoulder, pointing at Juni "Let's keep working on that 'situation'."

I nod at him, and we fist bump before he walks off to join Azalea and Wolf on the lounge to play video games.

Goldie pops her head out of the kitchen, "Guys come and decorate your pizzas!"

I grin. Only Goldie would call pizza toppings 'decorations'.

Thirty minutes later we are all spread out on Goldie's couch and across her floor, eating pizzas and watching a movie.

My phone beeps with a text. Balancing my plate on my knee, I click on the message.

Brax.

'I'm sitting in the bullpen drinking the worst coffee and all I can think of is, I wish it was yours.'

Two minutes ago, I was starving and now my food is all but forgotten.

I bite at my lip, thinking about what to write back to that. I write and delete so many times but make a split decision, deleting the message before sending it.

"Guys, I need to duck out for a little while. Zaylee, listen to whatever Aunt Goldie tells you okay? I'll be back soon."

I throw on my slippers and rush out the door, turning right at the end of the path towards the store, instead of left towards my house.

I rush to unlock the shop, racing through, flicking on lights as I go. I work fast and before I know it, I'm locking the shop door again and heading back down the street towards the station. I'm buzzed in by the nighttime clerk and I take the seat in the foyer while Brax is called out.

My leg bounces with nerves and I can't believe I'm doing this. This is so out of character for me.

The door to the bullpen swings open and I jump up. Brax walks over to me in that uniform, and it suddenly feels very hot in here. Why am I sweating all of the sudden?

He stops close to me, too close to be considered polite and not close enough for my liking. I'm breathless when I look up at him.

"Hey" is my response. It comes out breathy and I clear my throat.

"Hey" he says back, his own voice sounding slightly husky. He gives me a wry smile.

"I thought maybe you had ghosted me when you didn't reply. This is a nice surprise honey."

I remember that I'm holding a bag of baked goods and a coffee. I thrust it in his direction, hitting his chest.

"I brought you these. Can't have you drinking the station sludge coffee."

He smiles down at me before gently taking the bag and the coffee. His smile widens when he looks at my pyjamas. Crap. I had forgotten I was still wearing pjs and slippers. A warm blush spreads across my chest and coats my cheeks.

"Nice pjs," he says while taking a long, slow sip of coffee. It should be illegal to look like that while drinking my coffee.

I cover my face and the laugh that pours out is muffled. I'm wearing my easter pjs from earlier this year. The ones with bunnies all over them. And my slippers are hot pink and fluffy. My hair is a mess, thrown atop my head with a scrunchie. And I have zero makeup on. But when I open my eyes, Brax is staring at me as though he likes what he sees and doesn't care about any of that, and I forget all of it momentarily.

"I was at Goldie's doing pizza and movie night and forgot I was wearing them."

"I'm glad you forgot and didn't change. I like them. A lot. And I like that you came here to see me. My night was quiet and very boring till you got here. Suddenly, this has become the best shift I've had since I transferred here."

He gives me a genuine smile and I'm shy all over again.

"Well, I'm glad I could be of service officer."

He reaches out and tucks a loose strand of hair behind my ear. His fingers graze my cheek before he lets them fall. That's the second time he has done that, and I hope it continues. His touch is electric on my skin.

I clear my throat, but my voice is still hoarse when I speak again.

"I have to get back, but I hope this helps your night go a little quicker."

He nods. "Oh, it sure will. This visit is going to keep me distracted all night."

I gulp and it's so loud. God, I hope he didn't hear. But the meaning behind those words has me feeling like a wildfire has taken over me.

I take a step back, already missing the warmth from his body being so close. I take another few steps and he watches me with that intense gaze, before I turn and walk to the door. I glance back and give him a quick wave, before closing the door behind me.

I'm lost in my thoughts on the trip back to Goldie's. I faintly hear neighbours greeting me on the street, but I'm lost in my own world. I also can't wipe the smile off my face, I'm so giddy. I feel like a teenager again.

I get back to Goldie's and settle back into the couch. Thankfully no one asks where I went, throwing me absent waves when I return, too focused on the movie they are watching.

My phone beeps again like Déjà vu, and I eagerly flick it open, knowing exactly who it is going to be from.

'Lavender. This is the best cookie I have had in my life. Has anyone proposed to you over a cookie like this? It is THAT good. I might have to camp out in the shop to make sure your customers don't fall in love with you once they eat these cookies. Thank you again, you're amazing x'

My heart pounds as I read the message and butterflies fill my stomach. I forget all about the movie and instead spend the last half of it, reading that text, over and over again. Especially focusing on that single kiss, he dropped in at the end.

Chapter 17

Thank God, it's almost closing time. I'm on my sixth coffee and feeling buzzed. It was a really good day. Customers were in a great mood and there were lulls in the day where Goldie and Juni joined me in the coffee shop by the fireplace for an afternoon treat and of course, a cup of coffee. Any chance we can get for sister time, I'll take it.

It's quiet, so I'm slowly wandering Juni's book stacks sipping my double shot espresso from my mug, the rich taste lingering in my mouth. I'm helping her select next month's reading club book. I inhale the rich scent of the books, reminding myself how truly lucky I am. I get to peruse these aisles every day, choosing the perfect book to read. I get to make a hot coffee as I please and enjoy a warm, buttery croissant as I wish. I get to pick a sweet posy of bright, beautiful flowers to place on my kitchen table any time I want.

And I get to do all of that with my sisters by my side. I'm the luckiest.

I pull a few books from the shelf, turning them over to read the description. Although I don't get a lot of time to read, I love it, and I love Juni's book club nights. The cosy feel of the book shop at nighttime with the fireplace lit is incomparable. Juni decks out the space in pillows and cosy wingback chairs and I supply the coffee and cakes. Goldie makes sweet little posy arrangements for everyone who attends. It's one of my favourite nights every month.

"Coffee addict much?"

I practically spit my coffee out, caught by surprise. He reaches out and grabs my arm, steadying me. I turn to him and smile, the voice and face I have been dreaming about. If I'm honest, the body I've been dreaming about too.

"Oh absolutely. Coffee flows through my veins, nothing else."

He chuckles at that, and I love hearing his laugh. It's even better when it's me that's made him laugh.

He reaches just past me, his hand lingering on the shelf, his wrist and forearm resting against my shoulder. I'm cornered between him and the bookshelf. My heart rate speeds up, and I bite my lip, looking up at him. His eyes darken and he clears his throat, taking another step closer.

"Lavender," he says, his voice low.

I'm all breathy when I respond. For some reason I can't quite catch my breath whenever he is this close to me.

"Yes Brax."

"Would you like to…" but he doesn't get to finish what he is saying when we are interrupted.

"Hey Lala." Shit, it's Josh.

I quickly step under Brax's arm and turn to face Josh, taking a sip of my coffee to cover my embarrassment at getting caught. The hot coffee burns my tongue. I haven't told Josh about Brax. I mean, there's not much to tell just yet, but I hope there will be one day.

Josh and I made a pact when we separated that we would tell each other when we started dating. If it was serious. So, there's no reason I should feel like I've been caught out doing something I shouldn't be… except I do. Because my feelings for Brax aren't really feeling very casual and it's only just dawning on me now. I like Brax. A lot.

"Oh, hey Josh. Umm, have you met Brax?"

He raises an eyebrow, giving me a funny look that I can't read. I never was very good at picking up on Josh's facial expressions and now I wonder if that was a sign I missed all those years ago.

I look between them both. Where Brax is strong with a very well-defined body, tall and dark haired with dark blue eyes, Josh is my height, fair haired with brown eyes. Other than both men being kind and good, they couldn't be more different in personalities too. I really mustn't have a type.

Josh nods at Brax. "Hey, I'm Josh, Azalea's dad. She's told me all about you and Beth."

Josh looks to be studying Brax in his own way. Interesting.

Brax gives him a warm smile in return and shakes his hand.

"Hey Josh, it's nice to finally meet you too. Azalea is wonderful, we really love spending time with her."

I turn to Brax, surprised at his words and how comforted I feel by them.

He looks at me with a smile and it feels like a warm hug. What is this man doing to me?

Josh looks between us and narrows his eyes slightly. He reaches over, pulling me in for a side hug. "We are so proud of her aren't we Lavender?"

I nod, looking up at him. I lift my hand to my face, mouthing as discreetly as I can, 'What the hell are you doing?'

He looks just as confused by his actions as I am and drops his arm from my shoulder, muttering a hurried "Sorry" under his breath.

Brax raises an eyebrow at me, and I shrug slightly, not wanting to make Josh feel any more awkward than he already does right now.

Josh trying to make things less uncomfortable, starts asking Brax about work and they quickly settle into an easy conversation for a few minutes. I tune them out while I sip my coffee. What the hell is up with Josh? He has never been like this, even when we were together.

I realise they have said goodbye when Brax reaches out and lightly touches my hand.

"I need to get back to work. I'll message you later."

He lets his hand run through mine slowly, before dropping it.

I turn back to Josh, noticing his arms are crossed and his eyes are squinting at me.

"What?" I ask him innocently, pretending not to know what he is insinuating.

"You really like him."

I shrug my shoulders and walk past him, back to my now empty coffee shop.

"Goldie, hang the sign, it's five o'clock!" I call out to her.

Josh follows behind me laughing. "You do! I knew it. What happened to our rule Clemmy. We are meant to tell each other these things."

I whirl around and point my finger at him, calling him out on his hypocrisy, feeling only a little annoyed.

"Well J, you didn't tell me when you first started dating Amelia."

He sighs and rubs at his face before letting out another laugh.

"Yeah okay, you've got me there. But in my defence, that was three years ago, and it was my first serious relationship since we split. I had no idea what to do there."

I nod at him agreeing. He always was a little hopeless about these things.

I take a seat at the closest table, and he joins me.

"I don't know what this is J. We are just spending time together and I know he likes me… well I think he does anyway. And I know I like him too. But that's it right now."

He reaches out, patting my hand. I withdraw my hand and lean back in my chair, folding my arms.

"What the hell was that back there anyway? You putting your arm around me acting all territorial? That's not you J. And that's not us either. Spill."

He groans, leaning forward and resting his forehead on his hand.

"If I'm honest Lala, I've been a little jealous."

My head shoots up, surprise flashing across my face. We have always agreed that breaking up was the right thing to do and I would consider him one of my closest friends now.

"Not like that, I promise. You know I love you, but as the awesome mother of my child and my first love. Nothing more… I shouldn't have been like that with Brax. I knew as soon as I acted like that, it was the wrong thing to do."

I let out a sigh of relief and he rolls his eyes.

"Okay, you could be a little less relieved about it."

We both laugh this time. We are back on sure footing again.

"No, what I mean is, since our marriage ended, you've never dated anyone seriously. I think I just took for granted that would always be the case. I want you to be happy, I promise you that. And I don't want you to be alone. You're too wonderful not to share your life with someone Lavender. But I guess selfishly, I've loved that I can pop over to visit whenever I'm back in town. I've loved us being able to do family things together for Azalea. But I knew that would all change when you met someone, and it was serious. And I think it could be Brax. I know you and that back there, is serious for you."

I'm floored by his honesty, and at the same time, I think he could be right. I don't know when it happened, but I like him a lot. Thinking over what he said, I jump in to quickly reassure him.

"Josh, all of that won't change. I promise you. Anyone I'm with will need to understand and accept that you're a part of our family. You're Azalea's dad and always will be. She idolises you. That's never going to change. You will always be welcome to visit, to come to our family Christmas dinner and to spend time with us."

I take his hand in both of mine and squeeze it tightly. He smiles in response, the relief is clear on his face.

The bell over the door rings, interrupting us and I glance over to see my dad and Azalea walk in.

Azalea spots us instantly and her face lights up. "Daddy!" she shouts, tearing in through the store and launching herself at Josh.

He catches her in his arms, pulling her in for a hug, squeezing her. "Hey kiddo, I missed you," he says as he kisses her on the head.

I smile at their little reunion. Josh was away for two months this trip and it's their first time seeing each other since he left.

I realise then that Brax arrived a few weeks before Josh left on his latest work trip. That means we have known each other for two and a half months now. Wow.

I watch them chat away, catching up on what each other missed. Azalea stops every few minutes to take a deep breath and reach around for another hug. I'm all but forgotten, but I don't mind. Josh glances over the top of her head and gives me a content smile.

My dad leaves Goldie with a kiss to the cheek and walks over to Josh and I, patting him on the back. "Hello son." He makes his way over to me and leans down, kissing my head, "Hello darling."

I reach up and give him a quick cuddle before turning back to watch my girl and her dad.

Yep. Josh will always be a big part of our family.

Chapter 18

I'm just putting on my pjs and about to sit down to watch a show with Azalea when my phone rings. I pick it up and answer without looking. It's only ever my parents, my sisters or Josh at this time of night. I'm surprised to find Brax on the other end.

"Hey honey, I'm sorry to call so late and do this but I've just been called into work to go over an urgent case that has just come in. Eb is away for the weekend, and I didn't feel comfortable asking anyone else to look after Beth. If you can't that's completely fine. If you can, it would just be for a few hours."

I hear the desperation in his voice, but of course I say yes. I'm only too happy to help and I answer quickly, putting him out of his misery.

"Of course, Brax, Beth is always welcome here anytime."

I hear his deep sigh of relief.

"I'll be there in ten. Thanks so much honey."

Honey. I'm getting used to this.

Like clockwork, I hear a knock at my door ten minutes later. I had contemplated changing clothes, but this is my home and it's seven o'clock at night, so I stayed in my pyjamas.

Besides, Brax has already seen me in my most embarrassing pyjamas and slippers at the station. Tonight, is a step up from that at least.

Before I can reach the door, Azalea is there, flinging it open, squealing in delight.

"Bethy! Come in, mum is going to make us hot chocolate and she said we can watch a movie!"

Beth and Azalea jump up and down holding hands and it's the cutest thing ever.

Beth, breaking free, suddenly races over to me, throwing herself into my arms. Oh my. I squeeze her back tightly and she looks up at me with a huge smile. I pat her hair gently and glance up at Brax. His expression is thoughtful, while he watches our exchange. Beth disentangles herself and races over to the lounge to look through the movie catalogue with Zaylee. I watch them for a moment as they bounce in their seats, chattering away, the excitement rolling off them in waves. Just behind them through my large picture windows, I can spot the actual waves of the ocean as they gently lull to the shore.

Brax clears his throat, breaking my reverie and I turn back to him, as he leans against the doorframe, arms crossed.

"Thank you, Lavender. You're a lifesaver. I just don't trust anyone else to leave her with. She was so excited when I told her, and my chief of police maybe even more so, when I told him I could make it in. They just need fresh eyes to look at this case. I'm sure you have heard as there's lots of whispers around town, but there have been a few break ins lately. They think it might be a tourist passing through, as there have been a string of break ins up the north coast this past year."

Fear creeps in at his words and I shiver. I had heard the whispers about the break ins but not the part about the string of break ins up and down the coast, right near our town. Brax notices and reaches out squeezing my shoulder.

"I don't want you to worry Lavender, just be vigilant is all. They are targeting businesses only, never homes, and it's always when the store is closed so no one has even spotted them which makes identification hard. No one has been hurt either, thankfully. Just promise you won't close up on your own when you're at the shop and try to not stay after dark, okay?"

The concern on his face is real and it no longer surprises me. Brax is a good man. Contrary to what I first thought when we met in my coffee shop. I now know for sure that he is probably one of the kindest and most thoughtful men I have ever met. And the feelings that come with that scare me.

I smile reassuringly and give him a nod, pushing away the fear. He's right. It will be fine.

"If you ever need to stay late, call me please. I will meet you and walk you home. Promise me."

I nod again, touched by his concern, warmth flooding through me.

"I promise. I'll call you if I ever need to stay back late."

He searches my eyes for a moment before seeming reassured by my words and what he finds there.

"Call me if you need anything, I'll come straight back. I'm hoping to be done in a few hours."

Brax takes my hand in his and squeezes it. An electric current shoots up my arms at his touch.

"Thank you."

He glances over at the girls before looking back at me. "I wish I didn't have to go. It sounds like you guys are going to have a fun evening."

I squeeze his hand back and we stay that way for a few moments, lost in time. He stares into my eyes, and I feel a tingling heat travelling up my body. He eventually lets my hand slip through his slowly as he gently removes it from mine, looking reluctant to go, before turning to leave.

My voice is hoarse when I speak. "Bye Brax."

He gives me a coy smile and then he is gone.

It's eleven o'clock at night when I hear a gentle knocking on my door. I look around the dark room, slightly disorientated, realising I've have fallen asleep on the couch.

Both girls are curled up next to me, heads resting on my lap on either side of me. I gently move them onto pillows and stand. Pins and needles shoot through my legs, and it takes me a moment before I can walk to the door. When I reach it, I quietly pull it open.

Brax is on the other side, and he is frowning.

"Lavender, do you always open your door without asking who it is?"

He points at the door, not giving me time to answer before speaking again. He wouldn't like my answer if I did though.

"You don't have a peephole to check. Please do me a favour and just ask who's at the door next time."

He lets out a worried sigh, rubbing at his face with his hands. I can see the exhaustion on his face.

Remorse flows through me. The girls. I should have checked.

"Oh Brax, I'm so sorry. I promise Beth is safe and I wouldn't do anything to put her in danger."

He glances up at me, that frustrated look passing over his face again.

"Lavender, I trust you. Implicitly. I know you would keep Beth safe. But I want to keep you safe too. And Azalea. You're too trusting. Please just ease my mind and promise that if anyone knocks at your door again this late, or anytime, you ask who it is first."

I'm touched at his concern and instantly agree.

"Yes of course."

He's right. I do trust everyone that lives here, and that has probably made me a little lax over the years when it comes to basic safety issues.

I see my phone flashing with a notification on the hall table and grab it quickly. I see the text message he must have sent me earlier.

'Hey, I'm getting out of here in about ten minutes. I'll come straight to you. Let me know if you need me to pick you up anything on the way over xx'

It's then that I notice he has a brown paper bag in his hand. I glance at my phone again, rereading his text, loving those kisses at the end.

"Everything okay Lavender?" I glance up quickly, simultaneously locking my phone and throwing it on the bench.

"Yep, all good."

My words fall out in a jumble. I take a moment to pull myself together before continuing.

"Sorry, I only just saw your text. The girls and I fell asleep on the lounge. Well, they sandwiched me in, and I had no choice but to sleep. That's my story and I'm sticking to it."

He laughs. His voice is deep, and his laughter feels like rich, smooth whiskey.

I move aside and gesture for him to come in. He brushes past me, pulling the door closed behind him, setting the lock.

He holds up the brown paper bag, "Cinnamon donuts," before placing them on the kitchen bench.

I walk him through to the living room, and we stand in front of the couch, looking down at the girls. At some point after I left to answer the door, they reached out to each other to hold hands.

My heart melts. Brax's expression mirrors my own and emotions that look like a mix of wonder and tenderness cross his face.

He clears his throat. "I've never seen Beth connect with another kid like this. It's nice. Really nice." He looks over at me and smiles, the genuine love for his daughter so evident on his face.

I pick up Azalea and carry her to her room, declining his offer to do it for me. I'm so used to carrying her on my own, it doesn't even occur to me to accept. When I return, I see Brax sitting where I was sat earlier, Beth's head resting on his leg.

I sit on the arm of the couch.

"She's so tired Brax. Why don't you let her stay. Zaylee has a trundle pull out under her bed I can make up."

He glances over at me, before looking down at Beth.

"She would love that, I'm sure. Thanks Lavender."

I head down the hall and make up the bed before making my way back to the living room and gesturing for Brax to follow.

He follows behind me carrying Beth and gently places her on the trundle bed. He leans down and gives her a kiss to the forehead and tucks her in.

We make our way back into the living room and Brax settles into the lounge, making himself comfortable. I don't ask if he plans on staying, but I hope he will.

"I'm going to make myself a cup of tea. Would you like one?"

He nods, "Yeah that would be great."

As if an afterthought, he frowns and stops. "Wait, you drink tea?"

Turning my head to the side I smile. "Yeah, I do. Coffee flows through my veins but even I have my limit. Or at least, I make myself stop drinking it. I could drink it all day and night and I weirdly feel fine. I usually have a tea before bed though. It's a family joke that I was born in a coffee field. I love the taste, I don't get jittery or sick from it, and it doesn't affect my sleep at all. I'm an anomaly."

I can hear him chuckling, as I head to the kitchen to make our teas.

I hand him a cup of tea and place the donuts on the coffee table, before taking a seat on the couch next to him, our conversation continuing from before.

"I'm impressed. I love coffee but even I have a limit. If I drink coffee too late, I'm up all night. Which helps when I'm at work but not so much when I'm home and trying to sleep."

"Did you have coffee tonight at the station?"

Real smooth Lavender. It's my subtle way of asking if he is awake enough to stay up and hang out. Or if he is beat and needs to go home and sleep.

His head cocks to the side and I forget he is a police officer. He can read right through me. Busted.

"I didn't have coffee… but I'm feeling very wide awake."

I nod, blushing and grab my mug to take a sip, hiding my embarrassment.

While I'm hiding behind my tea, or doing my best to anyway, I look him over, realising he's dressed slightly different.

I hadn't realised that somewhere along the way, he had changed clothes. When he dropped Beth off earlier, he was dressed in jeans and a black t-shirt. Now he is in the same black t-shirt, but this time he has grey sweatpants on. Grey freakin' sweats. When the girls in book club would joke about them, I never got it. Now I do. I really do. And I can't wait to tell them about it at our next meet up.

He glances down at his clothes and back up at me, and I realise I must have been staring.

"I have spare clothes at work. I changed just before I left."

Embarrassment floods me again that he worked out what I was thinking.

I nod quickly, leaning forward to place my cup on the coffee table. When I sit back, I hadn't realised, but I had moved closer to him. Our legs practically touching now. I don't move away and neither does he.

I watch as Brax takes a sip of his drink and I've never seen a cup of tea look so sexy on a person. When did it get so hot in here?

Our knees still touching, he leans forward placing his cup down before leaning back, lifting one leg to cross over on his knee and turning on his side to face me.

He reaches out and squeezes my knee. I suddenly wish I had my cup to cover my face again. I realise I am so out of practice with this. It's been at least six years since Josh and not a lot in between.

"How were they?"

"Oh, they were perfect Brax. They had so much fun. I did too actually. Beth is so sweet, and they just had a blast together. I've honestly never seen Azalea laugh so much."

I smile, thinking back over the night. I'm being truthful when I say I had a lot of fun with them. I always wanted more children and for a brief moment, it was nice to imagine that both girls were my own.

"She's welcome any time, Brax."

That sultry smirk is back when he says, "What about me… am I welcome any time too?"

Another blush spreads over my chest and neck. Why am I always blushing around this man?

"You're always welcome too Brax… anytime."

I reach out for my tea again, holding it in both of my hands, letting the warmth soothe me. Brax reaches out and squeezes my knee again and electricity crackles between us. He reaches out, gently taking my mug and placing it on the table again.

Brax leans across the back of the couch one arm and with the other crooks his finger at me, gesturing to come closer. I shuffle up onto my knees, caught up in his spell.

We stare at each other for a few moments and without warning, I blurt, "I'm nervous Brax. It's been so long since

I've done… this." I gesture between us hoping he gets the picture.

He reaches out, gently again, tucking my hair behind my ear.

"It's okay Lavender. We can go slow, there's no rush. I mean, don't get me wrong, I want to rush. More than you know. But I'll wait for you. I'll follow your lead, okay?"

We stay that way for who knows how long, before I make a split decision.

I all but lunge at him and he catches me, our hands and arms tangling, pulling each other close.

Our mouths come together, and we kiss furiously, like we are starved and need this to survive. Brax dips his tongue into my mouth, and I moan. He must like that because he groans back and starts kissing my cheeks, my ear and down my neck.

He reaches behind my neck, pulling my mouth to his again and I bite his lower lip. He bites mine softly in return and pulls me onto his lap. I straddle his legs, and he groans again, his hands reaching under my top, stroking my back.

"Lavender, you feel amazing."

He softly bites at my neck and it's my turn to moan again. Our mouths meet again, and we are kissing furiously when we are suddenly interrupted.

"Mum… I'm thirsty."

We break apart, jumping back like we have been caught. I realise quickly that Azalea is still in the hallway, wandering out sleepily and hasn't seen anything.

"Of course, sweetheart," I call back to her.

I jump up from Brax and begin smoothing my top down, legs shaky as I walk towards the hallway. I hear Brax's chuckle behind me. I look over my shoulder at him and give him a sweet smile.

Who knows what would have happened if Azalea hadn't called out? I can guess that it would have been more than just kissing, and I can't decide whether I'm grateful it didn't, because I need to prepare myself more for that, or whether to be disappointed because I so wanted more to happen.

I get Azalea a drink of water and walk her back to bed. When I return, Brax is in the same spot. He pats the seat next to him and I slide in. He puts his arm around me, pulling me in tight to his side and squeezes my hand before lacing my fingers through his own.

"I won't rush you honey. I know you want to go slow, so that's what we will do. But I just want you to know that when you're ready, I want more of that. A whole lot more too."

I lean my head on his shoulder. Being braver than I thought I was, I look up at him, leaning in and gently placing a kiss on his lips.

"Me too Brax. But slow sounds good for now."

We spend the next few hours sneaking a few more kisses, talking and laughing about everything and anything, and it's the best date, if you could call it that, that I've been on. Ever.

I wake up, feeling a little disorientated. My head is resting on a leg. Glancing up, still half asleep, I see Brax and the events of the night rush back. He looks peaceful and I study his face for a moment. His hair is messy, the perfect definition of sexy bed hair and his thick dark lashes fall against his angular cheekbones. His lips are slightly open, and his arm is tucked behind his head resting on the lounge. The other resting on my shoulder. I slowly ease off him, hoping to not wake him. I would rather stay here and watch him a little longer, but I don't want him to wake and find me staring up at him.

I tiptoe quietly into the kitchen and turn on the coffee pot. The house is quiet except for the soft bubbling of the water and the coffee slowly dripping in. The scent begins wafting through the air and I sigh gratefully. It's my favourite way to wake up. Although waking up to see Brax's face might edge that one out for first place.

"Morning."

I jump back from the coffee machine, almost dropping the mugs I just grabbed from the cupboard.

Brax reaches out lightening fast, grabbing my elbow and steadying me.

"Oh my god, you scared me, Brax." I turn to him and laugh, placing the mugs down gently on the countertop. He drops my elbow and leans back against the wall in the kitchen.

"Sorry." He gives me a sheepish smile. His voice is raspy, and sleep ridden and it's glorious. He looks like he just stepped out of a magazine with that bed hair and sleepy expression I was admiring earlier.

I turn back to the coffee machine. Focus Lavender.

"Coffee?"

"Yeah, that would be amazing honey."

I wonder if I can ask him to call me honey permanently. It's becoming a regular occurrence, and it sends a thrill down my spine, every time he says it.

I make his coffee first, placing it on the bench in front of him.

"How did you sleep?"

I glance over at him and see he is massaging the back of his neck with one hand, the other still holding his coffee.

He rolls his neck from side to side. "It wasn't the most comfortable sleep I've had, but the company was nice."

He smirks at me, and I blush, quickly turning back to the task at hand.

I potter around for a few minutes making my coffee and getting out the ingredients to make pancakes. He stays by the doorway, mug in hand, one leg crossed over the other. Watching me.

I do my best to try and ignore him standing there. And to forget about everything that happened last night. Just for now at least. Later I will absolutely be replaying that in my mind.

I fail on both parts.

A quick glance at Brax, tells me he might be thinking about the same thing too.

An excited shout rings out from Azalea's bedroom and Brax laughs.

"Sounds like they have just realised they had a sleep over."

The girls come rushing into the kitchen. "Mum this is the best morning ever! Can Beth stay another night? Please, please, please?"

I laugh with them. "Not tonight baby girl. We are having a movie night at Aunt Juni's remember. But Beth is welcome any other time, okay?"

I smile over at Brax, and he returns it with a soft smile.

The girls rush off to the living room to put on cartoons, their giggling becoming the soundtrack to the morning. A feeling of peace settles over me. The combination of Brax being here, the girl's laughter, coffee, pancakes and a slow morning has me giddy.

"Thanks again for last night."

My head whips up at that, and he chuckles.

"Not that part Lavender… although that part was my favourite if I'm honest. I'm thanking you for minding Beth."

"Oh yeah of course. Anytime Brax," I mutter, a little embarrassed that I thought he meant the whole kissing part. I focus on mixing the pancake batter, hoping he doesn't catch my embarrassment.

I pour the batter in, and the aroma of fresh buttery pancakes starts filling the air.

"Are you hoping I would forget about the part where we kissed? Because there is no way I'm forgetting that."

I turn to him quickly, putting a finger to my lips, "Shhhh."

I lean over the countertop, looking into the living room, double checking the girls can't hear our conversation.

"There is no way they can hear us with the TV that loud."

He smirks at me. That damn smirk I found so infuriating when I first met him but now find incredibly sexy.

I clear my throat and focus on wiping down the bench, muttering, "I was thinking we wouldn't discuss it. I mean, we both know what a kiss is. What more is there to say about it?"

He laughs at that, but I still feel the need to explain.

"I mean, I loved it… a lot… but uh, I'm just out of practice talking about these things…"

He gives me a genuinely kind smile and I feel instantly at ease.

"I understand. I was just thinking maybe we could talk about a repeat sometime… or a date? One we both want to be at this time. Unlike our first date at the restaurant."

Internally I'm happy dancing at his words, but I try and maintain a cool facade.

"I would really like that… what did you have in mind?"

"I was thinking maybe we could give the Italian restaurant another try? I know it's your favourite and it's become mine too. What do you say to a do-over so we can give that place a nicer memory of the two of us?"

I'm blown away by the sweet thought. That he even wants us to change that restaurant memory to a nicer one means a lot. And that he remembered it's my favourite.

"Oh, I'd love to but… I was really hoping Nick might be free that night." I try to keep a straight face but burst out laughing.

Brax's expression moves from disbelief to relief, to finally amusement.

"I'm sorry, that was mean of me," I laugh. "But yes, that would be amazing. I would really love to."

"Well, it sure would be nice to leave the restaurant with you this time, instead of watching you walk out of it. I went to Ebony's house after, to sulk about that date."

A giggle escapes me, and his smile grows wider.

"I love that sound. You giggling. I could listen to that all day."

We stare at each other, the tension between us palpable.

The girls rush into the kitchen talking a mile a minute and the discussion is put on hold for now. We join in their laughter and conversation, eating pancakes together at the breakfast nook and it feels right. Like it's something we have done for a very long time, and it hits me. I can picture doing this for a long time. A really long time.

After breakfast, Brax heads home to get ready for work. Beth and Azalea run to the front gate together, planning their next play date. While they are caught up in their plans, Brax steps back in through the doorway and pulls me in for a kiss. Its fast, but gentle and sweet, and I want more of that. This is the most alive I have felt in years.

He takes a step backwards, towards the door.

"Dinner this week when you're free then?"

I nod, "Sounds wonderful Brax. Will I see you before then?" I ask him a little hesitantly. This man is under my skin.

"Every morning for coffee Lavender. It's my favourite way to start my day now… you and coffee. The perfect combo."

He walks backwards up the path a few steps and that smirk is back. Except now I see it for what it is, not what I thought it was when we first met, arrogance and ego. Now I see it clearly.

He's sexy, confident and kind.

Chapter 19

BOOK CLUB NIGHT. ONE OF my favourite nights of the month. We spend all afternoon setting up our cozy corner and I can't wait to hear what everyone thought about the murder mystery we started last month. Juni has already chosen the next month's book when I couldn't decide, and it's a contemporary romance novel. I can't wait to get into it.

We stand in the flower shop as our book club members start trickling in and we greet each person with a hug. Our little book family we call them. Everyone heads into the coffee shop to take their seat by the fireplace.

"Oh, ladies you have outdone yourselves again. Each month gets better and better!" Mary calls out.

I look around and I think she is right.

Twinkling fairy lights lend a soft glow to this corner of the shop and lamps shine a warm light that brightens the dark space, just enough to invite a comfy vibe. The fireplace is roaring, giving both warmth and light, and soft cushions and blankets are spread across the thick, soft rug. The tables and chairs have all been pushed behind the coffee counter, so the space looks big but also cosy. A few small chairs and tables are strewn about in between the blankets and cushions, in case anyone wants to sit at a table.

It's perfect.

I glance around, doing a head count and it looks as though everyone is here except for one.

"Juni did you say we had twelve people coming tonight?" I sing out to her.

She yells back that twelve people are coming and I double count to be sure. Our regulars are all here so the extra person must be new.

"We only have eleven. Who's the extra person?"

A voice much deeper than Juni's responds. "Me. Sorry I'm late everyone."

I swing around in surprise almost dropping my coffee mug.

"Brax. What are you doing here?"

Brax stands there in a black t-shirt, jeans and boots. Holding a book. Oh, dear lord. I hear an almost collective sigh from behind me. I guess I'm not the only person admiring this vision in front of me.

I realise then, that it's our book club novel he is holding. The one we were both reading at the beach.

A wry grin crosses his face at my shocked expression.

"After the beach that day, Juniper suggested I join the book club seeing as I was reading the same book. My first thought was no, but I don't know. It sounded nice to talk about the book with other people. I was going to tell you about it but then I decided to try the group out and surprise you. Plus, I didn't want you to feel like you had to talk about it twice – with me and then the group - so I decided to just come along here. With you. And your group. If that's okay?"

Oh, it is so much more than okay. I nod, a little speechless, wanting to reassure him. I can hear the hesitancy in his voice, but he needn't be. I'm a mix of excited, surprised and touched. Josh was never interested in what I was reading. He would always listen patiently to me talk about my books, but he was never invested enough to ask questions or ever come to book club. Juni walks over and grabs Brax's arm guiding him to a chair in the corner. She waves me over with a smile and I take the empty seat next to Brax.

Book club starts and before long everyone is chiming in about their favourite parts of the book. Including Brax. I'm surprised to hear his take on the book. It's refreshing. He speaks with such passion when talking about the story, and it's clear he really loves to read. Everyone here is enamoured by him and when he speaks, a hush falls over the room.

It's almost comical and I try hard not to laugh when they turn their puppy dog eyes to Brax.

As the evening winds down, Juni announces next month's book, passing the copies around. When one reaches Brax, he takes it and reads the back, looking thoughtful about what he finds there.

Everyone stares at him expectantly and he looks up, realising they are waiting to hear his reaction to what was chosen. Me included.

He smiles and its big and warm and genuine. He gives a little shrug, "It's not my usual read but yeah, I'll give it a go. It sounds nice."

With that, Brax has everyone practically swooning. Me included.

"Oh Lavender," Sandy calls out, "You mentioned in the book club chat you finally get the appeal of the grey sweatpants! You will love this month's book then!"

I quietly die inside and start silently gesturing at her to stop talking but she doesn't see. Her comment starts a conversation up in the group and Brax turns to face me, raising his eyebrow.

"You finally get the appeal of the grey sweatpants hey… seen anyone in those recently?"

His teasing tone has me grinning ridiculously.

"Nope, can't say I have."

He laughs, shaking his head.

As people say goodbye and make their way out, we thank them for coming. When I reach Brax, I pull him aside before he leaves.

"It was so nice to see you here. I don't expect you to read the next month's book… unless you want to of course. Or even to come back. I want you. I mean I want you to come back. But it's totally up to you."

I stumble over my words and Brax reaches out, taking my hand in his. His is warm and strong. I can feel the callouses at the base of his fingers and I want to ask if he plays sports or if it's from weights. Maybe from work. I realise there's still so much to learn about him and it excites me.

"I want to. And I want you too if that counts." He sends me a wink. Thankfully he is still holding my hand keeping me upright.

I grin cheekily at him. "Oh yeah, that totally counts."

He laughs before reaching out to take a copy of next month's book from me.

"I might get some tips from this," he says shaking the book. "I think I'm going to like this next book." And with another wry grin, he reaches up, carefully grabbing my chin and kissing me softly on the lips.

I'm still reeling as he walks out the door, left to float on cloud nine.

Chapter 20

It's the next morning after book club and Brax stopped by the store for some coffee and unashamed flirting. It was glorious.

I'm smiling thinking about it on my walk home. I'm so caught up in the memory that I don't even pay attention to the trip home. Before I know it, I've reached my house. I open my little front gate and am disrupted from my trip down memory lane, memory lane being this morning, by the sound of a screw gun.

I look up immediately to my front door in the direction of the sound and spot Brax, at my door, screwing in something at eye level.

I walk a little faster down the path.

"Brax?" The question in my voice clear. "What's going on?"

He turns, and I see the drill in his hand and a level in the other. I was not prepared for 'Construction Brax,' and it is not at all disappointing.

"Lavender. Hey. I was hoping to have this done by the time you got home." He looks at his watch, screwing his face up.

"I didn't realise the time."

He doesn't give an explanation as to what he is doing. I look at the door and spot the small hole he has drilled into my beautiful wooden door.

"There's a hole in my door Brax…"

He nods. "Yeah. Sorry, I should have told you. I saw Goldie on my way out of the shop this morning and she gave me a spare key to use when I told her what I had planned to do. But yeah, I should have checked first."

He still doesn't explain and I'm becoming increasingly confused.

"So, what is it exactly that you should have checked first?"

He points at the hole in the door. "I'm installing a door viewer for you. So you can see who comes to your door. I'm just about to install it, so there won't be a gaping hole in your door anymore. Please use it."

I stare at the door dumbfounded, a mix of emotions. One part of me feels annoyance that he didn't ask. The part of me that has had to do everything on my own for the past six years. But the other, the stronger emotion of the two, is touched by his thoughtfulness. That he wants to make sure I stay safe, means the world to me. This emotion wins out and without thinking, I launch myself at him. He catches me in time and gently places down his tools, his hands then circling me, rubbing soothing circles into my back. He rests his head on top of mine, and we stay like that until I hear Azalea calling out from behind me.

I step back and give him a small, watery smile. He stares at me, his eyes searching my face before mouthing, "Are you okay?" I nod quickly, before answering back quietly, "Yes, more than okay. Thank you, Brax."

Azalea joins us and we all chat while Brax installs the peephole. When he is finished, we test it out in turns, laughing. Before he heads off, Brax whispers in my ear that he will call me and with a longing look, walks off with that toolbox that I hope to see again sometime very soon.

It's a few days after Brax's impromptu appearance at my house to install the peephole. Since then, we have been texting nonstop. I feel as though the last few days have had me floating everywhere. It's a wonderful feeling and one I never had with Josh. There are so many firsts I am already experiencing with Brax, and I feel like a teenager again.

The evening is balmy and beautiful, and the lights down main street are lit up as my sisters and I walk home. We closed the shop a little later today as it was so busy with tourists, and we didn't want to turn anyone away. The downside is that we are headed home in the dark. The upside is the centre of towns pretty lights.

"Is lover boy coming around tonight? Seeing as Josh is back and you have the house to yourself with Zaylee at his house," Goldie asks in her sing song voice.

I roll my eyes at her choice of words.

"No, he isn't. He's working late tonight. And he's not my 'lover boy'. I like him. A lot. But I don't really know exactly how he feels… I mean I know he likes me but is it a casual like? Or a serious like? Or maybe somewhere in between. I mean, it certainly feels somewhere in the middle for him. Argh, I could be wrong though."

Juni chimes in on the conversation.

"Oh Lala, you've kissed. A lot. You text each other all day. You spend time with your kids all together. He showed up to book club for goodness sake. He installed a peephole in your door to keep you safe! I think it's obvious to everyone but you, exactly how he feels. I can't wait for the big, sweeping moment when he declares his love for you."

Oh, my sweet Juni. Forever the romantic.

She really is the best of us though. Goldie must have the same thought as she pulls Juni in for a big hug. I lean in joining them for a group hug. I'm hoping for that moment too, I think to myself.

We are almost home before I remember I need milk. I riffle through my bag, realising I forgot my purse.

"Oh shoot, I forgot my purse and I need milk. I'm just going to head back to the shop quickly and grab it. You guys go on ahead. I was thinking of skipping mum and dads for dinner tonight anyway. I have a TV show I'm desperate to catch up on, and a huge tub of ice cream to go with it. I'll see you both in the morning."

I blow them both a kiss and jog back to the store.

I unlock the front door, not bothering to hit the light switch. I could make my way through the shop with my eyes closed, I know the layout so well.

I'm almost at the counter when I hear some rustling from behind it. I pause. That's odd. I take a few more steps and hear the sound again. Adrenaline kicks in, sweat beading instantly on my brow. No one should be here. We must have left only twenty minutes ago. Who would be in here?

My voice is wobbly when I sing out "Hello?"

The rustling stops. I start to take some slow steps backwards into Juni's bookstore. I shouldn't have called out. Suddenly, a figure dressed in all black races past me and out through the front door. I'm so surprised and caught off guard that I fall backwards, my tailbone hitting the floor hard.

Fumbling for my phone, I quickly dial emergency services, hands trembling. My voice shakes when I tell them what happened.

I stay seated on the floor, legs too shaky to stand. I rest my head on my hands.

Within minutes of the call, I hear the sirens. The door is thrown wide open, the bell screeching almost as if in protest at being treated with such force.

I watch on, almost detached from what's happening. Brax stands in the doorframe, looking frantic. He spies me amongst the bookshelves, eyes searching me over, his chest heaving. Relief takes over his face and he rushes forward, dodging around the flower buckets that the intruder knocked over.

He reaches me, scooping me up in his arms and I fall apart.

"Oh Brax."

I sob into his arms, more in shock than anything else.

He pulls me in tighter. "I've got you honey. You're safe. I've got you."

Officers rush in around me and quickly start their fingerprinting and questioning. I just want to be out of here. I answer a few questions, and Brax stays by my side the whole time, tensing when I tell them about how I heard someone behind the counter and called out, instead of just leaving.

I hear a police officer mention that the window in the back was ajar, and they suspect that's how they must have gotten in. We never lock those windows and right now, I'm regretting that.

We get through the statement quickly, and Brax is ushering me out of the shop, holding my bag in one hand and gripping mine in the other. The trip home is a bit of a blur but on the way back, I call Goldie quickly to let her know I'm fine and ask her to let Juni know what happened. I promise to fill her in more tomorrow and reassure her a few more times that I'm okay. I tell her not to come over and that I'll see her tomorrow. I don't want them to worry.

I take a seat on the couch as soon as we are inside, still a little shaky but feeling better. Brax quietly takes a seat beside me.

I rub at my eyes and groan.

"I'm sorry Brax. I'm totally fine but it scared me. You don't have to stay, I'm okay."

I hear him shift closer to me and he takes my hand.

"Hey, look at me." He takes my chin and tilts my head up gently. "Do not be sorry. That would scare anyone okay. And I'm not going anywhere. So, do whatever you need to, to feel comfortable right now. I'm staying. I'm not leaving, okay?"

He picks up his phone and types in it for a minute. He gets an alert immediately and leans back, seeming a little more at ease.

"Would you mind if I have a shower? It's been a big day at work, and I would love to shower and get into my pyjamas."

"Of course, go ahead. I'll wait right here for you. I'm not going anywhere, okay." he reminds me again.

The relief at him being here is indescribable and I take so much comfort in it.

I have a super quick shower, but it does the job, washing away the grime and some of the stress of the day. I'm putting on my pjs when I hear a knock at the front door.

I hurry with my jumper, pulling my hair out of the neck of the sweater as I walk to the door, where I'm greeted by my sisters. Goldie and Juni, both dressed in their pyjamas too, rush in, launching themselves at me. We stay that way hugging, their muffled voices expressing their worry and apologising for not going back with me. I reassure them I'm fine when I'm interrupted by the doorbell again.

This time, it's Ebony. She rushes in and is welcomed into the group hug.

"Guys I'm fine I promise. I feel okay. A little shaken and my tailbone is sore from where I fell, but otherwise I'm okay. You didn't need to come."

Goldie scoffs. "Of course we needed to come. You're our sister and we were worried about you. You're crazy for thinking we wouldn't come really. And don't even bother telling us to leave. We are staying the night. I'm taking Azalea's bed."

Juni groans, "No, I wanted Azalea's bed. Fine, I'm sleeping with Lavender. Unless that spot is already taken." And she winks at me.

I hear Brax laughing behind me, but It's a little strained. I can tell he is still worried.

"Oh, I'm not going anywhere either. I'll take the couch. Sorry brother, looks like you're on the floor." Eb chimes in.

He smiles, and I notice it's a little subdued. Before I can check in on him, the door swings open again and this time it's my mum and dad. They rush in and fuss over me and

I let them. I'm so grateful for their support and everyone being here tonight. It means the world to me.

Everyone crowds around me to get the story of what happened. As I retell it, I see Brax pacing in the background, looking angrier and more upset than he did before.

When I finish my story, he speaks up "Lavender, I'm just going to run home and change out of my work clothes. I'll swing by your house Eb and just check on Beth, Ryder and the kids and then I'll be back."

Before I can answer, he is out the door.

An hour passes and during that time, mum and dad head home. Juni, Goldie and Eb all spread out on my couch where we start a movie. I'm grateful for the temporary distraction but I can't stop thinking about Brax.

The door eventually opens, and Brax walks through with an overnight bag. He has changed clothes and is back in those sweatpants I love.

He gestures for me to join him in the kitchen. My sisters and Ebony are so engrossed in the movie they don't notice.

I join Brax in the kitchen. He steps forward and pulls me in for a hug and I willingly fall into his arms. He strokes the back of my head, and I feel instantly calmer.

"I'm sorry I left like that honey. I just needed to clear my head. What happened tonight, scared me."

I nod, understanding. It scared me too.

"When the call came through to the station and I heard your voice, sounding absolutely terrified, I panicked. I've never felt like that on a call at work before. Or ever. The only other time I was that worried was when Beth was younger and got really sick and needed a short stay in hospital. I didn't even bother getting in the car with the other guys. I just ran to you. Seeing you on the floor, frightened, and not knowing if you were hurt was the most scared, I've ever been honey."

I'm at a loss for words with his honesty. I reach up and place my hand on his cheek and he leans into it, closing his eyes.

"I'm totally fine Brax, I promise. I really am. It shook me earlier when it happened but I'm okay now."

He doesn't look convinced, but he seems to accept what I tell him. His hand goes up to my cheek and he rubs his thumb across to my ear.

"I swung by the station when I was out and got an update. Because you interrupted the guy, he must have freaked and ran out the front door, when he should have gone out the back. We caught him on camera from across the street Lavender. We got him."

Relief surges through me at the news. I lean into his palm and close my eyes, quietly weeping with relief. Anguish flashes across Brax's face and he wraps his arms around me holding me tight. He rubs soothing circles over my back, holding me tight to him.

He kisses the top of my head. "I know I keep saying this, but I really am so sorry this happened honey. I wish I could have caught this guy before he did this to you."

I shake my head and pull back. "It's not your fault Brax. And you came as soon as I needed you. And you did all this," I gesture around to the wonderful, supportive people in my living room.

"I know you messaged Eb and told her to tell my sisters I was home and needed them. That means the most. That you're here for me when I need you and knowing that I need my family too."

He nods looking serious. "I'm staying tonight. To make sure you feel safe. If that's okay? If it's not and you would rather me go, I'll sleep in the car outside. Whatever you are comfortable with. But I'm not leaving you."

I curl into him for another hug. "Stay." He squeezes me even tighter, pulling me in even closer to his body.

We join everyone in the living room and spend the rest of the evening eating Chinese takeout and watching comedies on TV. Despite the events of earlier, I surprisingly enjoy the evening, my mind completely preoccupied.

We are onto the second movie when I realise Juni and Goldie are both asleep on the couch.

Ebony realises at the same time as I do and gets up quietly, leaning down to give me a hug.

"I'm going to sleep in Zaylee's room while she is away. I'll see you in the morning," she whispers.

She waves at Brax and makes her way down the hall. Exhaustion hits me. I grab two blankets out of the basket beside the couch and lay them over my sisters, before turning to Brax. He watches me quietly.

There's no space on the couch for him to sleep and Ebony has taken Azalea's bed. The only space left is the floor. Or my bed. I decide right then and there.

I hold out my hand and he looks puzzled but stands to take it anyway. Realisation dawns on his face as I walk him down the hall, turning off the lights. I take in a deep breath and turn to face him at my bedroom door.

"You can't sleep on the floor, I won't let you, and the only other place is my bed. If you want to, of course."

Brax smiles at me and pulls me in by the waist. "Did you think I would say no? I would never say no to that Lavender. Ever. I promise you that."

I rest my head on his shoulder, and we stay like that till I pull away, backing into the room, pulling him with me.

I point over towards the window. "I always sleep on that side. I know, it's weird. I should be sleeping in the middle of this huge bed, right? I know this sounds silly, but I've always wanted to sleep on the right side. When I was with Josh…" My words trail off. Why am I telling him this now? He doesn't want to hear this.

"It's okay. Go on," Brax replies.

"Well… He always wanted the right side, so I had to sleep on the left. But the right side just feels… well right." I laugh, embarrassed. Why did I tell him all of that? He is going to think I'm weird. I groan and cover my eyes.

Brax walks over to the left side of the bed and sits down on top of the covers, stretching his legs out and leaning his back against the headboard. He raises his arms, placing his hands behind his head.

"Funnily enough, I've always slept on the left side of my huge bed too. So, I think this fits perfectly, don't you agree?"

He pats the right side, and I hop up on the bed, mirroring his sitting position. We look out over the midnight ocean, the light from the moon illuminating the waves rolling in.

Brax's hand gently slips mine into his between us. This is nice. Really nice. I rest my head on his shoulder, and he rests his head on mine.

Without meaning to, I fall asleep. Sometime later, I wake with a jolt when I realise that Brax has moved me under the covers and is tucking me in.

When he realises I'm awake, he leans down and gently kisses me.

"Go back to sleep baby. I'm right here."

He settles down next to me and pulls me in close, my back touching his chest. He is warm and this is without a doubt, the nicest hug I have ever had. Josh hated cuddling in bed. All I think of as I drift to sleep, is that I could stay like this for a lifetime. Safe, and in Brax's arms.

Chapter 21

THE BRIGHT MORNING SUN, STREAMS through my window and warms my face, waking me from a restful sleep. The memories of yesterday's events, flood back to me.

I lay in bed a little while, looking out at the water, and a surprising sense of calm flows through me. I feel okay. They caught the person, and other than giving me a fright, nothing bad happened.

I roll over to my left, expecting to see Brax, but he's not there. A wave of disappointment engulfs me. Maybe he went home early. I push my disappointment aside and force myself to get up.

I stretch beside the bed, rolling my neck to work the kinks out, enjoying the burn it gives me in my muscles. I twist from side to side and wince, when a pain shoots down my leg from my tailbone. I fell on it pretty hard last night, and I bet it's bruised.

I need a coffee. That fixes everything.

I walk out to the kitchen, the floorboards cold beneath my bare feet. The sound of snores, and the smell of coffee roasting, soothes my soul. I love when my house is full. Looking over at the couch, I can see my sisters are still asleep. I remember then that Eb took Azalea's bed. I'm guessing she is probably still asleep too, with the house being so quiet.

Sleeping beside Brax, I slept soundlessly, considering everything that happened last night. Without a doubt, I know it was because he was there.

Walking quietly into the kitchen, I'm shocked at the sight of Brax standing in front of my coffee machine. I had assumed he left. I watch as he attempts to get it working. The coffee is brewing, but he seems to be having trouble with frothing the milk. I lean against the doorframe, wondering how long I should wait till I step in and help. I decide to enjoy the view of him in my kitchen, this early in the morning, for a little while longer.

He must sense me behind him, because he turns, giving me a wry smile.

"Please put me out of my misery and help with this."

I laugh, pushing off from the doorframe and making my way over. I adjust a few settings, while Brax's hands encircle my waist, meeting over my belly. Eventually I get it working, despite the distraction of him pressed up against me. I lean back into his chest and turn my head to rest against his neck. He smells like coffee and a surprising mix of vanilla and sandalwood. I could stay in this spot all day, soaking in this scent. It's warm and inviting, like Brax. We stay that way for a few more moments while the coffee machine hisses away, before I begrudgingly move out of his embrace, and let him finish making me a coffee.

He hands me the mug and I hold it in my hands, warming them.

I spy a large paper bag on the bench with Leo's bakery logo, and my stomach betrays me, grumbling.

I point at the tray of pastries. "Where did these come from?"

Brax picks up a scroll and takes a bite.

"I ducked out to the bakery this morning to grab breakfast for everyone. Unfortunately my favourite coffee shop was closed, so you will have to settle for my unskilled version."

I reach out and snag my own cinnamon scroll, inhaling the scent. My stomach grumbles again.

He smirks at me, "Don't worry, I made sure there was enough. I even got you an extra scroll and put it in the cupboard above the fridge so you can have another later."

This man knows the way to my heart is coffee and cinnamon scrolls.

I take a seat at the breakfast nook, taking a sip of my coffee.

I glance up at him in surprise. "This is actually pretty good Brax. I may be able to make use of you at the coffee shop yet," and I send a wink his way.

I'm loving this new flirty side I'm discovering about myself. Go me.

Last night hits me at his mention of the shop. My face drops when I think about having to clean up the mess from the intruder. It didn't look like a lot when I left, but it's the last thing I want to be doing right now. I check the time on the clock. It's 7am. If we are going to be opening at 9am, I need to get moving. I take another quick sip, placing my coffee down on the bench and sliding off the stool.

The worry must be clear on my face, because Brax reaches out, grabbing my chin lightly, tilting it up. "Hey, what's up?"

"I'm just thinking about the mess I'll need to clean up this morning," I grumble.

Brax shakes his head. "No, you don't need to worry about that. When I left last night, I organised a cleaner. They have already been in this morning and fixed everything. I meant to tell you last night but with everything going on, I forgot. I should have asked first before doing that. I'm sorry."

I'm absolutely stunned at his thoughtfulness.

I walk around the bench, launching myself at him.

He catches me, wrapping his arms around my shoulders. My voice is muffled in his shirt when I reply. "Thank you thank you thank you Brax. You're so wonderful."

He strokes my hair, and I hear him swallow. When he talks, his voice is filled with emotion.

"I would do anything for you, honey. Anything to make you feel better."

He rubs more soothing circles over my back, and I relax into his embrace.

His voice is husky this time when he speaks again. "So… last night. I could get used to that."

And in the spirit of his honesty, I decide to be truthful too.

"I was thinking that very same thing this morning. I was kind of missing you when I woke up and found the bed empty. I uh, thought maybe you had snuck out."

He pulls back slightly, and I can see his face this time when he speaks again.

"I wouldn't do that to you. Ever. Trust me, it was hard to leave but I wanted to make sure the cleaner had sorted everything, and I didn't want you to have to think about breakfast, so I grabbed the pastries from Leo when he opened."

He continues on, "Maybe we could do a repeat of that another night?"

I hear the hope in his voice, and I feel it in my heart too.

"Anytime," and I cuddle back into his embrace.

Brax kisses the top of my head. "I don't know what you've done to me Lavender, but I am under your spell."

Right back at you Brax Madox.

The shop looks exactly as we left it, and a huge sigh of relief that I didn't realise I was holding on to, escapes me. Juni and Goldie came with Brax and I to work this morning and have already taken a walk through to assess the damage. After realising nothing is missing and everything looks the same, we go about our business as usual. Other than a few regulars asking what happened, it doesn't cross my mind much that morning or for the rest of the day.

Brax walked me into work this morning and hasn't left the coffee shop all day. When I opened the store, I expected him to leave, but instead, he set up shop in the corner with a newspaper and his morning coffee.

Checking my watch, I realise its already three o'clock. Only two hours till closing, and he hasn't moved all day. It's the sweetest thing anyone has ever done for me. Every time I glance in his direction, I feel myself tearing up.

The afternoon rush has slowed, and my tailbone is still feeling tender, especially after being on my feet all day. I take my apron off and make my way over to his table, taking a seat opposite him.

"Hi."

He puts his book down and leans forward taking my hand. "Hi."

Using my other hand, I push the cookie towards him that I've brought over. I'm rewarded with a smile and a wink. I'm a sucker for both.

He takes a bite of the cookie.

"So, you're going to be here all day then?"

Smirking, he answers "Yep, looks that way."

He wipes his hands on the leg of his pants, his expression turning serious.

"I just didn't want you to face the store today on your own. I wanted to make sure you were okay. I do have to go back to work tomorrow though. We are short a few guys at the station right now. All I could get off was today."

My mouth drops open, "Brax you took the day off? I thought this just happened to coincide with a rostered day off. Oh, I'm so sorry."

I cover my face with my hands, before quickly moving them to the side, letting my eyes peak out.

He gives me a gentle smile. "Don't be sorry. I chose to do this. I wanted to. It was important for me to be here and I'm glad I did it. Anyway, I love watching you work Lavender. I can see how much you love your job and your customers. You don't need all these fancy lamps in here. You, light up this space. I was a fool to not see that the first time I came in here and met you."

Not wanting to waste any more time, my question comes out breathless.

"Come over tonight and let me cook dinner for you. Bring Bethy, I would love to see her."

"Lavender, I would love that."

Chapter 22

Date night. Ebony volunteered to have the girls overnight so Brax and I could have a proper date. Which means he can stay over without having to sneak in or out.

It's been a few days since the break in and Brax has stayed every night, but other than a ton of kissing and cuddling, that's been it. I know I told him I wanted slow, but slow is killing me right now. And from the look on his face each night, it's killing him too.

I have a feeling tonight might be a little different to the last few nights.

Tonight, I'm wearing a rust-coloured midi dress that wraps around and ties into a big, gorgeous bow on the side. The slit up the front reaches mid-thigh. I don't think I've ever worn anything this revealing, or this beautiful before.

The thin spaghetti straps lead down into a v neck front and the material is a soft chiffon. I do a twirl in front of the mirror. I feel good in this dress. And I'm so excited to wear something other than my jeans and a tee.

I've left my wavy hair out, cascading over my shoulders, instead of up in a clip or ponytail.

My makeup is light, just the way I prefer it. Most days I barely wear any. I hear knocking at the door and I grab my purse off the table and slip my feet into sandals, buckling them up around my ankles. I race down the hall. Shoot, perfume. I turn and race back into my bedroom and do a quick spritz. The racing around has given my cheeks a natural flush. I could have skipped the blush after all.

I race back down the hall again and practically skid to a stop when I swing the front door open, almost tumbling out into Brax's arms. His hands shoot out steadying my arms.

"Woah, Lavender. I've got you."

He laughs as he steadies me, and a giggle escapes me too.

Brax's laugh dies off when he looks down at my dress.

He swallows audibly and his hands that were steadying me only minutes ago slowly slide down my arms and circle my wrists gently.

"Baby you look… wow. I mean you're beautiful in anything you wear, and this could be a paper bag right now and I would love you in it, but you look unbelievable."

I smile a little shyly, my confidence soaring. It's been so long since I've had genuine comments like these, and I feel like I could take on the world right now.

"I'm glad I chose this one then. The paper bag was a little noisy."

A laugh bursts from him, and he shakes his head.

He runs his hand down my hip and the top of my thigh, turning serious.

His voice is husky when he replies. "This one Is definitely a lot softer that's for sure."

He touches the tie at my hip. "If I just pulled this loose, what would happen? Would the dress just fall to the floor?"

My heart speeds up and I boldly place my hand over his at my waist, bringing it up to where the dresses neckline dips into my cleavage.

I run his hand down the dip to my belly and shake my head.

My voice is husky now too. "No. It wouldn't fall to the floor. It would fall open here."

Desire pools in his eyes and his mouth gapes open.

"And what would I find under here?"

He gently slips his finger under the fabric that wraps around at the front.

I swallow, nerves setting in. I shake it off. This is Brax. And he's the reason I feel so at ease and confident to be this bold.

My response is so low, he needs to step closer to hear.

I lean in and whisper in his ear.

"Why don't you unwrap it and find out."

Before I can say another word, Brax wraps his arm around my waist, one hand holding my hip, the other grasping at the bow. He walks me backwards into the house and kicks the door shut behind him.

He crushes his mouth to mine; his tongue teasing entry and I open mine willingly.

His hand goes back to my hip, not breaking our kiss and he unties the bow. He pulls the tie to my left unravelling my dress and exposing my lacey black underwear and bare chest. I'm not wearing a bra.

He looks down and his chest rises as he takes in a deep shuddering breath.

He runs his fingertips lightly from the dip in my cleavage down my stomach, stopping where my lace underwear meets my skin. I squirm, wanting more.

"Lavender, fuck you're gorgeous."

His hands trail back up to my neck and he tucks his fingers under the edge of both straps and pushes them off my shoulder.

My dress ripples to the ground and I'm standing there in my heels, underwear and nothing else.

As his eyes make their way down my chest and below, his hands trail the same path.

His hands rest on my hips, and he squeezes, lifting me up to wrap my legs around his waist. I wrap my arms around his shoulders and gently kiss a path up his neck to his ear and across his jaw. He groans.

"Why weren't we doing this sooner honey?"

I giggle and shake my head. "Beats me. Seems like we should have been doing this from the moment we met."

He nods, grabbing the back of my head and gently pulling me in for another kiss.

"Oh yeah, we absolutely should have. Now I'm going to show you exactly what we should have been doing."

He slowly walks us into the hallway and pushes my door open, carrying me over to the bed and gently laying me down.

He stands there watching me and I've never felt more alive. Screw dinner, I'm suddenly not hungry for food. I crawl backwards up the bed, kicking off my shoes to the floor. Feeling bold, I slowly shimmy my underwear down my thighs and calves and kick them off with my toes. My skin feels like it's on fire with the way Brax is looking at me.

"Fucking hell," he mutters under his breath.

Brax lifts his shirt over his head and tosses it to the floor. He undoes his pants, kicking them off till he is standing in nothing but black boxer briefs. Heat pools at my core and I'm desperate for him to join me on the bed. Slower than I would like, he pushes down his briefs, and oh my. It has definitely been a while, but I've never been with someone so big.

He kneels onto the bed with one knee, the other leg still on the ground and without a single word, he kisses a path from my ankle up to my core, kissing and tasting me. My hands clutch at the bed, clawing at the sheets and my hips rise from the bed. He tastes and touches me like he is starved, just for me, and I've never been so turned on in my life.

I beg him for more, grabbing his hand and pulling him up towards me. His mouth finds mine and he tastes like me. We kiss and explore each other with our hands. Brax pushes gently against me, looking for entry and I open my legs wider, grasping at his lower back, encouraging him.

"Please, Brax," I whimper.

He leans down and nips at my neck and then my chest, his mouth circling my nipple, softly sucking it in as he pushes in. I feel his groan through me when he is completely inside of me.

He slowly pushes in and out, and my legs wind around his lower back, pushing him in deeper. The friction of our bodies meeting is too much, and I feel myself falling apart, stars dancing behind my eyes. Brax cries out, before finding my mouth with his own as we ride the wave together.

Brax pulls out gently and then rolls to his side, taking me with him. We lay that way, kissing slowly and softly for a little while before he gets up to use the bathroom, returning with a washcloth and wiping me down so gently, as if I was made of glass.

We drift off to sleep together, totally blissed out, listening to the waves crashing on the shore and I think this must be what heaven feels like.

The sunlight floods in the next morning, bathing the bed in warmth. I'm hot but not in an uncomfortable way. More like a cozy, I don't want to leave this space kind of way.

I'm spread out across Brax's chest, his arms wrapped around me, holding me tight. We are tangled in the sheets, our legs intertwined, and my head is resting on his chest, underneath his chin. I hear his soft snores fill the room.

I lazily trace circles across his chest, remembering last night.

I lean down and kiss his neck softly as the memories flood in. I pepper more kisses in a trail up to his ear and he lets out a groan, pulling me in closer. I can feel every inch of him, and I sit up, straddling him, while he runs his hands up my thighs, and over my waist to cup the sides of my breast.

"Perfection" he whispers to me, rubbing circles around and across my nipples. His hand trails down my belly and reaches where our two bodies meet. He lazily traces more circles, and I moan leaning back.

His hand reaches up to gently grab the back of my neck.

"Come here," he whispers pulling me down to him, his kiss lighting a fire in me.

I push him back on the bed slowly, and brush down on his body, lining our bodies up, guiding him in. He groans again and the sound is raw.

He leans up, kissing my chest and this angle gives just the right amount of friction. I wrap my arms around him, and we both come undone together. I'll have his moans, and his release etched into my memory forever.

Brax runs his hands up and down my spine and we lay there unhurried, gently kissing each other.

"Last night was amazing Brax. And this morning too… I didn't know it could be like that…"

His laugh is soft and hoarse. He pulls me in closer, murmuring into my ear.

"It's not baby. It's not always like that. I've never had it be that way with anyone else."

Warmth fills my chest, and I lay there staring at the ceiling with a ridiculous grin on my face. Six months ago Lavender, would be in awe of this.

Brax lazily runs his fingers up and down my arm. He reaches down with his other hand and threads his fingers through mine, lightly kissing my ear before whispering, "Ready for another round?"

Heck yes, I am. I nod, meeting him in the middle, pressing my lips to his. He gently bites my lower lip, and I moan into his mouth.

"Wait, let me just check the time," I breathe, reluctantly pulling away, turning to look at the clock.

It's eight thirty… eight thirty! Shit.

I sit up in bed pulling the sheet around me, leaving Brax uncovered and completely naked. If I had more time, I would stay to enjoy the view.

"Brax, it's eight thirty! I have to open the store in thirty minutes, and I still need to get ready and pick up Zaylee from your sister's house."

I scramble out of bed and Brax chuckles, lazily resting his hand behind his head, not caring that he is naked across my bed. I bite my lip. Hmmm maybe I could spare five minutes…

I glance at the clock again. Eight thirty-five now. Nope definitely not.

"It's okay honey, we can work it out together. You shower and head to work. I'll head over to get the girls. If you're comfortable with it, I was thinking Zaylee could hang out with Beth and I today. What do you think?"

I stop for a second, considering his offer. Josh and I have a rule that we always check with the other before leaving Azalea with anyone other than family and I don't want to break that rule now.

I smile at him, unbelievably touched by his offer.

"Give me one quick second, okay?"

I grab my phone off the bedside and leave the room, dialling Josh.

I chat to him for maybe all of thirty seconds and smiling to myself, walk back into the bedroom. Josh was totally onboard, and I couldn't be more grateful for his support.

"Brax… I would love that. That would be amazing. Thank you."

I lean down and kiss him, pulling away before he can grab me and make me think opening the shop late would be justified today.

I wave my fingers at him and walking away, I teasingly drop the sheet, smiling over my shoulder. He laughs, but when he calls out, his voice is deep and not at all joking. "Come back here."

I pop my head back around the door.

"Trust me Brax. I want to. It's taking everything in me to go and get into this shower when I would rather leave the shop closed for the day."

He lets out a groan and covers his face with the pillow. I hear his muffled reply. "Go before I change my mind and convince you to do just that."

I giggle and make my way to the shower, unable to wipe the smile off my face.

After a quick rinse, I get dressed and throw my hair up in a clip. I race into the living room, only stopping to toe my feet into some sneakers.

Brax is dressed and walking out of my kitchen with a to-go mug, handing it over to me.

I take a huge sip like my life depends on it, and liquid gold seeps into my soul. I close my eyes and savour the taste, moaning.

"You're too good to me Brax."

When I open my eyes, I see his are heavy with desire.

He grabs me by the waist and pulls me close.

"You deserve everything Lavender. Everything. And I intend on giving it to you."

I kiss him again, before reluctantly stepping back and grabbing my bag.

"I have to go or I'm going to have the town villagers standing at the shop door with pitch forks. Thank goodness it's the weekend and not a weekday. I would have had to leave here at like six thirty."

Brax grabs his keys and wallet and walks me out.

I pull the door closed behind him but don't bother locking it. He frowns, shaking his head.

"I know that most people around here don't lock their door, but you need to. Please. I won't be able to stop worrying till you do."

Even though I know it will be fine if I don't lock the door, I do it for his peace of mind. And honestly, it's so lovely to have someone care so much.

"If it helps to reassure you, I used the peephole yesterday before opening it to the mail guy. I think he heard me from behind the door because he looked really confused when I opened it."

A laugh bursts from me just remembering his face.

He gives me a quick half smile and nods his head. "It does reassure me. Slightly. Locking the door every time you leave would reassure me even more though."

We reach the pathway out the front of my house and mindful of the time, I give him a quick peck and turn left, towards the store. I walk backwards a few steps and blow him another kiss.

"Thank you for taking Azalea today! I'll call you once the shop is open!"

Brax stands there with his hands on his hips watching me race off, shaking his head with a huge grin on his face.

I turn around and start jogging. Five minutes till the shop is due to open. Crap.

When the shop is in my line of sight and I see no customers waiting out the front, I heave a sigh of relief. Both Juni and Goldie had to do a run into town this morning, so they had already told me they wouldn't be there on time. I finally slow down my jog and call Ebony. I let her know about Brax heading over to take Azalea for the day and she is ecstatic.

Reassured, I toss my phone back in my bag and throw open the yellow front door, setting about opening the shop.

Customers spend the day remarking on and off about how happy I look and that I'm glowing. I'm starting to wonder if I usually look like a grouch. But they aren't wrong. I can feel the good energy around me.

I get caught up daydreaming too many times to count. Remembering Brax's lips on my neck last night or the way he used his tongue. How tender and gentle he was but also how he didn't hold back when he was caught up in the moment. It was the best sex of my life, and I'm left wondering when we can do it again.

I'm daydreaming again at the counter when I'm interrupted by loud and very familiar giggling. A huge smile crosses my face. I would know that gorgeous laughter anywhere.

Azalea and Beth rush in the store up to my counter. Azalea runs straight around behind it and dives into my arms. Beth is not far behind her, and I'm almost bowled over by the two of them bear hugging me. I look up and spot Brax walking in at a more leisurely pace behind them. He raises his eyebrows at the sight of us and rubs at his chin with his hand, flashing a coy smile in my direction. He comes to a stop at the counter and placing his hands on the bench, he leans forward, almost as if to kiss me. He stops suddenly, likely realising where he is and pulls back.

I pat both girls on the back, "Why don't you both go help Goldie make some flower arrangements for the shop. I need some bright bouquets for the tables."

They jump up and down excited, before racing over to Goldie, chatting animatedly with each other.

Goldie greets them both with a warm hug and jumps up and down with them. She grabs them some aprons and sets them both up with some flowers and vases.

I turn back to Brax and step closer to my side of the counter. He gives me that side smile again and this time when he leans over, there's nothing stopping us.

He kisses me gently, lingering only a moment before slowly turning his head to reach my ear.

"I've been thinking about you all day. When can we repeat last night?" He whispers.

He drops a quick kiss there and leans back slightly. Our faces stay mere inches from each other as we talk.

"Every night from now until forever. How does that sound?" I joke, not realising what I just said. My face flushes. Brax gives me an indulgent smile and his expression smoulders, a sexy grin crossing his face.

"Sounds good to me. Do we do a blood oath to lock this in or something? I'll do whatever you want baby." Brax's voice deepens and that flush spreads across my entire body.

I shake my head and scrunch my face up, giggling. "I like the sound of that."

"And I like the sound of you. Here with me now, and last night in the bedroom."

I swallow, my hand lingering by my neck. I glance around quickly to make sure no one is listening. There's no one here, but we continue whispering anyway. It feels intimate.

I glance towards the flower shop and see the girls are too busy to notice us. He follows my line of sight, turning to look over his shoulder.

He turns back to me and sighs.

"When will we tell the girls? I'm ready when you are honey. I've been ready a while now."

He stares at me, his eyes imploring me to say yes. I've never done this before and I'm slightly freaking out. I'm sure Azalea will be happy, but what if she isn't? What if she doesn't want us to be together. That would be it for Brax and I, before we had barely even begun.

He must sense I'm internally freaking out because he takes my hand in his, rubbing it reassuringly.

"I know you're scared but it will be fine. I think you will find they are going to be excited. But if you need more time, then we can wait. I want you to feel comfortable. It's just getting really hard to not kiss you and not hold your hand. I want to tell everyone that you're mine."

He couldn't have said anything more perfect or reassuring than that. Worries still flood my mind but I feel a little better.

I nod, squeezing his hand in reply, before pulling back quickly.

"Okay let's do it. I just need to sort a few things first and then we can tell them. Sometime in the next two weeks for sure, okay?"

I'm stalling a little and he knows it, but he doesn't pressure me. Instead, he gives me a warm, knowing smile. "Sure baby, that sounds good. In the meantime, let me know when I can sneak over this week, and I'll organise for Beth to stay at Ebony's that night."

Giving me a wink, he reaches out, lightly grabbing my chin, and quickly planting a kiss on my lips.

"I need to head off to work shortly. Is it okay if Ebony swings by and takes Beth in about an hour or so? She said Azalea is welcome at her house too."

I nod, only too happy to have the girls here for a little while this afternoon.

I watch him walk over to the girls to say goodbye and notice for the first time that Azalea leans out to hug him. It's effortlessly natural. I realise then that my baby girl will be just fine with this news.

When I'm ready to tell her, and everyone else. For now, I just want to enjoy our bubble a little more before the twenty questions come.

Chapter 23

WE SPEND THE NEXT FEW weeks doing pizza and movie nights with the kids and lots of park play dates. In between our family catch ups, Brax and I take turns cooking for each other and we go on the occasional date alone. Brax sneaks into my house or I sneak into his late most nights, leaving early before the sun rises. It's blissful.

It's a glorious summers day and for the first time in years, I close the café early for no good reason other than I want to enjoy the last bits of sunshine of the day. I rush home with Azalea and grabbing her bike, we head to the coastal walkway to meet Brax and Beth.

The girls ride ahead while we walk behind them. Brax occasionally grabs my hand to give it a squeeze, before dropping it, so the girls don't see. We haven't told them about us yet, and I know we are running on borrowed time. I realise then that we haven't actually said what this is specifically. I know it's not casual and it's not just dating. I know what I want it to be, and I suspect Brax wants it to be the same too.

Brax stops suddenly, his hands going to his waist. He looks frustrated and I glance around. Did I miss something?

I call out to the girls, "Stop there, guys! We will catch up in a minute." They stop immediately in their tracks and sit down on the park bench, legs swinging, laughing at something the other said.

I touch his shoulder. "Brax is everything okay?"

He shakes his head and stares out at the water. It's crystal blue today and waves gently roll in, hitting the edge of the boardwalk. The sun beams down on the water, reflecting back on to us and my skin feels warm and toasty.

"Lavender, this has been weighing on me for weeks now and I thought it would go away but it hasn't."

A mix of intrigue and worry fills me. What is he going to say?

He turns to face me, and I wish I could see his eyes behind his sunglasses.

"Why did you stay in the shop. Why didn't you leave when you heard them there? Your life is never worth risking honey. Please promise you won't ever do that again."

Relief floods me at his words. I thought it was going to be something way worse than that. He continues on, and I hear the worry in his voice.

"I know I should have said something earlier. But it's been playing on my mind. Aside from Beth who I worry about constantly, I've never worried about someone else Lavender. Never. I've never felt this way about someone, and it's thrown me."

"So, you like me a lot huh?" I tease, trying to make light of the situation. I hate to see him so worried.

He smiles and shakes his head.

"Stop trying to distract me. You know I do. More than you know. Although I'm starting to rethink that right now."

I laugh, giddy at his words. "Hey!"

He lightly tugs on my ponytail.

"Has anyone ever told you that you are absolutely adorable Lavender Clementine?"

I scoff, "Only every single day."

"In all seriousness," I add, "I know that was silly. I should have left the minute I heard someone in the shop. I promise that will never happen again."

He looks a little less worried at my words, and dropping it, he throws an arm around my shoulders, squeezing me to his side, before I quickly pull away.

I really am looking forward to the day when we can hold hands or touch when we are out in public and not worry about anyone seeing us. I probably should explain to Brax that it's fear that's holding me back and not anything else. I'm scared that someone will ruin this bubble. That we will tell the kids and the world, and something will go wrong, and I'll have to mourn this loss publicly.

It was hard enough the first-time round with Josh. It clicks right then that I've never explained this to Brax. Even though it was the right thing for us, and we were both at peace with it, Josh and I still had to deal with the stares and the quiet whispers. Maybe even worse, the sympathy that flowed in for us.

The funny thing was, Josh and I were fine. It was the town that wasn't.

This time round, it would be the other way around. And I'm terrified.

I push the thought away for now. I'll tell Brax next week when Azalea is away with her dad, and I've had time to think through what I want to say.

We continue our walk, and the mood between us is light again. We laugh and talk about our week and it's easy.

We are interrupted when Azalea rides back to us, calling out to me.

"Mum! Can Dad come over tonight so I can show him this new trick Bethy taught me on my bike?"

I reach down and smooth the hair from her forehead.

"Not tonight sweetheart, Dad's busy."

"Oh man!" She calls back before running off, not seeming too fazed.

"Lavender, we can cancel pizza tonight so Zaylee can have her dad over." Guilt flashes over Brax's face and I reach out to touch his arm.

"No, please don't cancel. It's fine, he's busy."

He nods but doesn't look convinced.

We loop back around on the track, over to my house and order pizza. Brax is a little quiet the rest of the night, and I try not to worry. Did I say something? I try to pull him out of it a few times which works momentarily, but it doesn't last.

Just before he leaves, he seems back to his usual self, pulling me in for a kiss behind the door of my bedroom while the girls say goodbye to each other. We had to sneak off and pretend I was showing Brax something down the hallway.

I hear the girl's voices ring out, moving closer down the hallway to Azalea's room, and I panic, slamming the door. My heart beats uncontrollably and I lean my forehead against the door, laughing.

I turn to face him, my back sliding against the wood grain.

"That was close." The smile slides off my face when I see he isn't laughing.

His head tilts to the side, brow furrowing.

"If the kids knew… we wouldn't have to sneak around and hide in rooms honey."

He's right. I open my mouth to confess that I'm scared but close it again. I still haven't spoken to him about my thoughts from earlier today and If I tell him that, he will probably just tell me we can hold off. I can see it's paining him to have this be a secret.

"We can't put it off any longer. We need to tell the kids," I blurt.

He nods, a flash of relief on his face before its gone. He rests his forehead against mine.

"Yeah, we do. Want to meet during the week for lunch and to work out a plan of attack?"

"Yes," I tell him breathlessly.

We kiss for another few minutes before I walk him out. As we walk through the hallway, he looks at the pictures, stopping on one of Zaylee, Josh and I from when she was one.

Not wanting him to get the wrong idea, I jump in to explain.

"That was taken when we were still together. It's one of Zaylee's favourite photos so I keep it up for her."

He nods. "It's nice," is all he says.

I stare at the picture as he does. We do look very cosy and there is a lot of joy on our faces. We always did have fun together. I see the picture for what it is. A beautiful memory of a lovely time in my life but one I am very much over now and have been for a long time.

I begin to tell him about how Josh and I are great friends now, for Zaylee, but we are interrupted by the girls calling out.

"I better go. I'll see you for coffee tomorrow?"

I smile, but he seems a little off again.

After he leaves, I can't quite escape the feeling that there's something worrying him too. Suddenly, I'm looking forward to that conversation and getting everything out in the open.

The next day, I'm toasting a sandwich for a customer and checking my phone for what feels like the millionth time. Still no text from Brax and he hasn't come in for his usual morning coffee.

Unease grows as the day goes by with no sign of him. Did I say something last night? Or did he get scared after our talk on the walk. Thoughts flash back to his troubled expression last night.

I take the plate over to the customers table and make small talk for a few minutes. I glance up when I hear the bell ring, and relief washes over me when I spot Brax walking in. I politely excuse myself and wander in his direction. We meet in the middle of the coffee shop.

"Hey," he says quietly.

"Hey yourself. How's your day been?"

I'm doing my best to hide it, but I'm worried. Really worried.

He lets out a small sigh and grabs my hand pulling me in for a hug.

"Better now. I missed you today."

Neither of us care who sees right now. His words soften my worries, and I feel instantly lighter.

"Do you have time for a coffee?"

He shakes his head, "I'm already late for a meeting in town. I didn't even really have time to stop in here, but I had to see you. Did you want to grab dinner tonight?"

I nod but then remember my plans. "Oh shoot, I can't tonight I'm sorry. Josh is coming over for Azaleas birthday dinner. He will be away for the day on business for her actual birthday dinner, which I'm officially inviting you to by the way, so we are doing one tonight. Wanna sneak in later?"

I give him a wink, but he doesn't seem to be in a joking mood.

"Uh let's reschedule then. In case dinner runs late or something. I'll call you."

Before I can reassure him, it won't run late and I do want to see him, he leans forward and gives me a quick kiss on the forehead before turning and striding out. On a mission to get somewhere, or a mission to get out of here. I can't tell.

Chapter 24

BRAX IS DISTANT OVER THE following days, and I hate it. When I ask him about it, he just says work is busy and that everything is fine. But I know it's not. He told me he had to work for Azalea's birthday dinner and sent Beth over with Ebony and his apologies.

I decide then that I'm going to invite him over tomorrow night to talk, once Azalea has left. Azalea is heading on a road trip up the coast with her dad for the week and they are both so excited. I'm also excited to have Brax alone so we can get to the bottom of what's going on. I remember then that Brax and I never met up to talk about telling the kids about us. This week will be the perfect opportunity to sort that out and then tell them when Azalea is back.

The afternoon that Josh and Azalea are leaving, we go to the park and sitting on the park bench watching her play, I tell him about Brax and I. He gives me a big hug and tells me how happy he is for me. Azalea sees us hugging and races over to join us and we laugh in a group hug.

We stay at the park for another half hour before I head home after saying goodbye to them both, and they head off on their trip. I feel content for the first time in a few days. I'm excited to talk to Brax and resolve this awkwardness between us. Seeing Azalea so happy to go on this trip and having Josh be so happy for me, was also a nice way to finish the afternoon.

On my way back home, I decide then that I'm going to surprise Brax at the station with a pastry and some coffee to brighten up his busy shift. I remember how much he loved the last time I did that for him.

I reassure myself everything will be fine between us, and I feel lighter already.

I pop into Leo's to grab a cinnamon scroll for Brax and on my way back, open up the shop to quickly make him his favourite coffee to take with me.

I'm smiling wide as I reach the station. I'm going to miss my girl for the week, but I'm also looking forward to preoccupying my time with a certain sexy police officer.

I push through the front doors and wave at Betty the receptionist. Betty has worked here since before I was born and is the absolute sweetest. She still plays bingo with my grandmother.

"I'll bring you a coffee tomorrow, Betty. And one of those chocolate lava cookies you like."

She blows me a kiss.

"You're a dear Lavender Wild!"

I point at the door into the bullpen. "Is he in there?"

She gives me a knowing smile and nods.

"Yes, he is. I'll buzz you through."

I give her another wave and walk through the buzzing door. The fluorescent lighting shines brightly into my eyes and I can see how disarming this would be for any suspects getting interrogated here. I glance around the room and see Brax in the corner at his desk. He hasn't spotted me yet. I wave at a few officers I pass, having grown up with most of them.

I walk towards Brax's desk, admiring him in his uniform. He told me this morning when he stopped by for his daily coffee that today he would be stuck to a desk doing paperwork.

"Hi officer. I have a crime to report."

He glances up, surprise flashing his face. He looks me over, lingering briefly on the coffee and paper bag in my hands. I place it on the desk. He gives me a tight smile.

"Thanks Lavender. That's sweet of you. You didn't have to do that."

His words might be kind, but his tone is off.

"That's okay… I wanted to."

Silence stretches between us, and I stand there awkwardly.

"Umm how's the paperwork going?"

What is going on. He was so sweet and affectionate only a week ago, talking about telling the kids about us and planning a weekend away for the four of us. Today I'm greeted with frosty the snowman. Maybe it's been a hard day at work, and he is just tired. I can relate to that.

But intuition tells me its more. It's whatever has been bugging him these past few days.

"It's been hectic. I left the station a little earlier today to grab some pizza for lunch but otherwise I've been at the desk."

"Oh, I grabbed pizza for lunch today too. I took off earlier from work. I was right by there at the park too."

He frowns at that. Okay… that's odd.

"Hey Lavender, I'm so busy today. Thanks for bringing the coffee and the scroll, I appreciate it. I better get back to work though… Catch up rain check?"

He wants me to go. I look around and the place is quiet. Really quiet. I glance at his desk and see a file open with Brax's scribble in it. There's no phones ringing. Nothing here screams busy.

"Uh, sure Brax. I'm sorry, I should have checked first. Um did you want to come over tonight? I have the house to myself… Azalea has gone away with her dad. I could make us pizza?"

He glances away and clears his throat.

"I can't tonight… I'm pretty beat and will probably crash as soon as I get home."

Oh. An unsettled feeling comes over me and for reasons I can't explain, I feel like bursting into tears.

"That's okay, I understand. I'll leave you to it."

But I don't understand. What the hell has happened?

I slowly back away from his desk and bump into the one behind me. I'm flustered and teary. He is rejecting me.

"Oh, geez, I'm sorry Brax."

Pain flickers across his face and his mouth opens as if to say something. He quickly closes it and nods. I rush out of the room and with a quick wave to Betty, keep my head down as I leave the station.

Tears start to fall as soon as I push open the door to exit the station, and I don't even bother wiping them away.

A few days pass and I don't hear from Brax.

He doesn't pop in for his usual morning coffee either.

I'm busy restocking the glass cabinet with sugary treats and feeling sorry for myself when a sing song voice interrupts me.

"Hey Lavender, whatcha doing down there?"

I realise somewhere between starting to stack treats and her interrupting me, I ended up gazing into the cabinet space, lost in thought. I have no idea how long I've been crouched here, staring into nothing.

I straighten up.

"Nothing Eb, just restocking. Did you want a coffee?"

I start prepping her usual, knowing she will never turn down a coffee.

I don't look up at her or chat like I usually would as I prepare the coffee. If I do, I might burst into tears.

"Of course I do. But more importantly, I want to know what my butthead brother has done to hurt you. Don't say nothing. I know he has done something. Spill."

I sigh, shaking my head. I finish her coffee and start to make myself one. I'm going to need it. I flip the closed sign onto the counter and take our coffees over to the wing back chairs by the fireplace. It's warm outside, but we run the air conditioning just cool enough to allow us to have a lovely roaring fireplace most days. I take comfort in it today.

After dropping the coffees off at the table, I go back to the counter and pick out two sugar cookies. I need the sugar hit too.

Ebony takes a long sip, closing her eyes and savouring the taste.

"Ah, finally I feel human."

Then she places her mug down and leans back in the chair, staring pointedly at me, waiting for me to talk.

I sigh, filling her in on my visit to the station the other day and she looks more and more puzzled.

When I'm finished, we sit in silence. Eb looking thoughtful, tapping the tabletop. Suddenly she clicks her fingers.

"Okay. I didn't think anything of it at the time. But maybe it means something. You said he was fine in the morning and then weird later that day. He messaged me that day and asked me if I thought you and Josh would ever get back together. I didn't say no, but I didn't say yes. I was taken aback by his question. I asked him why he wanted to know that and why he wasn't asking you. I think I also added that you and Josh have a great relationship for Zaylee. That was all I said though. Do you think that had anything to do with it?"

Ebony looks remorseful and I reach over patting her hand. I think about what she just told me, but I can't make the connection, and my brain is tired from thinking too much about it the last few days.

I shrug instead. "I have no idea, Eb. But you did nothing wrong."

I rest my head in my hands. "He hasn't messaged me in days. I think he's done," I mumble.

My heart breaks and I can't stop the tears that trail down my face. Eb reaches across the table taking my hand in hers this time.

"Oh honey. I'm so sorry. But I'm so confused by all of this. I know Brax. And he really likes you. More than likes you. He also isn't someone who jumps in and out of things. Something must have happened. Have you messaged or called him?"

I shake my head. "I can't Eb. I went to see him at work and he all but pushed me out of there. He made it very clear he wanted me gone and then I didn't hear anything after that. I thought about messaging him but why should I chase him? He is the one running here, not me."

Eb looks thoughtful and takes a bite of her cookie. She eventually shrugs, her hands flinging out to her sides.

"I'm at a loss. But if it makes you feel any better, I knew he had screwed up somehow because he came over for family dinner last night and was the saddest, most miserable looking thing I have ever seen. You're a close second right now. But he wouldn't tell me why and I didn't want to push in front of Bethy. I could possibly ask him…"

I'm already shaking my head before she finishes. "No way Eb. I won't put you in the middle of this."

A look of sympathy crosses her face, and she holds her hands up under her chin.

"I really am sorry honey. I know you guys are perfect together or I wouldn't have pushed this. I never expected my boneheaded brother would ghost you. I know I keep saying it, but that's not Brax. But whatever the reason, it doesn't excuse this. You have a family and a business to run. You need reliability. Stability. Not this."

I take in her words. She's right. I straighten up in my seat. I resolve to not let this get the better of me. This isn't on me. It's on him.

"Just call him Lala. Ask him what the hell is going on. There must be some reason for it."

She takes another sip of coffee, smiling when she closes her eyes this time. Eb is a coffee lover like me.

I take a bite of the sugar cookie, but I can't find the same enjoyment from my cookie that she gets from her coffee. With how I'm feeling, it just tastes like cardboard right now.

I think over her comment, telling me to call him. I remember the way he looked at me at the station, and my heart jumps.

I'll pass.

Chapter 25

I'M JUST PUTTING THE LAST cup and saucer away for the night when the lights turn off and the fairy lights come on. We usually only put them on for book club nights and other special events at the store.

"I'm back!" Goldie sings out from the front of the shop. She left twenty minutes ago to drop the days takings in at the bank before they closed.

I call out my thanks before I'm hit with the most heavenly scent of pizza, wafting through the room. More specifically, a four-cheese pizza. My mouth starts watering at the smell of cheese and garlic. I can practically taste the stringy, gooey cheese on the bed of herb and sauce base.

I lean back from the shelves, craning my neck to see into the bookstore. I can hear Juni and Goldie talking.

Goldie is holding three pizza boxes on one arm and a tray of paper plates and napkins in the other hand. Juni has a bottle of wine and 3 glasses.

"Umm guys what's going on?"

Their heads swivel towards me. "Pizza night sister. What does it look like?" She sends a wink my way and I roll my eyes.

"I gathered there was pizza involved but some of us do have responsibilities and can't stick around. Mines about shoulder high, sweet as pie and relies on me to survive."

This time it's Goldie's turn to do the eye rolling.

"Like I would ever forget that plum pudding! Check your phone."

She sets about moving tables and making the cosy corner by the fireplace, even more cosy with blankets and pillows.

I grab my phone off the bench and find a text from my mum.

'Zaylee girl is here having a sleep over tonight so you can get drunk with your sisters. That's what Goldie told me anyway. Good for you darling. You forget about that handsome policeman. Your spirit is too precious to not be cherished. Love and light Lavender Clementine.'

Oh mum. The eternal hippy. I smile rereading her text message. It's a wonder we didn't turn out more unusual than we are really. Well, speaking for Juni and I, anyway. Goldie is definitely a girl after my parents' heart.

I throw the cleaning rag on the bench and take my apron off, before kicking off my shoes and shuffling in my socks over to the table.

I take the seat closest to the fireplace and warm my hands there a moment. This is exactly what I need. I watch the flames flicker and cackle, their bright amber and reds dancing around the logs. Goldie taps my arm, handing me a plate.

Juni pours a glass of sweet bubbly wine and Goldie slides two large pieces of pizza onto my paper plate. I take a sip of the wine, and the bubbles tickle my tongue. It's a mix of fruit, with the sharpness of champagne.

"No dishes for us tonight," Goldie tells me around a mouthful of pizza. I lift my hand for a hi-five, and she smacks it.

I take a huge bite of pizza and sink back in my chair. Pizza, bubbles and finally relaxing after a stressful few days is exactly what I needed.

I tuck my feet underneath me and curl back into the chair, letting the soft sides envelop me, cocooning me in their warmth.

Juni reaches over and takes my hand.

My sweet Juni all but whispers. "Have you heard anything?"

I shake my head, flashing her a weak smile.

Her face drops and her eyes fill with tears. One spills and she brushes it away.

Goldie tosses her pizza onto the plate and brushes the crumbs from her hands.

"Well, that's just shit Lala. What is his problem? I think we march over there and ask him what his deal is."

"No Goldie. No. Promise me you won't."

Brow furrowing, a wicked, mischievous smile grows. Uh oh.

"What if I don't 'say anything' as such? Maybe, showing is better than telling…"

I'm already shaking my head, giggling at the silliness of her comment. "No. You can't do that either."

She picks her pizza back up looking put out. Growing up, Goldie was always getting in trouble for toilet papering or egging the homes of people who did her wrong. Ex-boyfriends, mean girls and more. I have no idea what hairbrained scheme she was just starting to concoct but I can only imagine.

Pushing her chair out, Juni makes her way to her corner of the store. I can see the record player from where I sit. She runs her hands over the spines of the records before selecting one. Popping it in, she spins in place to face us, clapping her hands.

A popular melody from the seventies rings out from the player. It's a favourite of our parents and one we grew up listening to every Sunday. Our parents called them lazy Sundays and we would listen to music, bake cookies and swim in the lake. Now, every Sunday in our store, we play songs from the record player as a nod to our childhood. Once a month, we go over to our parent's house and do a lazy Sunday. Dad takes charge of the music and mum makes us pancakes, while we all laze around. It's the best.

This song gets us up and dancing every time we hear it. The song is part way through a verse and without meaning to, we all start singing at the top of our voices, at the same time. Goldie kicks off her sandals, her vibrant red toenails clashing perfectly with her lime green overalls and sunny yellow shirt.

She starts gesturing at me with her fingers and I laugh, letting her pull me up to dance. We move around the shop, dancing our way through bookshelves, grabbing a flower each as we pass Goldie's shop and stopping by the table to take another sip of wine. As the night progresses, another bottle of wine appears as if by magic and our laughter becomes more disinhibited, just like our dancing.

Goldie whips us up some flower crowns and even tipsy, they are the most spectacular things I've ever seen. A mix of green foliage, bright yellow, pink and purple flowers adorn each crown.

We are sitting crossed legged on the floor in a circle sharing a slice of mud cake when I reach up and pluck mine from my head to look at it closely.

"Marigold. One day when I get married, I want to wear one of these. Will you make me the biggest, most beautiful one ever. I want it so big I look like the queen."

I burst into a fit of giggles and she joins me.

I squint at the large peony on the front. I do love peonies. Maybe one day when Brax and I... and I'm instantly sobered at that thought. Brax and I aren't anything and it's looking like we won't ever be. Seemingly out of nowhere, a wave of anger rolls through me at what he has done to us.

I scramble to my feet, leaving behind the conversation about the queen and crowns between Juni and Goldie. I reach for my phone.

Entering my passcode, I bring up Brax's last message. Over a week ago before Azalea went away with her dad.

Without giving it a second thought, I start typing out a message.

'Brax. Why are you doing this? I deserve better than this don't you think?'

I don't allow myself time to back out, hitting send.

Crap. I don't want him to text back and ruin my buzzy vibe if it's only going to be to tell me he doesn't want to speak to me anymore.

I quickly type out another text.

'Don't text me back I'm drunk.'

Crap. Now that's going to have him asking questions I don't want to answer. Like possibly where I am, etc.

I let out a huge sigh. I pick up my phone again and write out another text.

'But I'm perfectly safe and fine.'

This time before I hit send, I quickly amend it.

'But I'm perfectly safe and fine. I'm with my sisters in the shop.'

A satisfied smile breaks out. There, that should do it.

I place the phone back on the table, impressed with how I handled that. Until I sit down and start eating mud cake again. Wait. Did I just text him and ask a question. But then tell him not to answer? I shake it off. I'll worry about that later.

I take another sip of bubbles and join my sisters in talking about which colour of the rainbow is superior.

Not even ten minutes later I hear a knocking on the front door. We stop our conversation, comparing our names and who's is the best, and stare at each other in silence. The knock comes again, followed by Brax's voice.

"I know you're in there. I just wanted to make sure everyone was okay. That's it."

Goldie turns to me accusingly, raising her eyebrows, angry whispering.

"You messaged him? You don't message him, Lala! He should be messaging you!"

I throw my hands up, "I know that okay. So maybe I messaged him. I didn't mean to. It was an accident!"

She rolls her eyes before struggling to her feet, giggling on her way up.

She stumbles to the door and throws it open.

"Brax my man. To what do we owe the pleasure?"

"Hey Goldie. I just wanted to make sure Lavender is okay. She seemed… drunk. I was just worried."

Worried enough to come here? Why on earth would he be worried?

A laugh bubbles up and bursts from me. Goldie moves to block his view, and I lay down on the floor, covering my mouth. Oh my god, I'm lying on the dirty floor. Oh, there's that notepad I lost a few weeks ago tucked under the bookshelves.

Goldie laughs awkwardly. "Yep, all good here officer. No need to worry."

She slams the door and turning her back to it, leans against it, covering her mouth with her hands.

"Shit. I just closed the door on a police officer!" She whispers.

Juni lets out a voracious giggle and rolling onto my back, I do the same. Suddenly I can't stop laughing. Until the tears come. And then I'm sobbing.

"Awww Lala," murmurs Juni, shuffling over on her knees to cuddle me where I lay. Goldie marches over from the door and falling to her knees, hugs me from the other side.

Between sobs, I pour my heart out. "I thought he was the one. Why isn't he the one?"

The tears flow in rivers, seeming like they will never end. My sisters hug me tighter. We stay that way until the tears subside.

I sit up, exhausted, emotional, tipsy and ready to go home to the comfort of my bed.

We don't bother cleaning up our mess. None of us are sober enough to do a good job anyway.

Goldie flicks off the lights and locks up behind us.

Juni's arm wraps around me, and she squeezes me tight, resting her head on my shoulder.

Goldie takes my other hand, and we walk home in silence. After saying my goodbyes to Goldie and Juni who live across the road from each other, I walk the ten houses up to my own home.

I stand at the door knowing that on the other side, is quiet. An empty house.

Nope, not doing it tonight.

Pulling my phone out of my back pocket, I fire off a quick text and march back up my garden path and down the street toward Juni's.

'Can I stay at your house tonight, Juni?'

The response flies in fast.

'The door is unlocked, and the kettle is on x.'

Later that night once I'm curled up In Juni's spare bed and sobered up after too many cups of coffee and cake, I let the tears flow. How on earth did I get here? From mentally planning my future with the most amazing guy, to sleeping in my baby sister's spare bed, crying myself to sleep.

Chapter 26

Brax

THE LAST FEW DAYS HAVE been hard. Worse than hard. Unbearable.

Since Lavender left the station, we have only spoken once, when she text me. I didn't even have the guts to message her back when she drunk text. I knew if I started writing back, I would cave and beg her to give me another chance. Fuck I miss her.

Getting that text was the highlight of the last few days, just seeing her name pop up. But getting that text and knowing she was out somewhere drinking and not sure how she would get home had me in a tailspin. I couldn't stop myself from tearing out of work and heading to the store to make sure she really was there and was okay. When Goldie answered the door, I wanted to march past her, pick Lavender up and carry her home. Back to my home where I want her to stay and never leave.

Leaning back, my head hits the chair, and I close my eyes.

I brought this on myself. But still, I hate that I haven't heard from her again.

After Goldie closed the door, I decided to stick around a little while and wait. I watched as the three of them stumbled out of the store and walked home together. I followed a distance behind to make sure they got home. I couldn't believe it when they all went their separate ways, and Lavender walked the last leg to her house on her own. I get that it's a safe town, but it drives me insane that she doesn't care more about her own safety.

But what killed the most was seeing her stop at her front door and stand there before turning around and heading back to Juni's house. She looked so fucking sad and lost.

I hate that I'm hurting her, but this is going to be better for her in the long run. Not better for me though. I know Lavender is my person. She's it for me. But she could have her family back if I wasn't in the way and I just have to remember that every time I almost cave and call or message her.

I groan, dropping my head to my desk. A few of the other officers glance over at me but I don't care. I know I'm being miserable, and I just don't give a shit. I am miserable.

I check the time. I'm due for lunch shortly. Screw it, I'm heading off to lunch early. I flick a quick text to Ebony, *'On my way.'*

She kindly invited me over for lunch with her and Ryder. I pack up the files on my desk and toss them in my drawer. Everything feels like an effort or a frustration right now. The other officers must be sick of me, and I don't blame them. I'm sick of my attitude right now too.

"See ya later guys," I wave goodbye and head out.

I can't sit at the desk without thinking about Lavender anyway. I can't get the image out of my head of her upset when she left the other day. I was a jerk. But I'm doing it for her and one day she will understand why I'm doing this.

I grunt just thinking about it. I'm going to have to move across the country when she gets back together with Josh. I feel sick to my stomach just thinking about it.

God, I hope I'm doing the right thing. I haven't slept properly in days.

I wave at Betty as I leave.

"I'll be out a bit longer today but call me for anything urgent."

She nods, a sympathetic smile on her face. Everyone around me knows how miserable I am. Even Beth asked me yesterday if I was feeling sad about something. I made up a story on the spot and she believed me thankfully. This morning, I made an effort to be happy and hide how unhappy I am before she headed off to school. Beth has asked every day when she can see Lavender and Azalea, and I'm not sure how much longer I can put off seeing them again.

I miss them.

I decide to walk to Ebony's and hope the fresh air will improve my mood. To get there though, I need to pass the store. Lavender's store. I stick to the other side of the road, but this is a small town. The road is tiny. I can't stop myself from glancing in the window. Lavender's corner of the store is at the back, so I don't expect to see her. Except just my luck, I can see her through the front window, sitting at Goldie's desk in the flower shop. She must be minding the flower shop for her sister. And she looks just as miserable as I feel. Her chin is resting on her hands, and she is absentmindedly twirling a flower in her hands. She looks sad. A pain shoots through my chest, and I guess this is what all those country songs Lavender and I love, are talking about. I rub at my chest, hoping to ease the pain but it seems to get worse.

My feet feel frozen in place. I need to keep moving before she sees me, but I can't seem to move.

I can't take my eyes off her. Even sad, she is stunning. She has her hair up in one of those messy styles that she always calls her 'mum hair' and makes fun of. She downplays her beauty all the time, but I've never met anyone more beautiful than her, in every possible way.

Before she looks up and catches me staring, I make myself leave. I just know if she looks over, I'll lose all my resolve and tear in there, begging her to forgive me and give me another chance.

Thankfully she never sees me.

I'm trying to do the right thing by her, but why does the right thing feel so bad?

I want her. And I don't want Josh to have her. Thinking about that, I feel like kicking something. Or myself.

Ebony greets me at the door and her happy expression turns puzzled and then sympathetic.

"Hard day at work Brax?"

I shake my head, kicking off my shoes.

"Am I that obvious Eb?"

I rub my eyes with the palm of my hand.

"Sorry Eb, I didn't mean to snap. I'm trying to pull myself out of this mood but it's not working."

She pats my shoulder, and we walk through the hallway into the kitchen.

"I did something you won't like," I blurt.

She looks at me over her shoulder, raising an eyebrow.

"Oh, I know. If you're talking about Lavender that is. You're crazy. Even without hearing the reason why, I know you're crazy. Why did you do it?" She asks me and I can hear the hesitation in her voice.

"Give him a second to sit down before you grill him babe."

Ryder walks into the kitchen and reaches over to squeeze my shoulder.

I look at the table filled with food, and it looks amazing. I was starving earlier today, but now I've lost my appetite.

I take a seat at the dining table, and they sit across from me. I feel like I'm a kid again, facing my parents after making a poor choice and I'm about to get interrogated. I deserve it I know that much.

"I've pushed Lavender away. Before you say anything let me explain."

I see Eb's mouth open and close, and she tries to look relaxed, but I can see she is anything but that.

"Maybe a week ago, Zaylee was asking Lavender if her dad could come around. We had plans that night so she told her no. She was upset. That's when it started, I guess."

"When what started Brax?" This time it's Ryder jumping in with the questions.

"Me realising that I was getting in the way of their family. I don't have that option for Beth with her mum. We weren't ever anything and I didn't want to be anyway. But Lavender was married to Josh. They had a whole life together. If she's with me, she won't have that again."

Ebony looks as if I'm trying her very last patience as I talk, but she softens when she sees how much this is hurting me.

"I knew something had happened when you were all mopey at dinner the other night Brax. And I will admit, I went to see Lavender yesterday. She's hurt Brax. Really hurt. I told her you must have a reason, but I admit I'm confused. Brax, Lavender didn't leave Josh for you. Lavender and Josh broke up years ago. So many years ago. They didn't want to be together anymore. And I know you didn't love Beth's mum, so you think that makes your situation easier. But Lavender doesn't love Josh like she did." She sounds sure but she hasn't heard the rest.

"There's more. A few days ago, I saw the three of them at the park. Lavender and Josh were hugging. Then Zaylee joined them. They looked happy. And whenever I brought up us telling the kids and everyone that we are together, she would find an excuse to put it off. I just figured that maybe she was scared to tell Josh because she isn't sure about where they stand. After seeing them at the park, I wasn't sure where I stood with her. It's a mess... I'm a mess."

I lean back in the chair. I wish I could wipe that memory from my mind. Watching the three of them hugging, looking like the perfect family. It wasn't just Azalea that looked happy. I had a clear line of sight to Lavender. She looked happy too. Content. Peaceful. I couldn't see Josh's face, but I imagine his was the same.

"I'm going to have to move. And I've already uprooted Beth's life once. I'm so fucking selfish."

Ebony laughs. I drop my hands and stare at her. What the hell?

"I've never known you to be this dramatic and I have to say I'm impressed. You like her a lot. Actually. You love her."

I scoff. "I'm not dramatic. But how can I stay here and watch her with someone else?"

I don't bother denying how I feel to Ebony. I do love Lavender. So fucking much. I had started to picture our life together and that's what hurts now. It would have been perfect.

Ebony laughs again.

"Eb, would you please stop laughing, it's not funny."

"No, you're right. It's not. It's ridiculous."

"What?"

"It is Brax. Josh and Lavender are friends. Friends. That's it. I promise you. Look I wouldn't normally betray a friend's confidence, but this calls for an exception. Just before I set you up on a date with Lala, I checked in again that there was no chance with Josh. I didn't believe there was a chance. This is my best friend. I know her. But I honestly believed you two would be a good match and I was right, wasn't I?" She smirks at me.

"Can you just get to your point?"

"Okay, okay. So, I asked her. And I know her. I would know if she was lying. She told me that there was no way she would ever get back with Josh. That she loves him because he is Azalea's dad but that's it. That she sees him more like a friend now. They are amazing co-parents. Just co-parents Brax, that's it. And I've never seen them act any other way than that. I promise."

I'm not entirely convinced but I listen when she continues.

"Brax, I didn't want to be the one to tell you, but she was terrified. She was scared of what would happen if you left her, if you made it public to the world. It was never about Josh. She told Josh about you two. He is happy for her. She wants this with you. But I'm afraid you have screwed up. I don't know how you fix this now."

Fuck. I'm an idiot.

"Brax buddy, I have one question for you that I'm confused about," Ryder jumps in. "Even if there was a small chance she considered getting back with Josh, why wouldn't you fight for her? I've known you a long time and you're a fighter. I've never seen you this way with a woman, but even this surprises me. I hate to say it and you know I love you, but you're an absolute idiot for not just talking to her and asking her about it."

I consider his words, and I know he is right. I am a fighter for whatever I want. And I want her. I just got caught up in my own worries and second guessing how she felt.

I check my watch. I've gone well past my lunch break.

"Eb, I've gotta go. I can't get out of heading back to work, but when I finish, I'm headed straight to Lavender's. I have to try and fix this."

I scrub at my face with my hand.

"I hope I haven't totally screwed this up."

Eb gives me that sympathetic smile again. The one that tells me she can't reassure me this time.

Dread fills me. God, I hope it's not too late to fix this.

Chapter 27

It's been days since I last saw him. Azalea is back on another short trip with her dad, and I have too much time to kill. And too much time to sit with my thoughts.

I miss him. I miss Brax so much.

I contemplate calling up Juni to watch a rom com and drink hot chocolate. Or see if Goldie wants to make pizzas and play board games, but I don't do either. Instead, I wallow.

He went cold, not me. Why am I feeling bad? It's him who should feel bad.

Who am I kidding? It's Brax freaking Madox. He is amazing. And I thought we were building something really special together.

Of course I'm feeling miserable. Who wouldn't be?

My pity party is interrupted by a banging on the door.

My sisters always let themselves in to my place and my parents would never bang. Ebony might, but she would be singing out something silly in her sing song voice while doing it.

I use the peephole. I've grown to despise it. Peering through, I all but jump back. It's Brax.

I take a few more steps back. Suddenly I'm angry. Who does he think he is, banging on my door.

"Go away Brax!" I yell out.

"Lavender, open up please," he calls out.

I already know I'll cave if I open the door, so I stay on the other side. I take a few steps forward and look out the peephole again. He looks good. Stressed and like he hasn't slept either. But so good. I press my face against the cold wood of the door.

I can hear him on the other side, and he sounds exasperated.

"Honey, please."

"Brax. You ignored me for days. I don't have time in my life for this. You made it clear at the station and then in the days after how you feel. I don't want to hear your excuses."

It takes all my willpower, but I push off from the door, walking away. I head to my bedroom and close the door. I slide down the door and cry till the room gets dark.

Well after he has left, I pull my phone out of my pocket and begin typing a message to my sisters.

'SOS – your girl needs a margarita. Anyone free?'
A reply comes flying in from Goldie.
'Get your butt down here. I'm turning the blender on x'

A few days go by after Brax's visit, and then the texts begin. Asking if we can meet up to talk. I delete them all and then block him. I don't read a single text.

Chapter 28

The Festival of Water, is my favourite time of year here.
But not this year.

This year I'm just at a loss. How to navigate living in a
town where I will inevitably see Brax all the time whether
I like it or not, is a mystery to me.

At least our store is my safe haven. There's no way he
will go there.

Maybe I'll have to become a recluse? Maybe I won't leave
the house except to go to the shop and the grocery store.

Except for today. Today, I'm headed to the festival.
The Festival of Water is exactly as it name suggests. It's
completely unoriginal, but totally fabulous. Everything is
water themed in some way and there's a ton of blue. Blue

rides, blue stalls, beach cupcakes, mermaid treats. It's the perfect day to celebrate our small coastal town.

It's a beautiful warm day, so for a change, I'm wearing a sundress. It's a short, butter yellow pinafore dress with a low back and it makes me feel cute. I bought it a few years ago on a whim and I don't get to wear it nearly enough.

I leave my hair out and for once it does what it's supposed to, falling in thick waves past my shoulders.

I keep my makeup light, and I throw on some sandals. After a few weeks of too many track pants and stained t-shirts, I needed to make an effort today. And surprisingly it has worked. I feel a little lighter already.

I make my way to the festival and already the sunshine and cool ocean breeze is working wonders.

I round the corner and spot my sisters, Wolf and Fox. Azalea is meeting us there later with her dad.

Wolf lets out a slow whistle and I roll my eyes.

"Laugh it up Wolfie boy."

He protests loudly, a deep laugh escaping him and he throws both hands in the air. "Hey! I think you're looking fine Clemmy."

He gives me chefs kiss and I cuddle into his side, appreciating the support and the sentiment. I didn't realise how much I needed my friends around me right now. He must sense it, because he squeezes me tight, not letting me go. We walk like that till we reach the beach park festivities, where games are set up and stalls dot the edge between grass and beach.

It's busy. Busier than ever. Five tourist buses stopped in this morning and on top of that, every local is here too.

Just as we walk through the blue ribboned arch, I spot a familiar black haired, man.

Just my luck. And why does he have to look so damn good today? He is back in that sexy uniform, patrolling the festival.

I hate him.

But I don't hate him. I just wish he hadn't broken my heart.

It hits me. I didn't even feel heart broken when Josh and I broke up.

But with Brax, I feel like my heart has been ripped from my chest.

Just as I'm about to turn away, he looks in my direction and I can barely make out the expression that crosses his face. A mixture of longing, frustration and heartache.

But then, it changes, sharpening, and he looks just downright pissed off.

Wolf leans downs and whispers in my ear.

"Ex alert. What do you want to do? Face him head on in that gorgeous dress or go hide in that crystals tent?"

I look over to where he is pointing.

"Definitely hide. Let's go."

I keep my face down and let Wolfie lead to me to the crystals tent. I pray that's the last time I see Brax at the festival, but I highly doubt it.

We get lost in the fun of the festival and when Azalea joins us, I forget about Brax for a little while. It's nice. Really nice. Maybe the festival was the distraction I needed. We went on a few rides, ate too much fairy floss and danced to local bands. I ducked in to see the tarot reader but quickly left when she started to describe Brax. I didn't want to know what was to follow that description.

After a few hours of wandering around, I guess that Brax must have left when I don't see him again, and I let my guard down a little more. Josh and Azalea join us for a few games and festival snacks. I share a sponge cake with Josh and we all reminiscence on previous years festivals. It's nice until thoughts of Brax pop into my head again.

Azalea and Josh eventually head home for pizza, but my sisters and I stay a little longer. We closed the shop for the day as is tradition, and we like to make the most out of it. Heart broken or not, that's what I plan to do today. I agree to meet up with Juni and Goldie later, wanting to check out the flower wreath station. They choose rides.

Just as I make my way over to the flower station, I come face to face with Brax, almost bumping into him. His hand shoots out to right me and keep me from falling. I pull my arm out of his grasp and take a small step back.

"Oh. It's you."

His eyes narrow and a look of disappointment crosses his face. "Yeah, me."

"I uh, thought maybe you had finished for the day. I hadn't seen you in a while."

Great. Now he knows I have been looking out for him.

We stand there staring at each other, neither caving. Is it my pride or his, that's going to be intact when the other leaves first?

I decide I can deal with my pride being crushed. I just need to get out of here.

I point over his shoulder. "I'm going to head over there. Bye Brax."

I turn to walk around him when I feel his hand reach out to grab mine.

"Wait. Can we talk?"

I pull my hand out from his, crossing my arms and turning back to face him.

"Now you want to talk?"

He screws his face up and he looks confused.

"I've been messaging you Lavender… I've wanted to talk all this time."

I scoff. "Only after you stopped talking to me. Remember that?"

He closes his eyes for a brief moment. "I can explain. Please let me explain… I miss you…"

I cut him off, holding my hand up. "No, you don't get to do that. I'm here to have a nice time not rehash this, Brax. I'll catch you later."

I can't miss the look on his face as I walk away. One of pain and longing.

I feel even more confused than I did before.

I make a wreath for my front door, planning on covering that annoying peephole, and I'm so impressed with how it turned out. Goldie ended up joining me, unable to stay away from anything flower related, and hers is of course a mini work of art. But mine turned out better than I expected it to. I leave it at the workshop with a promise to pick it up later before I head home.

Juni joins us briefly before I say goodbye to my sisters, who are off to meet our friends for dinner. I'm not in the mood to attend the catch up and decide to stay a little longer. I'm going to check out the chocolate stall and grab some last-minute treats before I head home. The sun has already set and the fairy and event lights at the festival are all brightly lit up. I gaze up at the stars and admire the lights as I stroll along. I haven't seen Brax in just over an hour and I hope to keep it that way. Although if I'm really honest with myself, I desperately want to see him again. I hate myself for it, but I miss him so much.

I reach a chocolate stall and pick up a few things that look good, as I go. I can see a lot of chocolate on the lounge nights in my immediate future.

I'm just reaching for the last bar of rocky road on the table, when someone else's hand reaches for the same.

"Oh, I'm sorry. Here, you take it," says a voice to my right.

I smile at the person whose hand collided with mine. He has a nice smile and an even nicer face. He' s tall, blonde and has brown eyes. A little like Josh the more I look at him. Any other time, before Brax, I would have been attracted to him. Now, I can recognise he is good looking, but I don't feel anything.

His smile widens and he holds out the bar.

I shake my head and smile. "No, it's okay, you take it. I have quite a few in my basket already."

He glances down at the small mountain of chocolate I have accumulated and laughs.

"Having a chocolate party?"

I blush. I had planned on sitting at home in my pjs eating at least half of this tonight and regretting it tomorrow.

I laugh too. "I was, actually. For a party of one."

He replies with a genuine smile. "I could help you out if you wanted to make it a party of two…"

Before I can politely tell him no, a stern voice cuts in from behind me.

"Sorry, she's not available for that party. Or anything else."

And before I can say anything, my basket is gently lifted from my arm, and Brax moves to stand in between us.

The guy looks at us both and holds his hands up, stepping back.

"I didn't realise. I don't want any trouble."

I let out a frustrated sigh and open my mouth to tell him it's nothing, but before I can, he leaves without a backward glance.

I turn to Brax and snatch the basket back.

"What the hell was that, Brax? He was just being nice!"

He runs his hand over the back of his neck and head. He looks furious.

"He was not just being 'nice'! The guy was asking you for a whole lot more. Look in the mirror. You are stunning Lavender. Everyone can see that."

I don't answer him, and he continues.

"Were you going to say yes to him?"

My blood is boiling before he even finishes that sentence. He looks even more furious with my silence.

"You are not going on a date with him or anyone else, Lavender. You're mine. No one else's."

Oh no. He doesn't get to say that.

"So, let me get this straight. You don't want me but no one else can have me? Ridiculous. Absolutely ridiculous. Brax, I don't even know the guy! I said a few words to him. That's it. And we aren't together," I gesture between the two of us, "So I can 'see' whoever I damn well like!"

He shakes his head, throwing his hands out to the side. "No, you can't. And if you would just hear me out, you would know how I feel Lavender. Do you want to know, or just guess?"

It's petty I know, but I'm so angry. "I'm fine just guessing, thanks!"

I spin and walk away, leaving my basket. I can hear him swearing to himself behind me, but I don't look back.

The next morning, I sleep in and it's a mad rush to get ready for work. I fling open the door, already running five minutes late. I stayed up half of the night, stewing on what happened with Brax yesterday.

I'm just stepping out the door when my foot bumps a brown paper bag on my doorstep.

I look around, expecting to see someone here who might have left it, but there's no one here.

I grab the bag and open it up.

It's my chocolate from last night. All of it.

I turn the bag over and see Brax's handwriting.

'I'm sorry Lavender. Please hear me out.' Is scrawled across the front.

I shake my head and toss the bag on the kitchen bench before heading out.

It's going to take a lot more than a little sorry to fix this mess.

Chapter 29

It's been a few days since the festival and I'm out the front of the store before opening. I'm carrying boxes in, from a delivery. Our usual delivery driver will bring the boxes in for me, but he is off sick, and today's driver obviously doesn't know this, because he left the boxes by the door. Unfortunately, my trolley is also out of action and my sisters aren't here yet. So, it's all up to me to carry them in before they spoil. And they are heavy and awkwardly shaped. The boxes bite into my hand with each trip in, and I'm cursing my sisters for not being here to help.

I stop and take a break, wiping a bead of sweat off my forehead.

As I gaze up at our sign above the door, a warm feeling spreads through me as I think back on our journey to get here. We have created an inviting, cosy, space for people to come and grab a book, some flowers and a coffee to enjoy. The perfect trio.

The Wild Flowers. Us three Wild sisters, each named after flowers. Although the running joke in our family is that our dear Juniper is usually known as a tree. But mum and dad have Juniper plants in their garden that flower, just to prove it's a flower too. They have all their daughter's name sakes, proudly planted in their garden, along with their granddaughter's, Azalea's.

Goldie always makes sure to keep stock of each of our flowers in the store, and at the start of the week, pops a vase of lavender on my coffee counter, some Juniper's on Juni's counter and some Marigolds on her own.

The milk truck roars by, and I'm shaken from my thoughts when the driver Pete, sings out hello. I wave back and look down at the boxes, sighing. I need to get the last of these in.

I'm leaning down dragging the last of the boxes in through the front door on my third trip, when I hear voices down the street. It's so quiet, that any voices ring crystal clear.

It's Brax and Ebony.

I duck behind the planter box at the front of the store.

It sounds like they are having an argument. Albeit a very tame one, but I would expect no less from Ebony. She's a sweetheart. And although I'm not Brax's biggest fan right now, he adores his sister and treats her respectfully always.

"Eb, I just need ten minutes of her time to explain it all to her. I can fix this."

I can practically hear her shaking her head.

"Brax, give her a little more time. She's hurt. I don't think she is ready to talk about it all right now."

I'm nodding along like they can see me.

"I get it, I really do. I hurt her. I wish I could take it back, but I can't. I can't lose her."

My heart is in my throat at that one. I didn't want to lose him either. But I can't imagine any excuse will be good enough for just ignoring me and shutting me out. I had too many years of an immature relationship with Josh, when we were younger. With us not talking about our feelings or issues in the marriage. I won't go there again with someone who can't talk to me when they have an issue or are upset with me. My pride, but mostly my feelings, are still reeling from that day at the station when he all but kicked me unceremoniously out of there, before ghosting me.

I peek around the flowerpot. Brax is scrubbing at his face with his hands. He looks remorseful. More than that, he looks devastated.

A pang hits my heart. Maybe I should give him a chance to explain. Even if it's just to let him speak so we can both move on.

Tears spring to my eyes when I think about moving on. About him moving on. It feels as if someone has punched me in the gut. I love him. I don't want to admit it, but I do.

They start speaking again and I lean back into my hiding space.

"I'm sorry Brax. I know you thought you did the right thing. Just give her a little more time and then try again. I know you won't ask me to pick a side or to talk to her on your behalf and I know she won't ask the same. But I just need to say it. I care about you both and I'm not getting any more involved than this, okay?"

She leans over and gives him a hug and he rests his head on her shoulder. He really does look like he is struggling as much as I am.

"I'm crazy about her Eb. Absolutely crazy about her and I don't know how to fix this, but I want a shot. I have to try."

She pats his arm reassuringly. "You will work it out. I know you will."

He nods, looking up the street at my shop. I lean back behind the pot a little further.

They say goodbye and Brax heads back down the street towards the water. Ebony heads in my direction. I'm caught off guard and I fall backwards, landing square on my backside.

Ebony glances down and does a double take, stopping in front of me.

She smiles. "Should I ask?"

I shake my head, embarrassment flooding my cheeks, but I smile back at her. "Nope."

I push off the ground and stand, dusting off the back of my pants.

I gesture towards the boxes. "Wanna help me get these inside?"

Together, we manage to get the remaining boxes inside and over to the coffee shop.

I go behind the counter and start making us coffees.

"So, did you hear any of that?" She asks.

She doesn't look in the least upset that I might have been listening to her conversation, but I apologise anyway.

"I would say I heard most of it?" I practically squeak out.

She laughs, "It's okay Lala, it really is. I'm not mad at all. The only person I'm mad at, is my big brother who has screwed this up. You and I," and she holds her two fingers together, "Were this close to being sisters!"

I laugh at that. "Not quite Eb. But that would have been nice."

She gives me a knowing, smug look but I don't grill her for information even though I would love to.

As if she reads my mind, she says, "I would love to tell you what's going on honey but it's not my place. I want to fix this but only Brax can. I told him you weren't ready to talk, but I know my brother and he is persistent when he wants something. And he wants to talk to you. I've never seen him this bent out of shape before. Ever."

She shrugs and I take her words in.

"I won't be ignored or made to feel like I'm not wanted around in a relationship Eb," I tell her gently, treading lightly. I have to remember that Brax is still her brother.

"I know love. And you shouldn't be." She says shaking her head. She pauses for a moment, looking contemplative, before continuing.

"I told Ryder and Brax I wouldn't get involved but I feel like that's what I'm doing. I'm sorry. I'll say this last thing and then that will be it. He's a good man. One of the best, other than Ryder of course. I know you know how good he is. I guess what I'm trying to say is that we all make mistakes, don't we…" She is so gentle in her delivery, but I hear her loud and clear.

He screwed up, but no one is perfect. I mean, I screw up all the time as a parent, but I always try my best to repair or to do better. Shouldn't I give someone else the same grace? Especially if that someone is Brax.

I nod, almost to myself. She's right. But I'm still terrified of getting hurt if I let my guard down again.

She looks at me, as if understanding what I don't say.

"I get it Lala. I really do," and she pats my hand reassuringly.

Time. Maybe a little more time will help me decide what to do.

A week later, I'm still thinking about my conversation with Ebony. It replays over in my mind, as well as the image of Brax looking upset outside the store.

He stays true to his word to Eb and doesn't reach out to speak to me again. But he leaves trails of his affections, in the following days. Somehow, and they won't tell me why, he has my sisters on team Brax.

The day after I saw him outside the shop, Juni brings a book to my counter, sliding it over to me. I pick it up and turn it over. It's the new mystery I was telling Brax about a few months ago, that hadn't yet been released.

"What's this?"

Juni gives me her sweet, innocent smile. "It's a book."

I roll my eyes, "Yes, I can see that, Juniper. Why are you bringing it over to me, all mysterious like?"

She smiles again. "Brax asked me about a month ago to put a copy aside for you when it arrived. It arrived."

She pushes the book back over to me.

I push it towards her again. "We aren't speaking Juni. He won't be needing you to do that anymore."

She pushes it back over to me before stepping back from the counter. "He called me two days ago and asked if it had arrived. When I told him it was here, he asked me to bring it over to you today. He said today's date is six months from when he met you."

She turns her head to the side, studying me, before giving me a finger wave and heading back to her part of the store.

I pick up the book tentatively like it might bite. I really wanted this book, and he remembered.

I try and focus on serving customers the rest of that day, but I can't stop glancing at that book. I get so many orders wrong, that I almost close up the coffee shop for the day.

A few days after Juni gives me the book, Goldie brings me a sweet bunch of flowers. The arrangement is bright and colourful and so happy. She hands it to me, and in Goldie's no-nonsense attitude, she doesn't make me wait to tell me who it's from.

"These are from Brax. He told me to make you a colourful arrangement that would bring a smile to your face. He asked me to drop them to you today and to tell you that these are the type of flowers he should have brought for you that first disastrous date you went on. Cute huh?"

Goldie walks away looking back over her shoulder and sending me a wink.

I'm speechless. And also, a little impressed with his gestures. I think back over the conversation I overheard between him and his sister. I had thought he was ghosting me because he didn't want to be with me anymore. But everything he has been saying, and doing, tells me otherwise.

I'm so confused.

I pop the vase on the bench for everyone to enjoy. I plan on leaving them at the cafe, not sure if I'm ready to take them home just yet.

Later that day, as I turn off the lights in the coffee shop and head to the door, I stop.

"Screw it."

I race back to the counter and grab the flowers, making my way back out. They are too pretty to leave behind and not enjoy. That's the only reason. Or so I tell myself anyway.

The next night, I'm curled up on the couch when someone knocks at the door.

I leave the blanket around my shoulders and sing out to Azalea that I'll get it. I open the door and it's the Amaretto's pizza delivery guy.

"Hey Michael, what's up? I didn't order pizza tonight."

He looks down at the box and up at me.

"It says it's for you. There's a note too. Enjoy Lavender."

He hands me the boxes and waves, walking back to the car.

I look down at the boxes as I kick the door closed with my foot. I pop them on the counter and open the note.

'The margarita and olive pizza I would have bought for you if our first date had gone better. Also, a plain cheese for Azalea. Brax x.'

Chapter 30

It's school holidays, and Azalea is at camp with Beth. It buys me a little time to work out how to navigate seeing Brax, when the girls want to have playdates.

With Azalea away, I'm in moping mode. Back when Brax and I were still together, we had talked about doing something special these holidays while the girls were away. Just us two.

Instead, I'm here eating ice-cream for dinner in my trackpants and a ratty t-shirt. My hair is unwashed in a knot on top of my head. I'm a real sight. But I just don't care.

I curl up on the lounge and flick through the channels, trying to find something interesting to watch. Nothing is appealing. I throw the remote on the lounge, disheartened. I can't stop thinking about the flowers, the book and the pizza.

Maybe I should text him. Just to thank him.

I'm startled by a banging on the door, and I almost drop my bowl. Placing it gently on the coffee table, with my phone, I head to the door. Before I can look and see who it is, a voice calls out.

"Lavender, it's me. Please open the door. We need to talk."

Brax.

I'm reminded of the last time he was here banging on my door.

"Don't even think about telling me to leave. I won't go this time. Not till you hear me out. I've given you weeks to cool down, and it's been long enough. It's killing me."

Weeks to cool down? It's been long enough? I decide when I'm done being mad, not him.

A few moments ago, I was considering texting him. Now I'm angry all over again.

"Brax, you ghosted me like we were teenagers dating. Not two adults getting serious, with children and responsibilities in the mix. I need someone I can count on. I spent years doing everything on my own while Josh was off traipsing around the world. I deserve better."

His reply is quick and sure. "You do deserve better. I let you down. But I had a good reason. Well at the time I thought it was a good reason. I thought I was doing the right thing. But I can promise you from this day forward, I won't ever let you down again Lavender."

I stay silent. My resolve is wavering again. Still, I don't open the door.

"Baby, please just open the door. I'm an idiot. An absolute idiot. I started out keeping my distance, thinking I was doing the right thing but then when I realised it was a misunderstanding, you didn't want to speak to me anymore. I'm literally going crazy missing you."

Misunderstanding? He mentions that word again, like he did when I heard him talking to Ebony. What does that mean?

"Lavender. I'm not leaving till you hear me out. And if that has to be with a door between us, then so be it."

It's silent on the other side for a moment, and I hear his weight lean against the door.

I wish I hadn't covered that damn peep hole with that wreath I made at the festival. I'm desperate to see what's going on out there.

"Honey, I pushed you away. And now you are pushing me away too. I get it. But please don't. Don't push this away because you're scared. I screwed up and you will never understand how sorry I am for that. Please give me a chance to show you and make up for it."

He's right, I'm terrified. Terrified this won't work, that he will go cold on me again. That I'll be alone and know that I'm missing something special. Him. The last few weeks have been torture, and I'm scared of going through that again.

He continues, almost as if he is reading my mind.

"A few weeks ago, I saw you, Josh and Azalea at the park. You and Josh were hugging and then Azalea joined you both. She looked so happy. You did too. I didn't want to get in the way of that Lavender. She adores her dad and you being with me means he won't ever live with her again. Not to mention I was damn jealous. I started to think that maybe I was getting in the way of you having your family back. Of Zaylee having her dad back in her life full time and I couldn't do that to her. Couldn't do that to you."

Before I can speak and tell him what he saw was innocent, he continues.

"It wasn't just that. It was also a few days before that, when Zaylee wanted her dad to come over but couldn't because I was there."

I'm speechless. His intentions might have been pure, but he was wrong. So wrong.

"Brax, you should have spoken to me about it. Not ignored me."

"I know, I know. I'm so sorry. Sorrier than you will ever know. Please tell me I can fix this?"

Can he fix it? Can I trust he won't do this again?

"Honey, I have been an absolute mess the last few weeks. No one wants to be around me, I'm so miserable. Beth practically hightailed it out of here to camp."

He doesn't let the silence creep in. "Then I sent you all those text messages and you didn't answer. I explained everything in those. But when I didn't hear back, I just guessed you knew and didn't care. Ebony told me today that you never read the messages. You just deleted them all. And I'm not trying to make excuses, but I let it get to me that you weren't ready to tell everyone about us."

Shit. No, I didn't read the text messages. I was too upset to read what I thought was going to be more goodbye messages or pathetic excuses. Damn, now I wish I had read them. But he is right to feel upset about me not being ready to tell everyone. I should have spoken to him sooner. I mean, I had planned to just as he ghosted me, but he didn't know that.

He starts to talk again but I cut him off this time.

"Brax, if you would let me get a word in, you would understand both of those things weren't what they seemed. I had just told Josh that you and I were officially together, and he gave me a friendly hug to say congratulations. He was genuinely happy for me. When Zaylee saw, she wanted to get in on it, so she ran over and joined us. That's it. That day on the walk when I told her that her dad was busy had nothing to do with you. He was out birthday shopping for her before they went away, because it was the only night he had free to go to the store."

I hear a thud against the door, and I'm guessing it's his head. I go to tell him the real reason why I wasn't ready to tell everyone about us, when my voice disappears.

Brax replies before I get a chance. "So, what you're saying is, if I had just been an adult about this and asked you, we could have avoided all of this?" He groans.

I nod, crossing my arms over my chest. It's my time to smirk now, even though he can't see me.

I hear his frustrated sigh.

"Not long after we stopped talking, I had spoken to Ebony, and she had told me in simple terms that I'm an idiot and that you and Josh don't want to be together. That you guys are great friends and that's it. But I didn't quite believe it. I came here that day to ask you and talk about it."

I'm nodding on the other side of the door, even though he can't see me. I'm still not quite ready to open the door. And my heart. I stay silent, waiting to hear if there is more he has to say.

"Look, I get it. I hurt you. And I am so incredibly sorry for that. I know you think if you keep yourself safe, you won't get hurt. But it's too late for that now. We can't go back, now that we have found each other."

"Can you please open the door? I have a warm cinnamon scroll here that's going to waste."

Sneaky. He knows the way to my heart is food. And coffee. For the first time since he arrived, I consider opening the door to grab the scroll and then close it again.

"I didn't bother buying you a coffee. You make the best damn coffee around any way."

Well, that's true.

"I'll bring you one of these damn things everyday of your life, if you'll let me, Lavender. And if the bakery runs out of them, I'll learn the recipe and make them for you myself."

My heart skips a beat at those words. Isn't that all I've ever wanted? Someone to support me and show they care through little acts like this. Like Brax has been showing me since not long after we met.

"And I can promise you honey, till the end of my days and beyond if you believe in that, I'm your guy. I'm not going anywhere. Before I met you, I was happy to do life exactly how it was. I had it all planned out. Beth and I were doing well. But then I met you and everything changed. I wanted more. I wanted a life with you in it too."

I'm thawing like a snowman in summer, hot and fast. I'm doing my best to keep my guard up, but it's not working. He drives the final wedge home.

"I don't like saying this with a door between us, but if I have to, I will. I love you Lavender Clementine Wild."

My heart leaps out of my chest at his words.

"Our start might have been rough" and we both laugh from our sides of the door, mine, tearily. "But the rest of your days won't be. I won't let them be."

I've heard enough. Tears roll down my cheeks and I can't stop the smile that spreads across my face.

I throw the door open and launch myself at him. He catches me, pulling me in tight. So tight I can barely breathe. I tuck my head under his chin and breathe him in. God, I've missed this. Him. After a few minutes, I pull back so I can see his face.

"The first time you tell me you love me, can't be through a door Brax."

He chuckles, "I know honey, I know. But that's the last time I will ever let a door, or anything else come between us."

He rests his forehead on mine, and we stay like that, both of us overwhelmed and smiling big.

He pulls back slightly, wiping the tears from my cheeks, his gaze smouldering.

"I want to spend every day with you, proving to you how much I love you. You, Beth and Azalea are everything to me. We're a team."

Oh, my heart. I never expected I would meet someone who would accept me and my girl like this. And here is this beautiful man, telling me he wants us to be a team. The four of us.

I nod so fast that he laughs tenderly.

"So, what do you say. Wanna join teams?"

I lean in kissing him gently on the lips. He responds with the same light pressure, touching his mouth to mine over and over.

"Yes, I definitely want to be on that team. Team Wild Madox."

He smiles, gently tucking my hair behind my ear. He kisses me again, a little longer this time.

"I was kind of hoping you might want to be on team Madox."

My hands cover my mouth, my heart almost leaping out of my chest.

"Are you... what I think... are you asking? Or suggesting?"

Chuckling, he pulls me in fast, our chests pressed tightly together. I look up at him, overwhelmed with every possible feeling I could have. But all the good ones this time.

"I am absolutely suggesting that. But I want to do it right, you deserve that. Give me time to do it. But this is my commitment to you that I'm in this for the long-haul honey. I'm all in. In every possible way."

Chapter 31

THE SUN ISN'T UP YET, but I need to be if I'm going to get ready for this race. It's not the biggest marathon I've ever done, but I'm a little rusty these days, so I need to make sure I prep myself. A hand finds mine in the dark and I remember that Brax is here with me. It's been a month since we told the kids about us, and it couldn't have been more magical.

The girls have not stopped bouncing with excitement each time we see them, which is every day. This past week, Brax and Beth have stayed over, and I can finally see exactly what our future will look like.

Excitement bubbles in my stomach just thinking about it.

Brax places a warm soft kiss to my palm, and I roll over, resting my head on his chest as his arms circle my shoulders pulling me in even closer.

His breath is warm on my forehead, and he places another light, lingering kiss there.

His morning voice is raspy and my favourite thing to wake up to.

"Morning, honey. How are you feeling about today?"

I stretch my legs out again before tucking them between his strong thighs. His leg hair tickles my legs, and his hand lightly strokes up and down my thigh.

"I feel good. Really good actually. I love the adrenaline rush I get from these marathons. I like pushing myself. Testing myself."

I feel Brax nodding against the top of my head. Brax has been joining me for the occasional morning run, and it's been wonderful.

"Yeah, I get that. I might even join you in next year's one."

I love when he talks about doing future things together. I get all warm and gooey inside. And I still can't believe this is my life.

Rolling onto my stomach, my chin rests on his chest. "I would love that, Brax."

I trace patterns on the smooth, muscled skin over his heart, and he raises his head to kiss my lips.

"I wish we could stay in bed all day, but you need to get ready for your race." He lightly swats at my butt, and I laugh, reluctantly rolling onto my back, and throwing my legs over the side of the bed.

He lets out a low whistle as I stand and I turn my head, looking back over my shoulder, blowing him a kiss.

He throws his arm over his forehead, laughing.

"Go before I drag you back into this bed."

A giggle escapes me.

"I love that sound."

Shaking my head at him, I can't wipe the smile off my face.

It stays there for the entirety of my shower and my breakfast with Brax and the girls.

I rush through getting dressed so I have time to stretch and hydrate. Sitting at the kitchen table to tie my shoes, I listen to the laughter coming from Zaylee's bedroom. I'll never get sick of that sound. I thought maybe it would take some time for the girls to adjust to being around each other so much, especially Azalea, but she has embraced Brax and Beth into our family so lovingly.

Brax walks into the kitchen like he has been doing it for years and I can't get enough of seeing him potter around my house. Since he is here so often, I gave him a crash course in using my coffee machine, and now he makes coffee almost as good as me. The guys at the station put in their daily requests for a Brax coffee and I love it. I joke every day that I'm going to steal him from the police force and keep him hostage at the coffee shop. What a dream that would be.

He leans against the door frame of the kitchen and slowly sips his coffee. I watch him take a few more sips and almost need to pinch myself.

"I've never paid much attention to runners before I met you Lavender, but you blow all of them out of the park.

Also, if I had known you look like this in your running clothes, I would have been running with you months ago."

He gives me a slow appraisal from behind his coffee cup, and my cheeks and chest flush with heat.

Today I'm wearing purple runners, black bike shorts and a white fitted crop top with my hair up in a tight ponytail. I can't afford to have my hair coming out during a race.

I slowly stand from my chair and walk over to join him. Holding his cup of coffee with one hand, he uses his other free hand to pull me in by the waist. I rest my hands on his chest and my forehead against his. To reach him though, I need to be up on my toes. It's also a good calf stretch, so I'm calling it a win win today.

"Baby, I will wear this for you anytime."

He raises an eyebrow, and his voice is thick and heavy when he answers.

"I look forward to peeling it off you next time you wear it."

My chest rises and falls in time with his deep breathes. I wonder if I'll ever get sick of this.

I place my hands around the back of his neck and pull him down into a kiss. My teeth gently bite down on his lower lip and I giggle, pulling back.

"Okay, I really do have to go. Are you guys coming with me now?"

A look I can't place crosses his face. "No, we will meet you there. The kids have a few signs they want to work on before the race starts."

I feel a little disappointed that I won't see them before the race, but I love that he is helping the girls to make signs and including them in the day.

I lean forward and plant another kiss before sweeping his mug out of his hand and taking a sip. I pass it back to him and sing out my goodbye to the girls before giving him a little wave and heading to the door.

I watch his smirk turn into a full-blown grin as he lifts the cup and takes a long sip from the side I drank. A thrill races through me.

I make it to the race in good time and spend thirty minutes warming up. I don't see Brax or the girls, before the race starts, but I know I'll see them at the end.

The first half of the race is easy, but my body is burning on this last leg. Sweat drips down my back, beading on my forehead and upper lip. I grab a paper cup of cool water from a volunteer as I run past, and it temporarily soothes my parched throat. I toss the cup in the bin as I push past. I'm slowing down, my body starting to cramp up and I feel so out of breath.

As I round the final corner, past the light house, I see the finish line in the distance. Finally. I get a burst of energy that pushes me on. I'm so close.

In the final straight to the finish, spectators begin lining the sides of the track. My eyes burn as sweat drips into them and the spectator's blur.

I swipe at my eyes to clear them, just in time to see my parents on the sideline waving. Mum is holding a big colourful, sparkly sign that reads 'Lavender.'

Nothing else written. Just my name. Odd, but I appreciate the effort she has made. Although the writing looks suspiciously like Azalea's.

I give her a wave and a smile as I pass her. A few metres up, I spy Juni and Goldie, each holding a colourful sign too.

In all the years my family has come to support me in this race, not once have they ever held a sign. Goldie once held a champagne bottle to celebrate with after, which was very much appreciated. But never a sign.

Their signs respectively read 'it was not love' and 'at first sight.'

Huh?

I don't spend much time thinking on it because I see another sign up ahead, and this one is held by Eb.

'but I promise you.'

What the hell is going on?

Standing a few people down from Eb, is Wolf and he has a big grin on his face. As I come to his sign, a laugh bursts from him. His sign is also colourful and reads 'I will love you.'

I mouth at him as I pass, "What the hell is going on?"

He shrugs his shoulders nonchalantly but laughs again.

I look around and spy Bear this time, holding another sign. This one reads: 'for the rest of my life.'

I piece the signs together so far and my feet slow. 'Lavender, it was not love at first sight, but I promise you, I will love you for the rest of my life.'

Oh. Brax.

I look around, searching through the crowd as I near the finish line. Where is he?

And what is happening?

I must be delirious and more dehydrated than I thought because it feels like… something big.

Suddenly I spot Beth and Azalea at the finish. With Brax. Just past the line.

And the three of them are holding a sign each. But I can't quite make out what they say.

The race all but forgotten now, I get an extra burst of energy. I need to reach my family.

As I cross the line, I beeline for them. But I can now read the rest of the signs, from where I am.

Beth's sign reads 'will' followed by Zaylee's sign 'you.'

My aching body is a thought of the past. Tears roll hard and fast down my cheeks, and I cover my mouth with my hands. I'm trembling and it's not from exhaustion.

Brax's sign is last.

'Marry me.'

A cry escapes me and as I reach him, he drops the sign, and I tumble into his arms.

I sob into his arms as he squeezes me tightly, and I feel little arms grasp me from behind. I turn, welcoming them in, and we all stand in one big, four-person group hug. My beautiful family.

I rest my head on Brax's shoulder, and he strokes my hair as my tears subside. I hear my parents behind me taking the girls, so we can have a moment together.

Brax pulls me in even tighter, which I didn't think was possible and I fold into his embrace.

We stay like that, and he holds me up, exhaustion and emotions now setting in.

He gently pulls back and reaches up to hold my face in his hands. He starts peppering kisses across my cheeks, eyes and mouth.

I open my mouth to speak, and the words are hoarse.

"Brax… I" and he silences me with a kiss.

Shaking his head, he starts talking.

"Please let me go first. Lavender Clementine Wild, I adore you. Beyond what I could have ever imagined in my wildest dreams. I'll be forever grateful that I walked into your coffee shop that day to interrupt you from checking out that guy," a laugh bursts from me and I shake my head.

He smiles and for the first time, I notice his eyes are watery. He sniffs and my heart skips.

"I love you. Forever and even more than that. I want to wake up next to you for the rest of my life. I want to make you coffee every morning before you wake, knowing it will never be as good as yours, but I'll bust my ass trying anyway. I want to cheer you on in this race every year till you can't run anymore. I want to make my shitty workdays better just by stopping in to see you for my morning coffee. I want us to do Saturday night movies with the girls followed by Sunday morning pancakes after a long sleep in. I want it all. Everything."

I'm stunned, lost for words. He reaches into his back pocket and pulls out a box. I don't see anyone else. All I see is him. The race is all but forgotten and I don't care about a medal or even my finishing time right now. All I see is this beautiful, wonderful, charming, sexy man, who is about to become my fiancée.

He opens the box and slightly shaking, takes out the ring. Gently holding my hand, he slides it on my finger.

I glance down to find the most beautiful ring I have ever seen. It's a stunning, oval shaped emerald, my birth stone, and a close match to my eyes. Surrounding the emerald are small diamonds and all along the band, halfway down, are more diamonds. It's perfection.

"Lavender, please put me out of my misery. Would…" and not giving him a chance to finish, I jump into his arms, as best as my wobbly legs will allow. Like I knew he would, Brax catches me effortlessly.

"Yes! Oh my god yes. Brax, of course I'll marry you."

He pulls me in tighter, laughing softly into my hair.

I rest my forehead against his and soak this moment in. I'm aware of our families crowding around us, desperate to congratulate us, but we stay in our bubble a moment longer.

In all the years since my marriage to Josh ended, not once did I ever dream, I would meet someone else. Let alone someone as wonderful as Brax.

Our family finally crowd us, no longer content to give us time.

As we are pulled apart by congratulating arms and voices, I find Azalea in the crowd. Taking her hand, I crouch down and give her a hug before pulling back and looking up at her.

I tuck her hair behind her ears and tap her lightly on the nose.

"Are you okay with this baby girl? With Brax and I getting married? With him and Beth moving in with us… or us moving in with them? With all of this?" I gesture around at what's happening and she gives me a quick nod. A wide, genuine smile breaks out across her face.

"Oh yeah Mum. Brax is awesome. And I get Beth as a sister! How cool is that! I've always wanted a sister and now I get one. And we are pretty much the same age!"

She does a little happy dance on the spot and overcome with emotion, I laugh, feeling so content I could burst.

I glance over to see Brax watching me with his hands on his waist, a look of pure joy etched on his face. His chest rises and falls deeply, and he shakes his head smiling. He looks elated.

I stand, taking Azalea's hand and walking over to Brax and Beth. I take Beth's hand, and he takes Azaleas. We stand there in our circle of four, hands all clasped together. A family.

Chapter 32

"No way. Definitely not. Can't we just go somewhere local? How about a pizza party, movie night in? Or a high tea at the shop?"

I want to do anything but, what they are suggesting to me right now.

"Juni help me out here. Wouldn't a nice high tea be lovely?"

I expect Juni to back me on this one, but she shakes her head.

"Normally I would say yes Clemmy, but this is your hens! You need to do something wild! Something you wouldn't normally do. I vote with Goldie on this one."

Marigold fist pumps to the sky, and I realise then, I'm outnumbered. There's no use trying to get Ebony on side. She will think this plan is brilliant too.

Marigold starts laying out brochures on my dining table and Juni rearranges them in order of hen's weekend events. Not even just one night. They have a whole weekend planned out.

Brax walks out of the hallway after putting the girls to bed and makes his way over to us.

Three months ago, he asked me to marry him and then shortly after, he and Beth moved in with Azalea and I. The girls love having a live in best friend and immediately voted to share a room. I've also loved having my live in bestie Brax, share a room with me too.

Brax stands behind me holding onto the chair and leans down to kiss my cheek.

He talks quietly in my ear so the others can't hear him. "Hi fiancée."

I turn my head and smile up at him. I'll never get sick of those words. But I'm most looking forward to, 'Hi wife' in a few months' time.

He leans over me to grab a pamphlet off the table. "What's this?"

"My hens. Apparently."

Brax raises his eyebrows in surprise. "Vegas, honey?"

I glance back at him, widening my eyes, silently begging him to save me and he laughs.

Goldie jumps in "So, this is what we are thinking. Weekend in Vegas. Best hotel on the strip. First night we go to a show. Shopping on the Saturday to get you something super cute and way too revealing for the club, and that night we go clubbing. Then spa day on the Sunday to recover. What do you think?"

I think it sounds like hell, other than the spa day but she seems super excited, and I don't want to rain on her parade.

"It sounds… fun?"

Juni bursts into laughter and Goldie gives me a wry smile.

"You will love it Lala, I promise. It's going to be so fun."

Fun for who? My idea of fun is a night in with a movie and snacks. It's definitely not a night of dancing in Vegas. I look over at Goldie and she is brimming with excitement. I don't want to let her down. And my sisters can make any location fun. Maybe it will be good for me.

"I'm stuck on the part where you guys are getting Lavender something 'cute' and 'way too revealing' to wear to the club… how cute and revealing are we talking here?" Brax says sounding a little concerned.

Juni pats his shoulder "Don't worry Braxy, we will fight off every guy who tries to get our Lavender's attention."

He groans, dropping his head to my shoulder. "You're not making me feel any better Juni. What about if we do a combined hens and bucks in Vegas instead?"

Juni and Goldie both shout "No" at the same time as I shout "Yes!"

Goldie and Juni look at each other as if resigning themselves to something they don't want to do. Goldie braces her fingers on the table, nodding to herself, hatching a plan.

"Fine. We can make this work. Friday night we go to the show – girls only – and then Saturday we shop – also girls only. Saturday night we can all hit the club together so Brax can go all caveman and protect Lavender from any advancing males. Deal?"

I'm already loving this plan way more.

Brax kisses my cheek again before walking over to the stove to boil the kettle.

"Sounds good to me. I'll let the guys know the plan. I look forward to fending off the 'advancing males'," and he sends me a wink. I giggle and wink back. Gosh I love him.

Brax makes us all a cup of tea, placing them on the table.

"You will all get to meet my best mate Callan. You'll love him. A real genuine, down to earth guy."

Goldie glances over at me, mouthing "He sounds boring," before bursting into a fit of giggles.

Brax sees our exchange and rolls his eyes laughing too.

"I'm off to bed honey, I have an early start."

He leans down and gives me a long slow kiss.

Goldie starts catcalling and I shoo her away with my hand.

She leans back in her chair and lets out a happy sigh.

"This is going to be the most memorable weekend, Lavender. Just you wait and see," she says.

THE END

Thank you

Thank you so much for reading Lavender and Brax's story.

I hope you enjoyed reading it, as much as I loved writing it!

Lavender and Brax's story is part 1, in a 3 book series featuring Marigold and Juniper.

Keep an eye out for Marigold's story later this year.

MJ xx